"I have until Hallow's Eve — when the past and present meet — when everything of yours becomes mine." Raven's reference to the midnight hour on Halloween was only four days away. She ran her tongue over her upper lip. "I know you want me, but you'll have to wait for Hallow's Eve." Raven's devilish laughter filled the bathroom. "You're so tempting lounging there in such a creamy red sauce."

Tayler looked down into the tub. The sight and smell of the blood surrounding her was appalling. She quickly stood, stepped out of the tub and reached for her necklace. Tayler held the crystal pendant out in front, her hand perfectly still.

Upon seeing the pendant, Raven retreated several steps.

"You're sick, Raven. When the clock chimes midnight on Hallow's Eve — I'll destroy you," Tayler's face was flushed.

Beware the Kiss

by

J. Alex Acker

Women's Work Press, LLC
P.O. Box 10375 Burke, Virginia 22009-0375

Dedication

Beware the Kiss is dedicated to
two very marvelous women:

Susan M. Schmid
for getting me started,
and
Rita L. Halbur
for keeping me going.

Acknowledgements

No writing could ever be done without the love and inspiration mentors and friends provide the writer. To these very special people, I would like to express my deepest gratitude for all the time, support, and encouragement you gave to me while I worked on this book.

Beware the Kiss could not have been published without the backing of my publisher, Women's Work Press; and written without my mentors—Deborah Keenan and Sandra Hyde; and without the continual support of my friends—Lisa Svac-Hawks, Ruth Baeumler, Diane Bauer, Mary Beth Buckman, Paulette DesJardins; and without my dangerous and adorable Ms. Demeanors group—Mary O'Harra, Joni Karl, Lori Larson, Sharon Pazlar and, again, Lisa Svac-Hawks. Louise and Don Van Hammond thanks, too, for being there when I needed you.

You're in my heart…

Alex

About the Author

J. Alex Acker has been a corporate communications writer and promotional copywriter for over 17 years. She also teaches business writing seminars.

Alex's writing accomplishments include several newspaper articles, poems, a personal essay, and a chapter in a professional textbook. In 2000, she was named a finalist in the Southwest Writers Conference writing competition.

She lives with her partner Rita and her dog Wylie in Saint Paul, Minnesota.

prologue

Raven Delaire closed her eyes, remembering the women who betrayed her. Slowly, her lids opened. She looked down at the floor and smiled. With a nine-inch blade pierced through her heart, her grandmother lay in a sea of blood. Her lifeless eyes, frozen with horror, were fixed on a distant object. Raven followed the gaze to the table where a small black book sat. Its worn leather cover encompassed an inch and a half of yellowed pages. She walked over to the table and ran her pale, white fingers across the leather.

"Ah, finally," she breathed deeply, "something to love."

She picked up the book, inhaling the musty scent of ancient knowledge and leather. It was the smell of power. From centuries of use and possession, it was smooth and malleable. She opened the book and leafed through the pages. An expression of displeasure spread across her pallid, angular face.

"Another obstacle?" Raven snarled at the body on the floor. "Even in death, Grandmother, you still try to keep these secrets from me. Foolish old woman. In my sixteen years, I am now wiser and more powerful than you."

She opened the book of black magic again. The text was written in Latin, a language Raven could not read. She tapped her index finger impatiently on the book's spine. Her full, red lips curved into a malicious smile.

Raven Delaire closed her eyes remembering the women who betrayed her. "Of course," she breathed, "I know just the woman to translate this for me. No one will dare to refuse me," Raven laughed. "No one will ever betray me again."

> *"Rejection mocks Love —*
> *Beware the Kiss.*
> *Pain a constant shadow —*
> *Beware the Serpent.*
> *Grief to shatter the Soul —*
> *Beware the Cry at Night.*
>
> *Darkness calls you and enthralls you,*
> *I await you with delight."*

one

The late August evening was filled with burning logs and decaying dreams. For twelve years, no matter where she went, Erica Kirsten-Laird stopped each night to read the curse. She did this to remind herself of the curse's tragic implications and destructive power. Though it had originally been written on white parchment, the folded paper was now torn from handling and yellowed with time. Its texture was as soft as a satin ribbon, but the words on the page were written with revenge. It was unnecessary for Erica to read the words since she had already engraved them on the walls of her soul.

With the curse held tightly in her hand, Erica eased out of her deck chair and stood stiffly. She placed the tattered paper on the table, walked to the edge of the deck and leaned on the wood railing. A spirited breeze rolled off Lake Mahala, feathering Erica's mahogany hair and blowing away the paper.

The waxing moon's reflection rippled on the surface of the water in the pool below. Erica looked away from the moon's watery image and focused on the brighter stars in the night sky. She located the Big Dipper and tried to identify other constellations, but when she caught sight of a falling star she quickly looked away. The prickling sensation of fear ran down her spine. She placed her hands over her eyes. Unable to rid herself of the feeling that this falling star was some ominous sign of her own impending death, Erica tightly gripped the railing.

The notes from George Benson's version of the Beatles tune "The Long and Winding Road" spilled gently on to the balcony. Erica sighed. The cherished melody could not erase the harsh words on the document and the signatures in blood on the bottom of the paper. After twelve agonizing years, the words on the yellowed paper were still haunting. She began to pace.

In the shadows of her mind an elusive demon stalked her. It was dictated in the parchment that if the curse was not destroyed, Erica would die on Hallow's Eve. Only two months remained.

The yard lights next door went on and lit the pool area. She stopped pacing and turned toward her neighbor's yard. A woman dressed in a short white robe slid the screen door open and walked into the light. From her second-story deck, Erica could clearly see her neighbor. At the deep end of the pool, the woman bent down and tested the water with her hand. She paused for a moment looking into the water's depth. When she finally stood, she walked toward the shallow end, where she hung her towel on a nearby wicker chair. Erica watched her new renter descend the steps leading into the cool, clear water.

When her attorney first suggested to Erica that she rent out the second house, Erica resisted. She had purposely designed and built the two houses close together so she could watch over her aging grandparents. She had been so fearful that they would die unexpectedly — just like her parents. When her grandparents did die six months apart from natural causes, the house had stood empty.

Built on six acres of land, wooded with large maple and oak trees and towering Norway pines, the houses overlooked Lake Mahala. The elaborate, contemporary structures provided Erica with quiet solitude. A wooden fence and bushes were the only edging between the two houses. Over the years, this property had become Erica's fortress, a place where she could let both her grief and her creativity flow freely. Her success as an architect, wealth and charitable contributions, and single status made her feel uncomfortable with a public that viewed her, ironically, as the most eligible woman in Minnesota.

While out of the country, Erica finally agreed to rent the house. She faxed her attorney detailed instructions. Erica wanted a renter who would respect her privacy and live a tranquil life. She was specific — no photographers, reporters, or news editors. After an extensive search the house was finally rented. That evening before walking out on the deck, Erica had taken a brief glance at her renter's file. Her attorney could not have caught the one thing that now unnerved Erica. She turned her gaze across the lawn, paying closer attention to her new neighbor.

The woman's hair was so light it seemed to glow. When she turned her head in Erica's direction, Erica stepped back into the shadows, afraid she had been seen. She silently reprimanded herself for not making a formal introduction earlier in the evening, but her flight had been late and she wanted to get home.

In her mind Erica scanned the woman's file again. It had to have been a dreadful trick of fate that her renter's last name was Windquest. She wrapped her arms tightly around her body and watched as Tayler Windquest began to untie the sash on her white robe. The wind grew stronger and a large dense cloud blocked the moon's light. Erica watched the cloud pass. When it did she looked back. Tayler remained in her robe silently transfixed on the steps.

In the shadows near Tayler's pool another movement stirred. A darkly clothed figure crept along the fence in Tayler's direction. Erica held her breath. For a brief moment she wondered if the image was a figment of her exhausted mind, but when the figure leapt from the darkness and the blade of a knife caught the glow of the moonlight, she yelled. With her heart pounding against her ribs, Erica pushed herself down the deck steps.

"This is Erica Kirsten-Laird," she shouted into the cellular phone, miraculously close at hand from an earlier business call, "at five Oaks Trail...my neighbor Tayler Windquest is being attacked...her address is seven Oaks Trail...please hurry."

Erica stretched her five-ten frame and dashed across the yard, reached the fence and threw open the gate. For a fleeting moment she wondered why it was unlocked. The dark figure at the shallow end of the pool leaned over the edge and held Tayler Windquest's head under the water. Tayler struggled in vain to free herself, but the loose-fitting, slippery material her assailant wore was difficult to grab. A cloudy substance swirled in the waves near Tayler's head.

"Let her go!" Erica shouted over the splashing.

The assailant looked up and eased the grip on Tayler.

"I said let her go — " Erica lowered her voice. She cautiously approached the shallow end of the pool.

Releasing the victim, the assailant grabbed the knife off the cement, stood and pointed it at Erica. The sight of the bloodied knife stopped her.

The assailant took several calculated steps toward Erica and then lunged toward her. She dodged the knife, barely missing its sharp, silver blade. The two turned and faced one another again. Erica's chest heaved for air, her breath coming in short, quick gasps. The black mask over the assailant's face concealed the identity, but there was something familiar about the mouth. The eye teeth were long and pointed. The wail of approaching police sirens cut her off mid-thought.

The assailant glanced toward the pool and Erica's gaze followed. Tayler's body was sinking deeper into the water. Erica looked back toward the assailant, but a black blur dominated her vision. She tried to recover her balance, but stumbled instead. The assailant's knife missed her chest by an inch, slicing deeply into her left arm. The knife was roughly pulled out. Erica grabbed her arm and fell to her knees. Blood seeped through her fingers and dripped on her jeans. She watched the assailant dash around the pool and disappear through the open gate. The sound of sirens warbled in her head and the concrete lurched in front of her.

"Oh God," Erica rose slowly and staggered to the edge of the pool.

She half-fell, half-dove into the water. The cool water helped to clear Erica's senses and she seized Tayler's robe with her right hand. She struggled to the steps and dragged the unconscious woman out of the water. She rolled Tayler over and saw the ugly gash in her neck. The numbness in Erica's arm abated and pain shot through her body.

Too dizzy to stand, Erica sat down on the top step and cradled

Tayler's head in her lap. She pulled the bottom of the robe and brought it up to Tayler's neck. She held the wet satin material on the gash to stop the bleeding. A noise from inside the house startled Erica as several police officers rushed through the door.

The emergency room bustled with activity. The phone rang constantly, people in white coats ran in every direction, and security guards tried to keep the cameras and reporters out of the lobby.

"Can you give us a statement?" a reporter yelled at the approaching figure.

"How bad is she?" shouted another.

A path was cleared for a fat, balding man in his late forties. His stomach was so huge that the two pieces of his tie parted around the unsightly mass like a divining rod. The reporters gathered around him, shouting out their questions.

"Detective, can you give us any information on the attack? Is Miss Laird okay? Who is the other woman?"

"We're just starting our investigation, boys. We'll let you know as soon as we've got something," Detective Lucas Steffan smiled for the cameras and walked into the hospital.

"Miss Laird, I'm Detective Steffan with the Lake Mahala Police Department."

He held up his badge for Erica, but all she could see was his pudgy, yellow fingertips. She leaned back and noticed several teeth were missing and those that remained were a dull gray.

"I'd like to ask you a few questions before the doc comes in. Can you tell me what happened?"

"I've already given the information to the Sergeant."

"I know. I'd just like to hear what happened in your own words." He ran his tongue over coarse dry lips. "Do you have any ideas on who might have wanted to see Miss Windquest dead?"

"No. Do you?"

"Well, we're still searching the area for clues, but it looks like our assailant just vanished into thin air."

"That's impossible. No one just vanishes."

"Miss Laird — "

"Ms.," Erica corrected.

"Yes, yes. Ms. Laird, we're doing everything we can." Steffan scribbled in a small black notebook. "We're looking at a couple of things right now, but two things are clear. First, the assailant attempted to cut Miss Windquest's throat and, second, there was the attempt to drown her."

"Yes, I know. I was there." Erica ran her fingers through her wet tangled hair. "What's your point?"

"My point being that whoever is after Miss — Ms. Windquest — has a major psychological inclination toward violence. In simple words, Ms. Laird, we have a killer with a vengeance." He scribbled another note. "Do you know what time the attack occurred?"

"It was around midnight."

"Did you notice anything unusual before the attack?"

"No — " Erica stopped abruptly.

Her stomach curdled and a strong feeling of nausea washed over her. She quickly reached for a blue plastic container and brought it to her mouth. Steffan retreated several steps. When she finally lifted her head he returned to his questions, but his eyes were focused several inches above her head.

"How about during the attack? Was anything out of place?"

"The gate," Erica took a deep breath. "The gate between the two yards was unlocked."

"Why is this so unusual?"

"Because that gate is *always* secured, Detective."

Intense brown eyes glared at Steffan. He began to fidget with his soiled tie.

"How long have you known Ms. Windquest?"

"I don't know her."

"Excuse me?" Steffan eyed Erica with suspicion. "Hasn't she been renting from you for the past," he consulted his notes, "two months?"

"Yes, but I've been out of the country the entire time. And, I didn't have a chance to 'officially' meet her before the attack."

"Where were you?"

"Spain."

"Nice place, good food." Steffan's stomach rumbled as if on cue. "When did you get back?"

"This evening."

"Great homecoming. Is there someone we could contact to let them know about Ms. Windquest?"

"My attorney has copies of the renter's application and reference forms. I've already given the number to the Sergeant." Erica's arm throbbed and she wanted to go home. The stench of stale smoke from Steffan's jacket permeated the room. When the door opened and a doctor and two nurses walked in, Erica could feel the fresh breeze on her face. One of the nurses hung up the x-rays of Erica's arm on the lighted viewer.

"Erica, how are you?" A short, petite doctor with graying hair walked in and put her hands on her hips.

Erica turned gratefully toward the voice. "Ev, how did you know—"

"I was just finishing an exam of another patient when I heard you were coming in. I'm sorry you had to wait." Dr. Susan Evans squeezed Erica's good hand. She peered at Steffan and looked back at Erica, her hazel eyes blinking in disbelief. "What a horrible thing to come home to."

Under the florescent lights Ev carefully removed the gauze pad and examined the wound. Erica winced. Ev walked over to the viewer and peered at the x-rays with the bloodied pad still in her hand.

"It's a deep cut, but luckily the knife missed the bone. It looks pretty clean. I'll use small stitches to reduce the scarring, but altogether, I'd say you're going to need about ten stitches." Ev turned to the nurses and gave them instructions. She turned back toward Steffan. "Lieutenant—"

"It's Detective Lucas Steffan, Doctor."

"Whatever. Detective, you'll have to conclude your questioning for now." Ev approached him with the bloody cloth. "Unless you don't mind the sight of blood."

Steffan's face went white and sweat began to bead on his forehead. "Fine, Doc, just one last question. Ms. Laird, did you see the knife?"

"Yes, I saw it on the ground."

"What did it look like?"

"It didn't look like something you'd use in a kitchen."

"What do you mean?"

"It had a black handle and the blade was curved."

"Here, why don't you draw me a picture." He flipped over a clean page and handed his notebook and pen to Erica.

"I think the blade was about six inches long. It looked like some kind of ceremonial knife."

Steffan eyed Erica suspiciously. "I take it you're familiar with knives?"

"Detective," the tone of Ev's voice warned him to finish his questioning.

"Okay, okay." Steffan flinched as Ev inserted a two-inch needle into Erica's arm. She slowly emptied the syringe filled with Novocaine. "Can you recall anything else about the knife? Did it have any markings or anything on the blade?"

"I don't know. It was covered with blood."

Ev withdrew the needle and placed it on the tray. She picked up a clean gauze pad to soak up the blood.

"Detective," Ev turned with the gauze still in her hand. "Now are you finished?" Steffan nervously peered at the bandage and swallowed.

"Yes, yes of course—for now. Ms. Laird, I'll talk with you

tomorrow." The door closed behind Steffan with a thud.

Ev bit her lip but her eyes couldn't hide her amusement. It was common knowledge among the hospital staff that the only weaknesses Detective Lucas Steffan had were his love for buffets and his fear of blood.

"Are you okay?"

Erica nodded. Ev had been her best friend since grade school and always knew when she was lying. Slowly, Erica changed the direction of her nod from vertical to horizontal. She took a deep breath, but when she exhaled, the air came out in short gasps.

"Oh, Ev. I can't believe this happened." Erica's fingers shook as she ran them through her matted hair. "How is she?"

"Tayler Windquest?"

Erica nodded again.

"She's doing okay. She's got a nasty concussion and two broken ribs. And, unfortunately, the knife nicked her vocal cords."

"Can she talk?"

"Eventually. For now we'll just have to give it time to heal. Her voice may be lower and she could lose it from time to time if she strains her voice."

"I hope she's not a singer."

"No, luckily she's not," Ev paused. "She's a writer for a national magazine."

"What?" Erica choked.

"A writer."

"I'd better have a talk with my attorney."

"Why?"

Erica waved her hand dismissing the comment.

"She's a lucky woman. It could've been a lot worse if you hadn't been home." Ev smiled, "By the way, welcome back. I missed you."

"I missed you, too."

Ev carefully gave Erica a hug.

"I'm scared, Ev."

"I know you are, but don't give up just yet. There's got to be a solution to this madness." Ev saw the wild look in Erica's eyes. "Were you able to learn anything more about the curse in Spain?"

Erica's eyes filled with tears. Unable to speak, she hung her head and leaned against Ev.

"We'll find a way, Erica. What can I do?"

Jet lag and the late hour made the attack and the curse seem like far away events. Erica pointed to her injured arm.

"Right." Ev picked up two instruments from the tray. Ev relaxed when she heard Erica finally laugh. "Do you want a bullet to bite on?"

Erica shook her head.

"Okay, then let's get this over with."

⤳⤳

"Beth said she'd be right over to pick you up and take you home." Ev carefully slipped Erica's left arm into a sling and fastened it around her neck. "I really wish you'd stay here tonight."

"I just want to go home," Erica complained. She bit her lip. "I don't know what I'd do, Ev, without you and Beth."

"We feel the same about you, Erica. You know we're here for you." Ev helped Erica stand. "Okay, well, at least let me walk you to the nurse's station so I can head off any meddling reporters."

"You know, I really just don't understand the media. Don't they have better things to do than spend the night in a hospital parking lot?"

"Dear, I hate to break the news to you, but it's not everyday that a beautiful, talented young architect saves the life of a Pulitzer Prize winner." Ev watched Erica frown. Her expression made Ev laugh. "And, I might add, a gorgeous writer at that."

"Gorgeous or not, she's still one of them." Erica rolled her eyes.

Ev chuckled again. "I understand your feelings toward the press, but you know they aren't going to leave you alone. You're too good looking."

"Yeah, right. Look at this hair, these clothes," Erica grumbled.

"Ms. Laird?" They stopped as a police officer approached them. "There's someone here who would like to speak with you before you leave."

Erica looked wearily at Ev.

"It's not the press, is it?" Ev asked as she watched Erica's face pale.

"No. Everything checked out okay." The officer pointed to a closed door.

"Do you want me to go in with you?"

"No," Erica grimaced, "I think I can handle it."

"Okay, but it's three o'clock in the morning and I want you to go home and get some sleep." Ev looked at Erica. "And don't forget to take the pain medication. It'll take the edge off." Ev kissed Erica on the cheek. "I need to check on our writer. I'll talk with you later."

"Bye, Ev. Thanks for the mending." Erica watched Ev stride down the hall. She walked to the door and knocked.

"Come in."

As she opened the door she saw a woman of average height looking out the window. With her back to Erica, the woman's face was hidden from view. She wore an expensive blue linen suit and gold accessories.

"The nurse told me you wanted to speak with me. I'm—"

"Hello, Erica," the woman slowly turned and faced Erica.

Erica blinked and leaned against the wall for support. Lightheaded and dizzy from loss of blood and shock, Erica put her hand on the wall to stop the room from whirling. Her body temperature rose. She felt on fire.

"Christina Windquest." The name was pronounced with hesitation. It had been eighteen years since Christina walked out of Erica's life.

"Erica," Christina's voice trembled. She walked around the desk narrowing the distance between them.

The years came crashing back to Erica in fragments—dinners wrapped in candlelight, conversations steeped with laughter, nights of passion. But it had all stopped without warning.

"You never told me you had a daughter." Erica clenched her teeth, the office now too small for comfort.

"I," tears fell down Christina's face. She reached for a tissue. "I almost lost her—again." Christina focused on the wall clock. When she looked back, she noticed the sling on Erica's arm. "You're hurt, Eri, no one told me that you were injur—"

"It's a deep scratch—nothing more."

The room grew silent.

"You saved my daughter's life." Christina came up to Erica and gently lifted Erica's hand to her face.

The years had been generous to Christina. Her eyes were still the same light blue, but she now wore twenty-five pounds she didn't have so many years ago. Erica did a quick calculation and realized that Christina had just turned fifty-five. To Erica, the only sign of age was the silver strands that sparkled in her hair. Erica wanted to run her fingers through the silver but stopped herself. She removed her hand from Christina's and walked to the door.

"How can I thank you?" Christina's eyes pleaded with Erica to stay.

"You can leave me alone." Erica's words were barely a whisper.

The door closed with a crisp swoosh of air.

two

A Lover's touch, a soft Caress –
the Dance of Lust, becomes Possessed;
Sighs fuel passion, a deep Embrace –
Twelve hours lost, a Life erased.

A crown of Light, a sea of Blue –
a Lightning mark, a darker Hue;
A brush of Air, lips of Fire –
a fragile heart, flame Desire.

The Mist betrays, and hides the Fool –
the Curse begins, adhere the Rule;
Beware the Kiss, Beware the Time –
on Hallow's Eve, your Soul is Mine.

The words to the curse seeped into Erica's dream. In her sleep, she kicked the covers off trying to run away from all that haunted her. Her dream was a mixture of disturbing images – her parents' death, Tayler's assailant and Christina's return. A knife flew from the depth of her nightmare. Bright red blood oozed from its silver blade. To escape it, Erica rolled to her left and on to her wounded arm.

"Arrgh!" Her eyes shot open.

Confused and disoriented, her eyes searched the room. It took her a moment to remember that she was back in her own bedroom. The desperate nights of Spain were replaced with a quiet Minnesota morning. She propped herself up with a second pillow and tried to ignore the pain in her arm and the agony in her heart. The silk nightshirt she wore clung to her, soaked with perspiration and tears.

The clock on the nightstand told her that she had slept for only two hours. It was seven o'clock in the morning. The bottle of painkillers Susan Evans had given her sat next to the clock untouched. She reached for it but her hand froze in midair. Underneath the bottle was the paper containing the curse. Erica shivered and pulled the blankets to her chin. Then she remembered that she had retrieved the yellowed paper from the balcony that morning and had put it on the dresser.

"How did it get over here?" Erica held her breath until she heard a knock on the door. She exhaled, "Come in."

"Good morning, boss," a woman with too much make-up, curly brown hair and large glasses walked in. "How's your arm?"

"Candace, what are you doing here?" Erica asked surprised to see her assistant and friend Candace Lanear.

"I thought I'd deliver the morning paper," Candace waved the newspaper and threw it on the bed. "So, how's your arm?"

"It's pretty sore. Good thing I'm right-handed."

Candace noticed the bottle of pain medication. "Why don't you stay home and rest today?"

"I can't. I've got too much to do before I leave again." Erica ran her fingers through her hair. "Okay, so who called you for information?"

"Your attorney, at least ten different television and radio stations, Detective Steffan, Ana and Ev — who made me promise to keep you home."

"I know I should and I'd love to, but it's a luxury I can't afford right now."

"Erica," Candace looked at the suitcases on the floor, "Did you find any clues to the stanzas in Spain?"

Erica shook her head. "I've lost so much time. It's already

the end of August and I've only got two months left."

"Do you think it's wise for you go to Greece?" Candace squinted and adjusted her glasses.

"I've got to go. I have to find someone to help me decipher the curse." Erica's words filled the room with an overwhelming sense of sadness.

"Ana doesn't seem to be doing much," Candace folded her arms. The past twelve years she had watched her friend struggle for freedom. As Halloween approached, she knew Erica was right—there just wasn't enough time. "She's the one responsible for all this."

"Candace, please," Erica held up her good hand. "There are moments I'm so angry all I can do is cry." She let her hand fall to the bed. "But, my life would be even emptier if Ana weren't in it."

"Love! How many civilizations, nations and good people have been destroyed because of love?" Candace held up Erica's bloodied shirt.

"It's greed that rips us apart, love puts us back together."

"Someone should tell that to Raven." Candace faced Erica. "What can I do for you?"

"You already did it," Erica smiled and picked up the folded newspaper. "I'll just have a cup of coffee, read the paper and be on my way. I'm already late."

Candace watched Erica's smile disappear.

Greeted by her own image on the front page Erica grimaced. "When in the world did they take this?" The color photo showed Erica getting out of the ambulance. Her hair was wet and her clothes were covered with blood.

"Oh, you know how the public loves stories of heroism." Candace offered. "Actually, it's not a bad picture of you. God knows I've seen some doozies."

Erica read the first three paragraphs and threw the newspaper on the bed. "I hate the inconvenience of this thing," she said trying to maneuver her arm in the sling. Giving up she held it out to Candace. "Would you help me?"

"Sure." Candace replied helping Erica out of bed. "Yuck, your pajamas are soaked."

"I know." Erica looked down at the crumpled nightshirt. Without raising her eyes she walked toward the bathroom. "Oh, before I forget. Would you remind me to order some flowers for Tayler? I'll be stopping by the hospital tonight after I'm done at the office." Near the bathroom door Erica stopped and leaned her head on the frame.

"You need help," Candace said.

"I need a miracle," Erica countered.

"You can be so damn stubborn." Candace loudly exhaled. "Would you like me to get Ana on the phone for you?"

Erica nodded. "Candace, if any reporters call while I'm in the shower, just do your magic, okay?"

"Okay."

The sun had set by the time Erica left her downtown Minneapolis office and headed west on Interstate 394. The twenty-five minute drive to the Mahala Community Medical Center was not enough time to calm her nerves. She hoped to avoid running into Christina.

Christina Windquest.

Though she had tried over the years, Erica was unable to forget her. Christina had been spontaneous, passionate and reckless. She had displayed the touch of a magician—her fingers easing aching muscles and awakening sleeping nerves. Life had been so different then. Erica slid her hand down the steering wheel and put the Jeep Grand Cherokee into fifth gear.

At the age of eighteen, Erica had viewed Christina as a goddess. Now, through the eyes of an older woman, Erica came face-to-face with reality. She was as captivating as Erica remembered, but that morning she had seen Christina—the goddess—as a stunned and frightened mother.

Erica knew she wasn't in love with Christina anymore. The

heart-ripping separation had stopped and the scar that remained was taut with indifference — or so she thought. She had her career, her close friendships with Susan Evans and Ana, and her solitude. Yet, she was very aware of how empty her life had become. What she missed most was the closeness and the intimacy of love. For too long she had lived without a lover's touch — not because she wanted to but because she had to, thanks to Raven's curse.

When she reached Tayler's room, Erica stood outside the door for several minutes. She took a deep breath and let it out slowly, raised her hand to knock but stopped. She tried again. After a number of attempts she gave up and turned to leave.

"Oh, hello," a nurse walked out of the room with a tray of medical supplies. "I'm finished. Please go right in."

"It's okay. I think I've missed visiting hours," Erica took several steps.

"No, no. I think Ms. Windquest would really like to see you. She's been asking about you, Ms. Laird."

For a moment Erica wondered how this woman knew who she was, but then remembered the article and photograph in the morning's paper. The nurse disappeared down the hall. Erica entered the room and walked to the side of the bed.

"Hello, Tayler, I'm your absentee landlady."

"Ms. Kirsten-Laird, it's a pleasure to finally meet you." Tayler's formal greeting was just above a whisper. She extended her hand to Erica.

Aware of Tayler's rib injuries, Erica avoided shaking Tayler's hand and held it instead. She was surprised to hear Tayler address her by her legal name. Most often, people referred to Erica by her father's last name, Laird, rather than her legal hyphenated name, Kirsten-Laird.

"I'm sorry it took so long for me to introduce myself."

"I think your introduction was perfectly timed," Tayler grinned.

Erica noticed the slight blush in Tayler's cheeks. "How are you feeling?"

"Much better." Tayler's voice was hoarse and scratchy.

"Thank you for the roses. They're beautiful."

"You're most welcome." Erica let go of Tayler's hand and put her purse on a chair. She noticed the colorful array of flowers that decorated the room. The long-stemmed red roses she had sent stood in an elegant porcelain vase on the table next to the bed. She removed a rose. "Have you thought about opening a floral shop with all these plants and flowers?" Erica asked holding the flower to her nose and taking in the sweet, sweet fragrance.

Tayler watched as the dimples on each side of Erica's mouth deepened. She pulled the blankets up around her. "I'm sending them to the children's unit first thing in the morning, but I'm keeping the roses."

"Why?"

"Because children love flowers."

"I meant, why are you keeping the roses?" Erica slowly rolled the stem between her thumb and index finger.

"They're my favorite flower." Tayler closed her eyes for a moment and then opened them. "My father used to give me a rose whenever I was sad or hurt."

"I would imagine he didn't give you many roses then," Erica inquired.

"Actually, I got quite a few."

Tayler's eyes were as blue as her mother's, but unlike Christina's, Tayler's possessed a translucence—like the blue coastal waters of Puerto Arista. Erica lowered her gaze and focused on Tayler's bruised neck. She could see several black stitches peeking out of the bandage. In the light of the sterile hospital room, Tayler's oval face and high cheekbones were a combination of strength and gentleness. Her age was difficult to estimate, but Erica guessed she was in her late twenties—a young age for a Pulitzer Prize winner.

"Thanks for your help last night." Tayler said softly. "I'm so sorry you got hurt."

Erica nodded.

"Mother told me that you two are old friends."

"Hm, yes. I met your mother quite a long time ago." Erica wondered how much Christina had shared with Tayler about their past.

"It's weird because I don't recall mother ever mentioning your name to me before."

Erica forced herself to smile. "I'm not surprised. We lost touch with each other."

She drifted off recalling the night she had first met Christina. Her rusted Mustang had broken down on a back road south of Minneapolis. Christina drove by, stopped, and offered her a ride. They meant to go to a gas station for help, but they never made it. That night Christina opened her house and her arms to Erica.

"Are you okay?" The low voice brought her back to the present.

"I'm sorry. Yes, I'm fine," Erica rubbed her temple. Her cheeks burned.

"When I'm released, do you think we could we get together and talk?"

"I—" Erica looked out into the dark night. "I don't think it would be—"

"Please, you saved my life." Tayler struggled to sit up. "At least let me take you out to dinner or something."

The overhead light behind Tayler's blond hair created the effect of a crown. Erica stared at the image. "All right, but only when you feel up to it," she said exhaling slowly.

A lone figure stood watching them from the doorway. Christina stepped out of the shadows. "Am I interrupting?" She asked as she walked to the opposite side of Tayler's bed.

"Hi, Mom. Look who's here."

"Darling, how are you?" Christina leaned over and kissed Tayler on the cheek. "Hello, Erica, it's nice to see you again." The level of tension rose sharply as the two former lovers faced each other. Christina avoided looking directly at Erica. She was still feeling the sting from the words Erica spoke several hours earlier.

"Hello, Christina." Erica picked up her purse. "I should be going." She looked down at Tayler and tried to smile, but the attempt failed.

"But you just got here," Tayler tugged on the hospital bracelet around her wrist.

"Erica needs to rest too, dear." Christina laid her hand on Tayler's shoulder then looked at Erica. "I'll be right back. I'm going to walk Erica down the hall."

Erica handed Tayler the rose.

"I was so surprised to see you this morning. I thought you moved to London." Erica said fumbling for her keys.

"I came back to Minneapolis a short while ago."

They continued to walk down the hall in silence. When they reached the entrance, Christina reached out her hand and stopped Erica. "You're still angry, Eri."

Erica found Christina's directness and the use of her old nickname unsettling. She tried not to look at Christina, but the magnetism Christina exuded made it too difficult. Her indifference turned to anger. "You left me," she said with dry bitterness.

"I never meant to hurt you."

"But you did," Erica retorted knowing she sounded like a spoiled child. "I tried to find out what happened, but you wouldn't even return my calls. I drove by your house—you were never there."

"I'm sorry, Eri, but I had to leave. I feared that if we went further I'd never be able to let you go."

"That was really nice of you, Christina," Erica replied hotly, "but I wasn't going anywhere."

"Yes, you were. That's exactly my point," Christina stopped and leaned against the wall. She was shaking. The tiny lines under her eyes deepened. She bit her lower lip. "You became my obsession. I wanted you with me for the rest of my life."

"And that's what I wanted."

"Oh, Eri, it was never that simple. You had just turned eighteen and were on your way to college. You wanted to spend your time in the library and I wanted to spend my time in Paris, the Caribbean—anywhere. I couldn't stand the thought of only seeing you on the weekends. I was too old for that. I just didn't know how to bridge the years between us. It wouldn't have worked. Don't you see?"

Christina's words tore at Erica's heart. She knew Christina was right. "I do now, but I didn't back then."

"I'm so sorry. I was only doing what I thought best."

Erica turned toward the door. "So, why didn't you tell me you had a daughter?"

Christina looked out the door into the dark night. When she looked back at Erica there were tears in her eyes. "It's such a long, complicated story." Christina searched Erica's face for compassion. "If you can give me a little time I can try to explain."

"Time is something I don't have right now, Christina." Erica struggled to find the words, any words, to explain the hell she was living—but there were none. Every moment she lived the curse drew closer.

"I have to go." At her car, Erica leaned her head against the door and clenched her fist. "Damn you, Raven. Why don't you make a move?"

three

"I don't understand why you created this foundation," Erica's accountant said fidgeting with his pen, "but your dad was the same way. I think he gave to every charity in town. You're a lot like him."

"I'm not sure that's a compliment, Tony. He had a size 13 shoe." Erica smiled at the gray-haired man sitting across the desk from her.

"I...I meant to say that you have his generosity and genuine concern for people," Tony Fittipaldi blushed. "Your dad and I were roommates in college."

Erica nodded. She had heard this story a number of times before, but nonetheless, loved the mood of reverie the discussion created.

"He was a bright student and a tremendous athlete. He was a handsome boy — tall, muscular and lean, dark brown hair, blue eyes — I practically had to be his bodyguard. The girls wouldn't leave him alone. At first I couldn't figure out why he didn't date. Then I realized that Weston was shy. By the end of our senior year, your dad wasn't acting like himself. I told him to see a doctor, but he said what he had no doctor could cure." Tony scratched his head.

"What was wrong with him?"

"Rebecca Kirsten—your mother," Tony laughed. "She was the most incredible woman I have ever known." He peered out the window lost in his memories. "The night your parents died I headed to the nearest bar. I had lost my boss and best friend, and the woman I would've married if your dad hadn't married her first.

"You take after your mother," Tony continued. "You got her dark brown eyes, cheekbones and figure. I couldn't help but fall in love with her." Tony smiled sheepishly. "Your parents were so sad when they were told they'd never be able to have children, but they never gave up hope. The day you were born your dad was so happy he gave everyone in the company the day off. He was so proud. A fine man to work for—your dad. What a tragic end to a fairy tale love story." He wiped his eyes on a white handkerchief.

"I know you were a good friend to my parents, Tony."

"Well, anyway, I guess I've taken enough of your time," Tony stood. "I really just came up to have you look over these reports on the merger and to sign this check."

"Why didn't you sign it?" Erica raised an eyebrow.

"Because the bank needs your signature on this amount." Tony handed the check to Erica.

The quizzical expression on Erica's face froze. She stared at the check.

"Is something wrong?" Tony stood and switched from one foot to the other. When she didn't respond he added, "I know you're busy. Why don't I just come back later?" He started to remove the check from Erica's hand.

"No. No, it's okay, Tony."

Erica's hand shook as she signed her name. The normally healthy color in her face turned a ghostly white. When she finished, Erica snapped the cap back on her pen and laid it down on the desk. "There. That should do it for another year."

"Thanks, Erica." Tony took the check, collected his things

and turned to leave.

"Oh, Tony, before I forget, I'm meeting with my attorney this afternoon to have my will updated." She saw the concern in his eyes.

"You're not ill are you, Erica?"

"No, but I suppose my timing is pretty poor considering we were just talking about my parents. I'm sorry. It's just that I want you to oversee the financial arrangements for this charity. It's very important to me that their work continue." Erica rubbed her eyes.

"You're not—" Tony blushed, "I thought your dad was ill until he told me he had fallen in love. You're not in love are you?"

"Oh heavens, no." Erica rose from her desk and walked Tony to the door.

"You know, your dad waited for the right woman to come along. Maybe you're just waiting for the right man."

Erica smiled. "It's an interesting thought, Tony. Thanks for stopping in." She shut the door and leaned against it.

With her eyes closed she fought against the memory of Patricia Locksley's senseless death. The guilt she still felt scorched like white hot steel. Her tears burned with remorse. She grabbed a tissue from a nearby table and blew her nose, walked to the window and looked down at the world fifty floors below. From her south window, Erica could see the lakes—Calhoun, Harriet, Nokomis and Lake of the Isles. She longed to be outside enjoying the weather, but the sands of time were running out—just as they had for Patricia Locksley.

The Patricia Locksley Foundation was a charity she had established in honor of an innocent woman who had been brutally murdered—twelve hours after she and Erica had made love. Raven's curse went immediately into effect and had a fatal implication for Patricia.

She looked down at her hands, but all she could see was the emptiness they held—all because of Raven, the evil enchantress who had seduced Ana and made Erica's love for Ana a sheer mockery. Raven, the green-eyed demon who had trapped Erica's life in her cold, jealous heart. No matter what end of the earth

Erica ran to, she could not escape what Ana had done.

Erica walked back to her desk and looked around the room. Her office was elegantly furnished with a large mahogany desk, rich shades of blue fabric on the cloth furniture, and silver lamps and picture frames. She placed her hands on the desk and closed her eyes. With increasing horror, Erica feared she would lose all that she had created in the loving memory of her parents.

The Kirsten-Laird Architectural and Design Company was known worldwide, and Erica had a reputation for designing buildings that were not only breathtaking, but also sensitive to and protective of the environment. She was both a gifted architect and an intuitive diplomat.

Her success in business caused problems of their own. When *The San Francisco Chronicle* made the mistake of publishing an article with readers' responses to their idea about a dream date with "the country's most eligible female architect," however, she was livid. The newspaper published the letters of the top three responses. In public Erica laughed, but in private she was outraged. She threatened to cancel all of her projects and charitable donations in the state of California. The governor, an old friend of Erica's father, ordered the paper to print an apology. As a goodwill gesture, Erica had dinner with each of the three contest winners. Patricia Locksley was one of the winners.

The dinner with Patricia couldn't have come at a worse time in Erica's life. She had just learned that Ana had slept with Raven. In her hurt and anger, Erica had refused to talk to Ana, Ev or anyone else about Ana's betrayal. No one was able to warn her about the curse. Recklessly, she acted out her anger by sleeping with Patricia.

When Patricia was found in an alley with her heart removed, Erica went to the police, but they sent her home. If the press found out the real reason why Patricia Locksley died, Erica knew they would prey upon her like vultures. This terrifying fear drove Erica from the spotlight. In the rational world of the '90s, few people believed in curses, but Erica knew differently and vowed to never be sexual again. She could not and would not let Raven claim another victim.

To cope with Patricia's death, Erica began to funnel her business profits back into the communities where her projects were located. She created jobs, contributed to educational programs, funded the arts, and did hours of volunteer work. But her professional and volunteer work could not replace the one thing she wished for the most—to share her life with the "right" woman. Time was running out and she had to destroy the curse before she became Raven's next victim.

"Help me—" she whispered, raking her fingers through her thick black hair.

The intercom buzzed.

"Erica," it was Candace, "I hate to bother you but Christina Windquest is on the line for you. It's the fifth time she's called this morning. Do you want me to keep stalling?"

"No, I'll take it Candace, thanks." After taking a deep breath, Erica pushed the button down. "Christina, what can I do for you?"

"Eri, I really need to talk with you."

"You've caught me at a really busy time, Christina. I can't take the—"

"I know you don't want to see me and I've given you good reason not to. I can't change what I've done and I know I can't apologize enough," Christina paused. "At least give me the chance to repair some of the damage. Please?"

"It doesn't matter anymore. Let's leave the past in the past." Erica wished she felt as strong as her words. She drummed a pencil on the desk.

"It does matter. It matters to me and I believe it matters to you, too."

"It's too bad it didn't matter to you eighteen years ago." The pencil snapped.

"I didn't call to fight, Eri. I'm asking for a chance to explain my actions. I don't want to go to my grave with this dagger in my heart."

Erica winced at Christina's choice of words. "All right. When?"

"How about lunch tomorrow?"

"I can't. I'm leaving for Greece in the morning."

"When will you be back?"

"In three or four weeks."

"Is there any chance you could meet me today for lunch?"

Silence filled the air as Erica brought up her calendar on the computer. She frowned at the canceled lunch appointment. "I've got an hour from two to three, but that's all. Where do you want to meet?"

"How about the downtown Hilton?" Christina paused, "Cafe Vienna?"

"Okay. I'll see you at two o'clock."

"Erica?"

"Yes, Christina?" The line hummed as Erica waited for Christina to continue.

"Thank you."

"Good afternoon, Ms. Laird, please follow me," the hostess led Erica through the crowded restaurant to a secluded table in the corner.

Erica smiled in an attempt to hide her nervousness. "Hello, Christina," she sat quickly to prevent her knees from buckling.

Christina reached across the table and wrapped Erica's hands in a fragrant embrace. Her pale lavender suit flowed over her well-pampered body. Her nails were freshly manicured. Perched on her left hand was a one-carat diamond ring with rows of diamond baguettes. It glittered in the sunlight streaming through the floor-length windows.

"Thanks for meeting me." Christina looked directly into Erica's eyes. "It's been a long time. How are you?"

"I'm fine. And you?" Erica placed the napkin on her lap and took a drink from her water goblet.

"I'd be great if that insane psycho who attacked Tayler had been caught." The formality of their conversation unnerved Christina. She fixed her gaze on Erica's hands and her long, slender fingers. "You have the hands of an artist." She sighed. "Tayler does too."

"When can she leave the hospital?"

"Tomorrow. I spoke with her this morning, but she seemed rather preoccupied. I guess I can't blame her with all that she's been through."

"Is she going to be staying with you while she recovers?"

Christina laughed. "That's the last thing she'd want to do — she wants to go home." Her blue eyes widened. "I must admit that it gave me a start when she told me she was renting a house from you."

"Why?"

"Well," Christina paused, "it's just that she's one of the reasons I ended our relationship. And now, she's the reason we're here — " Their server approached the table interrupting Christina. When they ordered and were alone again, Christina continued. "I was afraid you'd find out I had a daughter."

"Really, why?"

"I thought you'd think I was a horrible mother."

"I don't know why you'd think that." Erica leaned forward and put her chin on her hand.

"You used to talk about your mother a lot. After awhile it got to a point where I wished I could've been the mother she was. But I wasn't." Christina straightened in her chair. "Tayler was such an exceptional child. When she was very young she'd make up stories according to what she saw in her picture books. Her tales were always about some adventure and they always ended happily ever after. Unfortunately, our little family's story ended in divorce."

"Back then you told me very little about your ex-husband. I often wondered why you were so secretive. What happened?"

Christina knotted her napkin. "I lost custody of Tayler because my ex-husband convinced the judge that I was an unfit mother."

"On what grounds?"

"It's all so complicated. I'll try to keep it brief." Christina looked at her watch. When she looked up she found Erica staring at her. "I only wish I had told you this years ago."

"We can't change the past."

"I know, but there are times when I wish we could."

"You're not alone in that wish." Erica's thoughts flew to the curse. She clenched her fist.

"I'm sorry, I didn't mean to upset you." Christina reached across the table and unbent Erica's fingers. "Are you okay?"

"Yes."

"You look so pale." Christina leaned toward Erica.

Her blouse gaped partially revealing a lavender lace bra. Erica looked away and took a deep breath.

"Really, I'm fine. Please go on."

"Well, after Tayler was born I lost all interest in J.T. He sent me to a clinic in Paris where they specialized in treating 'female' sexual problems."

"Really?" Erica's eyes grew wide. The thought of Christina losing interest in sex seemed absurd to her.

"It's amazing what you can find in Paris. But I did realize something while I was there."

"What's that?" Erica asked.

"That my lack of interest was not due to some genetic problem or neuroses. It was due to the fact that I was married to a self-indulged, spoiled little boy," the words came out in a rush. Christina laughed. She relaxed her grip on her napkin and smiled. "While I was being treated at this clinic, I fell in love with my doctor."

"Hm, this is beginning to sound like a Harlequin novel."

Christina lowered her voice. "Ah, but my doctor was female."

"Okay, cancel the novel. Is that why J.T. felt you were an unfit mother?"

"Yes, but first he needed evidence. He had me followed by a private investigator. I must admit this guy got some rather sizzling photos of my activities. They even made me blush." Christina wrinkled her nose. Erica laughed. "The judge awarded custody to J.T. even though I had evidence that he, too, was having an affair."

Their server returned to the table and placed a leafy green salad in front of Erica and a grilled chicken salad before Christina.

When they were alone again Erica asked, "Did you appeal the decision?"

"Yes, but it didn't change things. Unfortunately, the judge believed that I'd recruit my own daughter to my way of life. I believe he used the term 'perverse'." Christina took a sip of her water and took a deep breath. "I even lost all visitation rights."

"I'm sorry."

Christina's laugh was forced. "Through the years, J.T. convinced Tayler that I was some horrible monster. I was really depressed." She paused again as if the words were becoming more difficult to say. "After his death she finally contacted me. Tayler is only six years younger than you. I was old enough to be your mother."

"And that's why you left me."

"As I said the other day, I didn't know how to bridge the years between us. When I saw you the night Tayler was attacked, I knew I had to tell you the truth. I'm so sorry for leaving you the way I did." Christina swirled her fork around in her salad. Finally, she pushed it away unable to eat. "I've never been able to forget you or what I had done to you."

"All these years I thought you ended our relationship for another woman. Had I known that the other woman was your daughter, maybe it would have been easier for me to accept. It's difficult to say." Erica shrugged her shoulders. The pain in Christina's eyes made Erica's heart soften.

"We had wonderful times together, Eri." As Christina took a sip of her water, her hand shook. "In the hospital you told me to leave you alone. I want you to know that I'll respect your wish, but I had to explain. I'll continue to see Tayler, but wouldn't it be easier for you if she didn't live next door?"

"No. Tayler may stay as long as she wishes. I haven't been home very much lately and it's comforting to know she's living next door. I've had a security system installed around the perimeter of the two lots and hired a guard to keep out unwanted visitors." Erica's eyes darkened.

"Tayler was so excited when she found out she'd be renting from you."

"Why?" Statements like this always threw Erica into a spin.

"I think it's called 'awe'." Christina smiled. "Tayler told me the other day that she's been following your career for years. I'm not surprised, really. She's always loved mysteries."

Or a news story, Erica thought to herself. "I don't see myself as mystery."

"Of course you don't, but others do."

Erica shrugged her shoulders again.

"Tayler tells me you donate not only your money but your time to several charities here in the Twin Cities, and that your company contributes to the construction of housing for the poor."

"It sounds like she did her homework." Erica frowned.

Christina reached across the table and held Erica's hand. "She won't expose you, if that's what you're thinking."

Erica withdrew her hand and placed it on her lap. "Christina, I've spent a lot of energy in keeping my personal life out of the media. All I've ever asked is to be respected for what I do at the office, not what I do in my bedroom."

"I understand completely. If it's any reassurance, she'd be exposing me if she exposes you."

"Good point." Erica sat back in her chair.

"She's really not that kind of person. She has a lot of compassion and sensitivity for people. That's why I think she does so well. I know I'm biased, but she's a wonderful woman."

Since the night in Tayler's hospital room, Erica was finding it difficult to forget how blue Tayler's eyes were, or their depth and intensity. She had never seen such beautiful eyes.

"I really need to get going," Erica reached for her purse. "Thank you for lunch and," Erica rose from her chair and walked over to Christina, "thanks for letting me know why you left."

"I'm sorry, Eri." Tears streamed down Christina's face.

Without turning back, Erica walked quickly out of the restaurant. As her car appeared and the attendant jumped out, Erica put on her sunglasses to hide her own tears.

four

The following evening, Christina walked into the house and put her coat and purse on a bench in the foyer. She peered into the living room. The lights had been dimmed for the night. As she turned toward the open staircase she suddenly stopped. The oak banister triggered a long ago memory — a memory she would never forget.

The night Christina first brought Erica to her home seemed so long ago. Erica's car had broken down and Christina had stopped to help. While Erica was in the den talking to her grandparents, Christina leaned on the banister waiting to take Erica to a gas station.

Christina smiled at the memory. She had no intention of seducing an eighteen year old, but when Erica walked into the lighted foyer, a strong magnetic force seemed to draw the two of them together. Erica was as intense as she was beautiful. The old pair of black jeans and her father's leather bomber jacket simply drew attention to Erica's beauty. Her long dark eyelashes, deep brown eyes and dimples made it impossible for Christina to keep from staring. Instead, she stood on the stairs unable to speak.

"I'm ready," Erica walked to the stairs and put her left boot on the lower step. Her hand encircled the newel.

Christina laughed to ease the growing tension.

She recalled how weak and vulnerable she had felt. No one — no woman — had ever caused this type of response. Christina tried to control the trembling that seemed to start at her feet, but she knew if she didn't have the banister's support, she would have fallen to her knees. She watched Erica slowly unzip her jacket without removing it. She simply pushed it aside and put her right hand on her hip. The grandfather clock in the hall chimed the hour — it was eleven o'clock.

Christina glanced at the clock in an effort to steady her voice. "The gas station is probably closed by now."

"I really should be going." Erica didn't move.

"You can take my car —" Christina held out her keys, but when Erica reached out for them, Christina dropped them down her blouse, "if you dare."

Erica slipped out of her jacket and let it drop down to the floor. She then unbuttoned her cuffs and rolled up her sleeves. When she was done she raised her eyes slowly until her face was only inches from Christina's. Her voice was a whisper. "Never say 'dare' to the hungry."

Her hand felt cool against Christina's hot, feverish skin. The keys were removed but were now somewhere on the floor. Christina caught Erica's hand as it emerged from her blouse and brought it to her lips. She placed light, airy kisses on Erica's wrist and hand. One by one, Christina took Erica's fingers into her mouth. Her tongue encircled each finger and as she gently sucked them, Erica moaned. Christina smiled as Erica lowered herself on to the steps.

The memory, even eighteen years later, still caused shivers to run up Christina's spine. She knew that Erica's passion for making love was only matched by her passion for life. As she walked to the den, Christina was troubled. Though many years had elapsed between them, she sensed that Erica was running away from something. The thought made Christina sad.

"Mother?" The voice startled Christina. She turned to find Tayler sitting in the shadows of the den. "Are you okay?"

"Oh, hello dear. I thought you'd be in bed by now." Christina shivered. "Is Catherine upstairs already?" she asked about her partner.

"Yes. She said she'd wait up for you."

"Well, I'd better turn in." Christina looked back at the staircase.

"Mother," Tayler paused, "You look like you've seen a ghost."

"I did." Christina walked past Tayler to the bar and poured herself a drink. She couldn't see Tayler's eyes hidden in the late night shadows. "It's been a long day. You should be in bed."

"I couldn't sleep." Tayler sighed. "Every noise in the house makes me jump."

"Would you like me to sit up with you?" Christina took a sip. The brandy slid down her throat and warmed her stomach.

"No, but I think I'll go home tomorrow. Would you drive me home in the morning?"

Christina nodded.

"Are you sure you're okay? You look really pale." Tayler got up from her chair and walked over to her mother. "I've never seen you have a drink this late."

Christina sat down in a chair but said nothing. She took another swallow from the glass.

"Catherine told me you had lunch with Erica yesterday. Was it difficult for you to see her again—I mean, is she your ghost?"

Christina tilted her head back and looked at the ceiling. "Oh, I think it's a combination of my moving back here and your being attacked by some weirdo. I was shocked to learn it was Erica who rescued you."

Tayler hesitated, "You were lovers, weren't you?"

Christina took another swallow of her brandy before answering. "Yes."

"I shouldn't be surprised but I am. She's very beautiful," Tayler added.

"Yes, she is. And she seems to have grown more so."

"Are you still in love with her?"

The room grew quiet while Christina tried to find the right words. She had never talked to Tayler about the women in her life, even Catherine, whom Tayler adored. She had been too afraid that Tayler would not approve of her lovers or friends.

"I don't know if you can understand this, Tayler, but Erica's a difficult woman to forget." Christina looked at her drink.

"Did she leave the relationship or did you?"

"I left." Christina saw the surprise on Tayler's face. "I was too set in my ways. What I wanted and what I got were two very different things. Erica was young and just starting to sample life's delicacies." Christina tried a weak laugh. "I wanted someone to be there for me—night and day. And, I was beyond making out in the library."

Tayler raised an eyebrow. "I happen to find libraries very appealing."

"Leave it to a writer." Christina laughed.

"Is her lifestyle the reason why she's so private about her personal affairs?"

"Probably. Like other women in her position, she has a lot to lose if her personal life were to become public knowledge."

"But don't you think it makes more sense to 'come out' and fight for what you believe is so natural?"

"Absolutely, but I don't want to start receiving death threats because of who and what I am." Christina got up and poured herself another drink.

"When I found out that I would be renting from Erica I thought I'd learn more about her. But she's never home." Tayler squinted her eyes.

"Darling, Erica is an enigma. She's the type of woman who you'll never really fully understand. She's elusive and she prefers it that way."

"But it's that very quality that makes such a great story."

Christina's eyes grew wide. "You're not going to do a feature on her for your magazine, are you?"

"It would sell a lot of magazines."

Christina got up from her chair and walked over to where her daughter was sitting. "Tayler, let me give you some advice. Keep Erica as your friend because you don't want her as your enemy." She raised her index finger. "Hurt her and she'll haunt you the rest of your life."

"I'm teasing, Mother. I had no plans to do a story on her. Although I know many writers who'd love the chance."

"I feel sorry for the writer who tries." Christina walked across the room and put her glass down on the bar. "There's more to Erica than even I could ever imagine."

"She is definitely one of the most intriguing people I've ever met." Tayler said more to herself than to her mother. "As I said in the hospital, I've done a lot of research on her—or maybe I should say on what I could find out about her. She reminds me of a crystal."

"A crystal?" Christina searched her daughter' face. "Why?"

"Years ago, Father gave me a crystal for my birthday. I still have it. Anyway, when you take a crystal away from the light it basically reflects the things surrounding it. But when you shine light through it, a crystal reflects a rainbow of colors." Tayler paused. "I used to get out of bed at night and hold the crystal up to my eye. The moonlight created a brilliant background."

"I'm not sure I'm following you. So, why does she remind you of a crystal?"

"As beautiful as crystals are, they're also cold and lifeless. But they can also be extremely dangerous. If you hold a crystal at the right angle it can start a fire."

Christina noticed a strange look in Tayler's eyes. "In that, dear, you're right. Erica can seem cold at times, but I think that's a defense for her. She can also be extremely confident and self-assured. She's always been able to read people like an x-ray machine." Christina smiled remembering people's reactions to Erica. "I think that's why people are both intensely attracted to her and immensely fearful of her. She's black velvet personified—soft and secretive."

"I take it that she didn't agree with your decision to end the relationship." Tayler said. "She seems to still be holding a grudge."

"After our lunch yesterday I can only hope she'll understand and accept what happened." Christina waved her hand uncertainly.

"Has seeing her again made you wonder if you made a mistake?"

"No, I still stand behind my decision. We did, however, have some fun times." Christina cocked her head to the side. "Oh, Tayler, all I can hope is that some day she'll find what she's searching for and stop running around. I can't believe it's all because I left her. I'm good but I'm not that good." Christina threw Tayler a seductively evil smile.

"Mother, you're such a tease. Now I know why all those women keep calling. Doesn't that bother Catherine?"

"Catherine knows I'm not about to stray. She trusts me and I wouldn't do anything to endanger that trust."

"I knew I should've gone home tonight." Tayler laughed. "I was beginning to feel like a switchboard operator."

Christina smiled. "It's just my way of getting you back for all those calls from macho high school boys."

"Well, Mom, my phone isn't ringing off the hook anymore." Tayler rubbed her eyes and stretched.

"You're intelligent, successful and you've got your mother's good looks. What man wouldn't want you?"

"I think I've convinced myself that there's something wrong with me. I feel more passion playing the piano than bowling with the boys. Maybe I'm really the crystal." Tayler's voice got softer.

"Are you dangerous?" Christina shook her head. She had made the same comments to herself years ago.

"Only when I'm face-to-face with an adversary—like the tight-lipped source who has the information I need and won't divulge it." Tayler growled.

"Just be careful, okay?" Christina walked toward Tayler and bent down to examine the stitches in Tayler's neck. "There's a nut out there who tried to kill you. Don't give him another chance. And as for Erica, I think I'd focus my attention on something a little more tangible."

"Mother, you make her sound spooky," Tayler chuckled.

"Tayler, I'm serious. Don't tangle with her." Christina stood. "All I want to do is take her out to dinner as a thank you. She saved my life—it's the least I can do."

"Well, you won't be able to for awhile."

"Why not?" Tayler asked.

"She left for Greece this morning." Christina replied.

"How long will she be gone?" The smile on Tayler's face disappeared.

"A month." Christina helped Tayler from her chair. "Darling, please be careful—especially around Erica. Her beauty and charm create a seductive appeal. You'll get hurt if you're not careful."

"Mother, come on, now she sounds like a witch who goes about casting love spells."

"She is a witch," Christina's words echoed in the quiet room.

"Well, I guess I'd rather be under the power of a love spell than that of a curse." Tayler chuckled again.

Christina's expression did not change.

"Did she place a spell on you?" Tayler's eyes teased.

"Yes." She saw Tayler roll her eyes. "I know you don't believe me. Listen, I've known many women in my days and none, including Catherine, have obsessed me more."

"Oh, Mother, how can you believe such baloney? This is ridiculous. I can't believe that an educated, intelligent woman like you would believe such nonsense."

"It's true, Tayler," Christina sighed. "Hours turned into weeks and years trying to forget her."

"That's quite an accusation. Do you have proof?"

"Erica is a member of a coven." Christina shook her head as she spoke.

"How do you know this?"

"I have my sources, dear."

"Oh, Mother, this is absurd. I'm going to bed." Tayler shook her head and got up from her chair. "The next thing you're going to tell me she wears a decoder ring and has a secret handshake." She turned toward the door almost colliding with Catherine. "Oh, Catherine, excuse me."

"Where are you flying off to in such a hurry?" Catherine asked.

"I need to consult the Ouija board," Tayler's laughter filled the hall. "I have this sense that life is about to get really strange."

five

"You look tired this morning," Jane Fischer, Tayler's editor, sat across the table from Tayler.

"I feel tired." Tayler took a sip from her coffee cup. She wrinkled her nose.

"I know it's strong but you looked like you could use the boost. You haven't been sleeping, have you?"

Tayler shook her head. "It's been a month since the attack and I still feel edgy."

"I take it the security system and full-time guard isn't helping?" Jane was trying not to stare at the dark red, jagged scar on Tayler's neck. "You know you can stay with me. I've got plenty of room."

"Thanks, but I've got to learn to deal with this whole thing. Otherwise, I'll be running from every shadow and stranger I meet. I can't live my life like that." Tayler stretched her arms. "Dad never let this stuff stop him. He taught me to look danger in the face and then act—very, very quickly."

"Do you want to lie down?"

"No, that's okay." Tayler eyed the pile of correspondence on the table. She cleared her throat. "And stop staring at me. We've known each other for a long time, but you're looking at me like I'm some aberration."

"I still think you sound like Kim Carnes." Jane watched Tayler roll her eyes. "Hey, what woman wouldn't want your low, sexy voice?"

"And you look like Amy Grant with red hair." Tayler retorted. She often teased Jane that she could be Amy Grant's double, except for the voice. Jane couldn't carry a tune.

Dr. Evans had told her that the low, strained texture of her voice might be permanent and that only rest could help her vocal cords heal. But Tayler wasn't resting. She, in fact, had increased her work hours. She almost never made it home before midnight, was up by four most mornings, and worked weekends.

"Are you ready?" Tayler cleared her throat again and looked at the first assignment. "I think further research is needed on this one. It could turn into a great series. There are too many barbaric practices going on in third world countries." Tayler handed the file to Jane. She opened another file and began to read. "Oh, this is interesting." Her grin was malicious.

"I'm not sure I like the look on your face." Jane leaned forward. "What's up?"

"What would you think if I did a feature on matriarchal societies for the January issue?"

"Interesting. What's the angle?"

Tayler leaned back in her chair. "How about the reactions of men living in this type of society?" Tayler squinted while she concentrated. "You know, sort of a sex reversal thing. What are the parallels between matriarchal and patriarchal cultures? How do these men cope?"

"Do you want a male or female team to work with you on this?" Jane asked jotting down notes.

Tayler paused. "Actually, let's wait. I'd like to personally look into this first."

"Well, it'd be a good excuse for you to get out of here for a while." Jane lowered her voice. "At least until things die down."

"I'm not sure I like your choice of words." Tayler shuddered.

"God, Tayler, I'm sorry—I," Jane shook her red curls. She drummed her fingernails on the glass table top.

"It's okay," Tayler replied. She went back to the story. "Do you think it's a crazy idea?"

"No. Sometimes your suggestions are out to lunch but not crazy," Jane gave Tayler a reassuring smile. "Oh, I'm glad you mentioned lunch."

"Did I?"

"You haven't forgotten about the awards luncheon today at noon."

"Damn, that's right. Well, I guess I'd better dig in then."

As a writer for *The Narrator*, a biweekly national magazine, Tayler frequently attended award lunches and dinners for colleagues and friends. Today's lunch was different though—this time she was the guest of honor.

It took nearly two hours to go through the list of story possibilities. At the bottom of the files was a manila envelope. Tayler gave Jane a puzzled look. It was stamped "Personal and Confidential." She ripped it open and removed the single sheet of paper. As Tayler read the contents the color drained from her face.

"What's wrong?"

Tayler squeezed the bridge of her nose between her thumb and index finger. "It's a death threat."

"What?" Jane jumped up from her chair. A confused expression spread over her face. "You haven't written anything lately that would cause such a response."

"I think it has more to do with the attack." Tayler's hand shook as she laid the letter down on the desk. She rose from her chair and walked to the window in her office.

"Should I call security?" Jane's eyes followed Tayler.

"No. I'll call Detective Steffan."

"In my opinion he's been really ineffective in the case so far. Maybe you should think about hiring a private detective. You know, 'B' is for 'Bungle'."

"Is that a new Sue Grafton mystery?" Tayler tried to laugh.

"Very funny." Jane walked up to Tayler and put her hands on Tayler's upper arms. "I don't want anything to happen to you. I kinda like working with you."

"I'll call Steffan, okay?"

"Okay. Is there anything else I can do?"

"Yeah. Would you call Dayton's and order me a bullet proof bra in a 46D — I think that will work very nicely. Then I'll be protected and have a place to keep my Kleenex and pocket thesaurus." She smiled weakly.

"Why don't you forget about your luncheon today."

"And not give my inspiring, sensational acceptance speech? No way."

"Do you want me to go along?"

"No. Just order the bra and I'll be fine." Tayler watched as Jane shut the door shaking her head. She returned to her desk and picked up the letter.

> *"The Flames are hot, and fuel the Fear —*
> *a Storm at bay, clouds disappear;*
> *A gift of Black, to kill the Fool —*
> *a frightened Soul, a Game so cruel.*
>
> *The Cave is dark, the Air is thin —*
> *the Night is long, your Life will Dim;*
> *Beware the Kiss, Beware the Time —*
> *on Hallow's Eve, your Blood is Mine."*

six

When Tayler arrived at the Hilton Hotel and entered the grand ballroom, she was amazed to see so many familiar faces. Of the five hundred women in attendance, Tayler recognized local and national newsmakers, leaders in the health care field, lawyers, lobbyists, bankers and business executives, artists, writers and social welfare advocates. She anxiously searched the room for Erica, certain that Erica Kirsten-Laird was a member of this eclectic group. Unable to find her, Tayler wondered, for the millionth time, when Erica would return from Greece.

"Tayler, it's nice to see you again." Dr. Susan Evans met Tayler at the door and gave her a hug.

"Dr. Evans, what a nice surprise," Tayler returned Susan Evans' affectionate hug. Without her white lab coat, Susan Evans reminded Tayler of the absent-minded doctor. Her wool jacket looked one size too large, dwarfing the good doctor in a sea of dark chocolate material.

"You look absolutely wonderful." Ev ran her eyes over Tayler's stylish red suit and draped white blouse. Her long blond hair was pulled back and held in place with a silver clip. "Let me take look at that scar." Ev tilted Tayler's head back.

While Tayler was in the hospital, she had the opportunity to learn more about Dr. Susan Evans. She had graduated from Harvard Medical School with honors and did her residency at a clinic in Harlem. As a general practitioner, Ev preferred the chaos of the emergency room over the expensive suites of private practice. Ev had grown up in south Minneapolis and had lived next door to Erica's family.

"Erica and I have known each other for so long." Ev had told Tayler. "We tease each other that we were twins separated at birth."

Tayler laughed at the memory. Dr. Susan Evans and Erica Kirsten-Laird were complete opposites in looks. "So what's your professional opinion, Doctor?" Tayler returned to the present.

"Well, I must say I did a fine job." Ev lightly touched the scar with her finger. "It's a bit red but it should lighten with time. There aren't a lot of people who can sport a lightning bolt like you can." Ev smiled and then frowned.

"What's wrong?"

"It just occurred to me that you might be starting a new craze."

Tayler saw a twinkle in Ev's eyes. "What do you mean?"

"I can just see large numbers of women coming into my office wanting the Windquest 'lightning bolt' look." As Ev and Tayler laughed two women walked past them.

"I told you she was busy. Look, she's even doing medical examinations at award lunches," said one of the women.

"I've often wondered how Elizabeth puts up with it," the other woman said in a caustic tone. "Rumor has it she takes her patients along with her on their romantic evenings."

"That's disgusting," replied the first woman.

Ev turned. "Very cute you two. I happen to be conversing with our guest of honor. Tayler Windquest, please meet Channel Seven's anchor, Parris Shepard, and weather forecaster, Diana Ford."

"It's a pleasure to meet you, Tayler," Parris and Diana said in unison. They shook hands with Tayler and exchanged hugs with Ev.

"Ev, how do you rate? Diana and I never get to sit with our attractive guests of honor," Parris pouted. "We always get left out."

"Hey, speaking of being left out, Ev, is Erica back yet?" Diana looked around the room.

"Not yet but, hopefully, soon." Ev called over her shoulder. She ushered Tayler to the head table.

While she sat in her chair, Tayler was surprised by how vulnerable she had been feeling since Erica left. Though she technically had only met her once, Erica had become Tayler's safety net. If Erica was back home, Tayler knew she'd sleep better. It was a strange feeling — and hard to admit — that she missed Erica terribly. The month had gone so slowly since she left for Greece. Tayler had overworked herself to fill the time. She had called Erica's house several times but left no message with the answering service. Late at night, with sleep still hours away, Tayler found herself waiting for a phone call. A phone call that never came.

She even went to a psychic to see what the future held for her.

"Don't be afraid. You'll soon be faced with a series of very serious challenges. Be patient, the knowledge and skills you need will be revealed to you as you deal with each obstacle," the psychic had said. The woman's dark gray eyes rested on Tayler's scar. "Someone wants the power you possess." The woman's final words were, "Before you know who you really are, you will feel the hunger of an empty heart and the flames of a soul on fire. To find love you must first come to know yourself — only then can you face your enemy."

Tayler was skeptical, but the psychic's words followed her continually. She became more fully aware of a buried interest in things strange and unexplainable. She knew that her sudden interest in precious stones, spells and rituals was due in part to her mother's comment about Erica being a witch.

Her thoughts were brought to a abrupt halt when Ev got up from her chair and stood behind the lectern.

"I'd like to welcome you this afternoon to the Crystal Society's annual benefactor's luncheon. I'm Dr. Susan Evans and

I'll be your host for today's award presentation." Ev put on her glasses. Before she could continue, an unknown woman walked up to the dais and whispered something in Ev's ear. Ev nodded and wrote something on a piece of paper. She folded the note and handed it to the woman who immediately left the dais.

"It never fails. Whenever I'm asked to speak there's always someone who wants my autograph." A wave of groans rolled from the back of the audience to the front while Ev's laughter rang through the public address system. "Okay, back to business. Our guest of honor and award recipient has made a profound impact on the lives of the poor in our cities. Through her professional and volunteer efforts, she helped to raise the funds needed to build three hundred homes for single mothers and their families. Mothers have been given educational opportunities to help support their families while child care is provided at facilities located within their neighborhoods for a small fee. Classes and on-the-job training for these mothers are paid for by corporate contributions. This year alone, two hundred and fifty companies have participated." Ev stopped for the applause.

"Follow-up studies have shown that the participants in this project have reduced their welfare and health care costs, reduced their use of alcohol and drugs, and increased their literacy rate and employment level. This project has not only provided families with shelter, but has given three hundred families a place they can call home." The audience's applause thundered through the room.

"The project is named after our guest of honor and is known simply as the 'Windquest Project'." Applause interrupted Ev for the third time. She looked over the crowd and began to conclude her remarks. "We're honored today to have with us two of Minnesota's most gifted women. I'd like to ask Erica Kirsten-Laird to come forward to present the award."

The applause was deafening. From all the hugs and greetings she received, it took several minutes before Erica could make her way to the front of the room. When she reached the dais, Erica warmly hugged Ev who had walked to the edge of the platform to greet her. As Erica walked to the lectern with Ev, she stopped and held out her hand to Tayler.

"Hello, Tayler, I'm happy to see you," Erica's smile was mesmerizing.

Tayler rose slowly from her chair and accepted Erica's hand. The noise in Tayler's head seemed muffled as she stood too stunned to say anything. Erica's hand was warm against her own cool palm. Before she could respond, Ev spoke into the microphone. Tayler took her seat.

"From the look of that tan it appears Greece was exactly what the doctor ordered." Laughter rippled through the audience. "I'd like to officially welcome you back, Erica. You've been missed."

Erica stood behind the lectern, her cheeks red from the attention. She looked directly at Tayler and smiled.

Dazed by Erica's sudden appearance, Tayler struggled to regain her composure. The speech she had so painstakingly memorized came back to her in fragments. Dr. Evans was right, Erica looked absolutely fabulous. The Greek air and sun undeniably had an incredible effect on Erica. Her eyes seemed darker and more mysterious than Tayler had remembered. Against the bronzed skin her teeth shone a brilliant white. Tayler closed her eyes and etched Erica's image in her memory. She never wanted to forget this moment.

"Thank you. It's good to be home," Erica paused. "I have the pleasure of presenting the Crystal Society's highest award to a woman I met only a month ago. With my extensive out-of-the-country traveling these past several years, I'm embarrassed to admit that I had to be updated on Ms. Windquest's activities. Though our first meeting was rather chaotic, I have since come to admire and respect her strength and courage.

"Born in Minnesota but raised in San Diego, California, Tayler Windquest has spread her energy and ambition far and wide. She holds a Master of Fine Arts degree in writing and a Master of Business Administration from Stanford University. She is a member of the President's Literary Council and has received hundreds of awards and citations for her volunteer efforts, and, of course, received the prestigious Pulitzer Prize for outstanding literary achievement." Erica paused, lowered her voice and then slowly said, "It is my pleasure to present to you Ms. Tayler Windquest."

Again the room erupted in applause. Tayler pushed back her chair and stood. As if she were in a trance, Tayler walked toward Erica. When she reached the lectern, Tayler gratefully accepted Erica's hug. She was ill-prepared for the stunning effect Erica's perfume had on her. The exotic fragrance seemed so familiar, but she could not place where she had smelled it before. Her mind swam in the scent.

"Ms. Windquest, I would like to present to you our society's most prestigious honor — the Crystal Award. This award recognizes your commitment and devotion to the 'Windquest Project,' our city's finest endeavor for single parent families in need. Congratulations." Again the room exploded with applause. Erica reached below the lectern and handed the ten-inch crystal pyramid to Tayler. When Erica's eyes noticed the scar on Tayler's neck, her smile froze. Erica took a step backward.

The strange look on Erica's face upset Tayler. She wanted to reach up and cover the red mark with her hand, but gripped the award instead. She turned and approached the microphone.

"I'd like to thank the members of the Society for this incredible honor. The check that you have presented to the Windquest Project will build three new homes and provide an education for as many families — families that would not have this chance without your noble contribution." Applause interrupted Tayler. When it died down, she gave the audience a brief overview of the selection process, the education program and the ten-year strategic plan. With her voice beginning to falter, she decided to conclude her speech. "This honor is very special to me since the woman who saved my life a month ago is also the same woman presenting me with this award. I'd like to take this opportunity to publicly thank Ms. Kirsten-Laird for risking her own life to save mine." Tayler could feel the tears stinging her eyes. "Thank you."

Erica reached for Tayler and the two women embraced. The audience stood and filled the room with applause. When the noise abated, Erica sat down at the table with Tayler. She leaned over and asked, "Will you have dinner with me tonight?"

Tayler mutely nodded her head.

"I'll pick you up at seven."

"Hi, Maria, it's Tayler. I just wanted to let you know that I won't be home for dinner tonight. I'm not sure how late I'll be." Tayler loved the Spanish accent in her housekeeper's voice. Christina had hired Maria right after the attempt on Tayler's life. "No, by all means use my car. Mother gave me a ride to work this morning and I don't need it tonight. Have the service station pick up your car at the house. Okay. You're welcome, Maria. I'll see you later tonight." Tayler hung up the phone.

"Poor Maria, she has so many problems with that car," Jane laughed. "So, it sounds like you have a date tonight."

"It's more like a dinner engagement," Tayler answered, engrossed in the research files Jane had placed on her desk.

"Sure," Jane folded her arms across her chest. "I've been around. It starts out with that 'damn' luncheon, then progresses to the 'it's just' a dinner engagement, which leads directly to the infamous nightcap. The rest, my dear, becomes bedroom politics."

Tayler ignored Jane's comment.

"By the way, I ordered that 46D bullet-proof bra for you."

"Great," Tayler laughed, looking up from her papers.

"Hey, I figured that thesaurus could come in handy tonight."

"Why?" Tayler asked trying her best to return to the files in front of her. Her mind kept drifting back to the awards luncheon.

"I thought it might help if…if the evening goes well and you want to use some new words. You'll blow your credibility if you say 'Oh, baby, you make me so hot.'"

Tayler rolled her eyes. "Very funny. Say good-bye, Jane."

"Good-bye Jane."

In the evening air, Tayler shivered. October had announced its arrival with heavy gray clouds that threatened to drench the city. She carefully pulled her raincoat closer so as not to crush the long admiral blue jacket and short skirt she was wearing. Tayler smiled to herself as she recalled Jane's comment.

"Whew, look at those legs. You look exquisite. I only wish I could be a fly in your soup tonight."

"Have a good evening, Ms. Windquest. I'll see you tomorrow." Benjamin Ezri, the magazine's security guard, opened the door to Erica's Grand Cherokee for her.

"Thank you, Ben." The door closed. Tayler sat back and watched Erica get behind the wheel. Erica's coat was open and Tayler could see that she wore a starched white shirt with a stand-up collar, black wool pants and a multi-colored vest. Her long silver earrings sparkled against her dark skin. "Thanks for picking me up tonight."

"My pleasure." Erica started the car and pulled into the night traffic. "It gave me a chance to see a real writer at work."

"I was surprised you actually walked into the building."

"Why?"

"Rumor has it that you're not very fond of the media nor anyone associated with it."

"Let's just say I'm not very fond of inaccuracies in the media." Erica's smile was both cool and seductive. A long moment passed. "So, what exactly does a Pulitzer prize-winning writer do?"

"I meet strangers in dark alleys for tips, smoke cigarettes two at a time and guzzle coffee in Styrofoam cups. Oh, did I mention that I stand on corners with a hole cut in my newspaper so I can get a realistic view of life on the streets." Tayler grinned.

"Now there's a good use for the media."

Tayler coughed. "Actually, I research topics to be covered in each issue of *The Narrator*, I make recommendations to the editor-in-chief about who should write what article, I rub noses with local and state legislators to get a better idea of the political climate, and I have dinner with famous architects to convince them that the media isn't so bad."

"And are you successful in convincing them of that?"

Tayler lowered her already low voice. "I guess you'll have your answer by the end of dinner. By the way, where are we going?" She noticed they were heading east on Interstate 94.

"To my favorite restaurant. Unfortunately, it's a little ride out of the cities."

"Duluth?" Tayler laughed.

"Hm, they've got some very nice restaurants up there, but no, we're only going as far as Stillwater."

Tayler was about to ask the name of the restaurant but Erica's car phone rang.

"Excuse me for a moment. Hopefully, this won't take too long." Erica picked up the phone.

To Tayler's dismay, it did last too long. Erica's phone conversation ended thirty-five minutes later when they arrived in the parking lot of the Harbor Cafe located on the banks of the St. Croix River.

≈ ≈

They were seated at a table in front of a large window that overlooked the dark and fast flowing river. The candle on their table cast a warm glow on Tayler's face. Soft music added to the warm ambiance.

"Hello, Ms. Laird. A sparkling water with a twist of lime as usual?"

"Yes, thank you. Tayler, what would you like?"

Tayler scanned the beverage menu. "I'll have the same." She smiled at the young woman.

Erica looked out the window at the river and sighed. She could see Tayler's reflection in the glass. She knew her silence was making Tayler uncomfortable but she was having a problem finding her voice. Tayler looked stunning, and the cozy atmosphere made her even more appealing. Erica wondered if she had made a mistake by bringing Tayler to this cafe. Finally, she turned her head back to Tayler. "I love this view. It's so peaceful."

"I can see why you do. The view alone is worth the ride."

"Not to mention the company," Erica noticed Tayler's cheeks redden. Their server returned with their drinks. "Here's to your courage and your recovery—"

"And to luck for bringing you to my door," Tayler added to Erica's toast. They clinked their glasses.

Erica's eyes fell on Tayler's neck. The red scar was two inches in length and began near Tayler's Adam's apple. It extended in a jagged line to the right.

"It's pretty ugly, isn't it?" Tayler lowered her eyes.

"Your scar makes me sad. It reminds me of the violence in our world and the people who use it to get whatever they're after." Raven's image cut through Erica's thoughts.

"But don't forget they are often destroyed by the violence they create." Tayler picked at a nonexistent piece of lint.

"We can only hope." The heavy conversation was not what Erica had planned. "I would imagine that my staring doesn't help. Is it uncomfortable for you?"

"The scar?" Tayler asked.

Erica nodded.

"Actually, I don't see it unless I look in the mirror. Mother told me the other day that it looks like—" she paused.

"A lightning bolt." Erica's hand shook as she took a sip of her water.

"That's exactly what she said." Feeling self-conscious, Tayler tried to ease her discomfort with humor. "Good thing I live in Minnesota. I can wear turtlenecks practically year-round."

Erica brought her napkin to her lips. "Have there been any new developments in the case?"

"Not really. Detective Steffan believes that the assailant was only trying to scare me." Tayler studied her hands.

They were beautiful hands, Erica thought to herself—hands that belonged to a painter, pianist or lover. "But you don't believe his theory."

"I don't. Why else would he have gone for my jugular? An amateur would have just sliced anywhere to get the job done fast. Professionals are more calculated, more precise and definitely more successful. If it hadn't been for your surprise appearance, the attack would have had a very different ending."

Stinging tears threatened her composure. Tayler looked away, but the touch of Erica's hand brought her back.

"You sound as if you're no amateur in these things."

"I wish I were," Tayler paused, "my father was murdered eight years ago by a professional killer."

"I'm sorry, Tayler," Erica squeezed Tayler's hand. "Was the person ever caught?"

"No, unfortunately."

"Does Steffan think your father's murder and the attempt on your life are somehow related?"

"Not really—there aren't a lot of similarities to connect the two."

"Were there any suspects in your father's case?" Erica asked.

"My mother, but her alibi checked out." Tayler sat back and withdrew her hand from Erica's. The server appeared with their dinner.

"You really don't think Christina would have been capable of that, do you?" Erica's eyes reflected her disbelief.

"At the time of his death I didn't know my mother. I did know that there had been a lot of discord between my parents. I didn't know what to think back then. But it wasn't her. She may be cruel at times but she would never do something as awful as that."

"What about other possibilities?"

"Like me, my father tended to make more enemies than friends." Tayler suddenly remembered the death threat she had received. She chose not to mention it. Death threats were common in her line of work. "I'm curious about one thing, Erica."

"What's that?"

"How did you know I was in trouble that night?" Tayler thought she saw Erica smile but she wasn't sure in the candle-light.

"I was standing on my deck taking in the night air. I missed my home and I wanted to smell the pine trees. When I saw what was happening I flew over." Erica noticed Tayler cringe. "If this is making you uncomfortable, Tayler, we don't have to talk about it."

"It's not that, it's—" Tayler's voice was so soft that Erica had to lean closer to hear. "Erica," Tayler avoided Erica's eyes. "Did you notice anything unusual about the assailant?"

"I'm not sure what you mean."

Tayler slowly exhaled. "It was a woman who attacked me."

Silence engulfed the table.

"I know," Erica replied.

Tayler looked back at Erica astonished. "You knew?"

"It's difficult to hide the curves of a woman, even if she is dressed in loose fitting clothes. Though it's been done, it really is difficult to hide hips and breasts. But it was the mouth that convinced me the attacker was a woman."

"In the hospital I thought I was hallucinating. I actually thought I was going crazy. But she was so strong and so," Tayler paused to find the right word, "deadly."

"You're not crazy, Tayler. In our American culture, we hate to admit that women are capable of evil." Raven's image again invaded Erica's thoughts. She shuddered.

Tayler tried to lighten the heavy conversation. "Well, at least we can rule out my mother. The only knife she's ever held was a butter knife."

Erica laughed. She was grateful for Tayler's sense of humor. When their eyes met, Erica refused to look away. Her skin ignited and her throat ached for the pools before her.

"Mother told me that the two of you were lovers."

Erica looked out the window. "So, you know about that. What else did she tell you?"

"Well, she told me that you're very intelligent, talented and..." Tayler paused.

"And?" Erica prompted.

Tayler looked around the room and lowered her voice. "And that you're dynamite in bed."

"Tayler," Erica cried, " She didn't!" She tried to continue but Tayler's laughter cut her off. Erica found herself joining in. After they calmed down she asked, "Does that upset you?"

"That you're dynamite in bed?" Tayler smiled wickedly. "No."

"I meant your mother's and my past."

Tayler grew serious. "Part of me is sad that it didn't work out for you two. The other part is glad you escaped my mother's possessive ways. Catherine has her hands full."

"Catherine?"

"Mother's partner. Didn't she mention her when you met for lunch?"

"No, she never mentioned she was in a relationship." The mystery of the one-carat diamond ring on Christina's finger was solved.

"Oops, I get the feeling I just revealed a significant detail."

Erica found Tayler's embarrassment endearing. "Don't worry, Tayler. The past is the past."

Tayler cleared her throat. Her voice was beginning to falter. "I know I should mind my own business, but it was difficult to avoid your phone conversation in the car. Are you serious about a merger?"

Erica squinted her eyes as she contemplated Tayler's question. "I really can't talk about that right now."

"Ms. Laird, is there something wrong with your meal? I noticed neither one of you have touched your food." The server nervously eyed the two women. "Would you like something else?"

"No, everything is just fine. We've been too engrossed in our conversation. No need to be alarmed." Erica took her fork and tasted the trout. "It's wonderful, thank you."

When the server left, Tayler placed both of her hands on the table. "Is it because I'm a writer and you don't trust me?"

"Tayler, I can't." Erica said. She saw Tayler raise her arms above her head. "What are you doing?"

"I'm trying to convince you that not all writers are monsters. I have no tape recorder, I'm not electronically wired, and I'm not doing hand signals to anyone outside." Tayler said defensively.

"I know. And I have no reason not to trust you. It's just…it's just that there are things I can't talk about." Tayler's sudden show of emotion touched Erica. "So, why are you so interested in my plans anyway?"

"I don't know," Tayler would not look at Erica. "Well, at least it's not what you think. I mean, I'm not out for a story."

Erica could only guess Tayler's real intent, though the truth was difficult to hide. She found Tayler's innocence both intriguing and alluring, and if she didn't watch herself very carefully, things could get fatal.

Tayler slowly turned her hands over on the table. "Allow me to get myself out of this awkward moment and see what other damage I can do." Tayler bit her bottom lip.

Erica leaned forward. "In my lifetime, Tayler, I've done more damage than you could ever do."

"I can't see how that would be possible. What damage could you have possibly done?" Partially recovering her exposed feelings, Tayler added, "Was your trip to Greece for strengthening U.S. business ties or for pleasure?"

"I'm impressed, Tayler. You really do your homework. To answer your question, it was personal. I went to Sparta and Athens to consult some experts. While I was there I took advantage of its dry heat and 80 to 100 degree temperatures."

"You're not ill, are you?"

"No," Erica shook her head. She squeezed Tayler's hand. "Thank you for your concern."

Tayler shifted in her chair. She hated being denied information. "I'd love to see the ruins in Athens. I studied Greek culture and mythology in college."

"The ruins are beautiful. Unfortunately, Athens is the most polluted city in Europe and it's taking its toll on the ruins."

"What are the people like?"

"Greek men are chauvinistic, but on the whole, the Greeks are a very passionate people. They're very proud of their families, politics and traditions."

"I heard recently that the island of Crete is the birthplace of matriarchy." Tayler watched Erica's expressions.

"Yes, the 'Green Island' as it's known."

"That's one place I'd like to visit."

"I'll keep that in mind. Maybe the next time I go you could come with me." Erica slid her index finger down her glass.

"Sounds great. I can be packed by tomorrow." Tayler slowly lifted her eyes off the table and looked directly at Erica.

"Don't play with fire," Erica warned. "You might get burned."

"I'm not afraid," Tayler smiled.

seven

The windshield wipers on the Jeep moved to the cadence of the falling rain. Lightning flooded the sky while thunder filled the air with the sound of its fury. The green lights from the dashboard made Tayler feel like she was in the cockpit of a plane. She was warm and dry and snug in Erica's company. Few cars were on Interstate 694. Tayler noticed that Erica had reduced her speed and wondered whether it was because of the stormy weather or to prolong their inevitable separation. Tayler was sure that she didn't want the evening to end.

The lightning outside the car was nothing in comparison to the electrical surge Tayler was feeling in the car. The intensity frightened her and she began to wonder if Erica was feeling it too.

She's probably got her mind on the merger and not on her hormones, Tayler thought but quickly reprimanded herself for her behavior. I've made a complete idiot of myself tonight.

"You're frowning," Erica turned down the volume on her compact disc player.

"How can you see, it's so dark?" Tayler watched the drops of rain stream down Erica's side window. Her profile was dominated by the darkness of her eyes.

"I see better in the dark," Erica chuckled.

"I suppose that's quite an advantage for an architect." And, a witch, Tayler thought. She rubbed the button on her coat between her fingers. "I mean, it would make it easier for you if the lighting wasn't the greatest at a construction site."

"Hm, I wasn't thinking of that situation exactly, but you're right, it does help at construction sites." Erica laughed. She concentrated on her lane change before continuing. "You seem tense, Tayler. Is it my driving?"

Tayler shook her head no.

When they circled around the northwest corner of the Cities and got on Interstate 494, Erica glanced over at Tayler. "I know it's late, but I'm wondering if I could interest you in a cup of tea before taking you home?"

"It's really out of your way," Tayler's heart jumped.

"I know, but I think there's enough time to go an extra 1,000 feet."

"If it wasn't lightning I could run across your lawn to my front door." Tayler smiled at the image of running through the rain soaking wet with Erica.

As they drove up the long and winding driveway a crash of thunder shook the car. Tayler looked through the intermittent darkness and light for Erica's house. Neither Erica's nor her own house could be seen from the street. Large oaks loomed before them. A strong wind came up and caught the Jeep.

"Wow, this is quite the storm," Tayler shouted over the thunder.

Erica drove the Jeep around the circle and parked it in front of the house. "Ready?"

Tayler nodded. She heard Erica's door slam. The rain picked up just as she opened her door. She was soaked before her feet hit the pavement. Erica stood on the porch laughing. By the time Tayler reached the stoop she was wet and out of breath.

On the porch, Tayler turned toward Erica. She started to tell Erica what a good time she was having, but Erica's closeness made her stop. For a long moment she gazed longingly at the raindrops clinging to Erica's eyelashes. Her own senses exploded. She reached up to wipe away a drop on Erica's face, but her hand froze in midair.

Tayler's eye grew wide. She gasped, "Erica, it's burning."

"I know —"

"No, no Erica," Tayler interrupted, "look, my god, my house is on fire!" Erica turned around and saw the flames.

Tayler pulled off her shoes and bolted toward the burning house. "Maria. She's in the house. We've got to get her out." She screamed, running and slipping in the wet grass.

Erica sprinted after Tayler and caught up with her in front of the house. "Tayler, wait here," she barked.

"I'll help." Tayler's eyes darted back and forth. Flames were spewing out of the first floor windows.

"No, I want you to stay here. I designed this house. I'll find Maria." Erica commanded.

"Hurry, Erica, hurry." When Erica disappeared, Tayler quickly ran to Erica's Jeep to use the car phone and dialed 911.

Minutes seemed like hours. As Tayler ran back to the burning house, she could hear sirens between claps of thunder. Tayler nervously paced back and forth watching for some sign of Erica and Maria. Out of the storm came three fire trucks with their lights flashing and horns crying.

A firefighter jumped out of a truck and quickly approached Tayler. He shouted over the noise. "Is anyone in the house?"

"Yes, yes, it's Maria," Tayler choked, "Erica, Erica went in to find her —" Her voice faltered.

Between the claps of thunder a loud explosion shook the ground. Wood, bricks and glass flew in every direction. The firefighter threw his body in front of Tayler to protect her from the flying debris. A chair crashed through a window on the second floor. Two firefighters hurried over and quickly hoisted a ladder to the front window. Erica yelled and helped Maria through the window. A firefighter assisted Maria down the ladder. As they reached the ground another explosion was heard. Erica disappeared from the window.

"The stairs have collapsed. The whole second floor is giving out," one of the firefighters yelled above the roar of the flames.

"Get her out of there!" The firefighter standing next to Tayler was sweating profusely under his helmet.

"It's an inferno in there. We don't know where she is," the firefighter's words seared through Tayler.

"Erica!" Tayler silently screamed running toward the house.

"Hey, you can't go in there!" The firefighter ran, catching up with Tayler and bringing her to the soaked ground. Tayler struggled to get up, but the firefighter was too big for her to fight. He pinned her to the ground. He saw that she was going into shock. "Chuck, get me a blanket quick! We've got to move her out of this rain. Pete, what have you got?"

"We're going to have to let it go," the firefighter yelled back, his face black from the smoke. His boots were covered in mud.

"Where's that goddamn blanket?" the firefighter bellowed. Someone ran up with a thick wool blanket and covered the struggling woman.

"Please get her out of there, please, I—" Blackness began to flood Tayler's vision and she drifted into a deep abyss. It echoed with the voices of the firefighters and the sound of the rain.

Just before the abyss swallowed her completely, Tayler heard a far away familiar voice say, "Tayler, everything's going to be okay."

"When you noticed the fire, where were you standing, Ms. Windquest?" Detective Steffan snapped. He had arrived shortly after Tayler regained consciousness. She was sitting on a sofa in Erica's library, wrapped snugly in one of Erica's thick robes, and trying her best to answer Steffan's questions. It was now the third time Steffan had asked her the same question.

Tayler looked at Erica from across the room. Erica paced back and forth with black soot on her hands and face. Her wet clothes were caked in mud. Tayler reached for her tea cup with trembling hands.

"I was about to enter Ms. Laird's house when I saw the flames." Tayler's voice was a whisper. She cleared her throat to gain some volume, but her voice was gone. Her hand went to her neck and she touched the scar.

"Did you see a streak of lightning hit the house or a flash of light?"

Tayler shook her head.

"How about anything unusual, like someone running away from the house?"

"No." What Tayler did recall was that she had wiped a raindrop from Erica's face and that they were about to kiss. It was only then that she saw the flames.

"Detective, I think Ms. Windquest has had enough for tonight. Is it possible to finish this in the morning?" Erica intervened.

"You're right, it is late," Steffan looked at Erica and then back at Tayler. "Where can I reach you tomorrow, Ms. Windquest."

"Here," Erica avoided Tayler's eyes. "When can I expect the fire department's report on the cause of the fire?"

"It'll take a few days, Ms. Laird, and they'll make sure your insurance company gets a copy of the fire inspector's report. But from the weather conditions tonight," Steffan looked at his shoes, "it looks like lighting was the cause."

"Lightning? That's impossible!" Erica stated emphatically. "I designed that house to withstand lightning strikes. Fires caused by lightning never spread that quickly."

"But we're not certain how long the fire was going before Ms. Windquest saw it," Steffan tried to dodge Erica's growing wrath.

"What about the gas odor?" In her earlier years as an architect Erica had redesigned and rebuilt houses destroyed by fire. Lightning wouldn't cause this type of damage — arson would.

"Miss Laird, one of the explosions was the gas line leading into the house, which explains the odor. But the fire inspector will check it all out before filing his report." Steffan began to leave but turned back to Erica.

"Ms. Laird?" Steffan straightened his tie and rubbed his chin. The day's growth made a scratching sound in the silent room.

"What is it now, Detective?"

"The fire inspector will be out tomorrow to begin the investigation. He may find something that supports your position, but until then, I have no reason to believe it was arson." Steffan picked up his hat.

From where she sat, Tayler could see Erica clenching and unclenching her fists. Her face was flushed and she stood solidly in one spot. Erica's body was so rigid that Tayler expected Erica to explode. She saw Steffan turn at the door.

"Ms. Laird, I spoke with the firefighters before they left. They told me that, in all their years on the squad, they have never seen anyone walk away from that kind of fire." Steffan ran the brim of his hat through his fingers. "They said that there was no way you could've gotten out."

Tayler could see he was both awed and skeptical.

"Obviously, Detective, there was a way." Silence filled the room.

When Steffan left and Tayler and Erica were alone, Tayler noticed a strange look in Erica's eyes. She seemed distant. Tayler was glad when the door opened.

"Erica, I got over here as soon as I could. Are you okay?" Candace put her briefcase and cellular phone on a chair. She saw Erica nod her head. "What the hell is going on?"

"Tayler Windquest, meet Candace Lanear, my assistant and friend." Erica gestured to the new arrival.

Candace shook Tayler's hand. "On my way over, I called the hospital. Maria's doing fine. When she's released she'll be staying with her sister. I've got the number."

"Thanks," Tayler whispered hoarsely.

"You both look exhausted. Why don't you get some sleep?" Candace looked at Erica. "I'll handle your calls. Oh, before I forget, Ana tried to reach you earlier this evening. She'd like to talk to you."

"Okay, I'll talk to her when I get Tayler settled in. Would you put the call through in about thirty minutes for me?"

"Sure, anything else?"

Erica shook her head. "I'll take the call in my room."

Candace closed the door quietly behind her.

Tayler heard the rain against the windows. The wind had lessened but thunder could still be heard in the distance. As Erica passed the sofa, Tayler reached out and caught Erica by the hand.

"You don't believe lightning caused the fire, do you?"

"Not for a moment," Erica looked down at Tayler. "I've seen too many buildings destroyed by fire. Houses don't go up in flames that quickly with lightning."

"You think it was set?" Tayler searched Erica's face, already knowing the answer.

"Yes."

Tayler let go of Erica's hand and shifted uncomfortably in the dark blue bathrobe. She was finally warm and dry, but she shivered from the possibility that someone had tried—once again—to kill her. All she could think about was the first sentence of the death threat she had received just that morning. *"The Flames are hot, and fuel the Fear —"*

She put her face in her hands trying to think of what she'd done to cause this type of peril. Death threats were often acts of revenge—angry people trying to get their points across—or acts to scare their intended victims. But this logic didn't calm her overwrought nerves. Death threats were carried out. Her father was proof of that. Frightened and confused, Tayler stood unsteadily.

Erica wrapped her arm around Tayler's waist to support her. They stood transfixed. A flash of lightning lit the night sky and the lights in the room blinked off. Seconds later they were back on. The thunder seemed to crash around them.

Tayler leaned her head against Erica's shoulder. Her shirt was still wet and smelled of smoke, but Tayler didn't care. She found comfort in Erica's embrace, but she couldn't stop shaking. The violence of the fire and the attack were still too vivid in her mind. She raised her head and looked into Erica's eyes.

"At the restaurant, you warned me not to play with fire," Tayler whispered, "but it wants to play with me."

"Are you afraid?" Erica threaded her fingers through Tayler's hair. It was soft to the touch and smelled of rain water.

"No," Tayler lied. She raised her hand and brought her thumb and index finger a half an inch apart. "Okay, maybe a little."

"I think we've both had enough excitement for one day. Let's go upstairs."

Tayler followed Erica into the foyer. The house was a beautiful, contemporary home with vaulted ceilings, wide open spaces and elegant floor coverings. Several large Robert Mapplethorpe and Devin St. Ives photos, set in silver frames, hung on the stairwell and hallway walls. Wooden plant stands were filled with exotic plants in exquisite pottery. The windows were covered in cloth, pastel-colored blinds. As she ascended the stairs, Tayler held on to the oak railing and Erica's arm for support.

When they reached the top of the stairs and walked down the hall to the last two rooms at the end, Erica stopped and ushered Tayler through double doors. The room was done in a deep, forest green. Tayler felt as though she had walked into a lush, tropical paradise. She noticed the sheets had already been turned back on the bed.

Erica faced her and saw Tayler scan the windows. "Will you be okay tonight?"

"Ye—yes."

"Yes?" Erica prompted.

"Erica, I never meant for this to happen. Some psycho is out there trying to get me and now has hurt you and destroyed your property. I can't, I won't—" the words squeaked out of Tayler's mouth, "I'm so sorry, I can't believe this is happening. I don't understand any of this—"

"Tayler," Erica took her into her arms and lowered her voice. "Tayler, you need to rest."

"But, but I thought I'd never see you—again." Tayler looked away. Fear magnified her exhaustion.

"I'm sorry you thought that. My biggest concern tonight was getting Maria out. I also had to retrieve something I'd left in the house."

"Something so important that you'd risk your life?"

"Yes, but we all survived." Erica watched Tayler get into bed. She walked to the door and turned. A smile graced her lips. "By the way, I'm still not convinced."

"Convinced about what? The lightning?" Tayler cocked her head.

"You realize that the media is going to have a field day with the fire tonight. Therefore, this architect is still not convinced that the media isn't bad and that writers aren't monsters."

"I must be losing my touch," Tayler raised her hands in front of her. She looked back at Erica. "How about another chance?"

"We'll see." A phone rang somewhere. "Sleep well, Tayler. If you need anything, I'm just across the hall."

To Tayler's disappointment, Erica slipped out of the room and closed the door behind her.

It was four-thirty in the morning when a shadow moved toward Tayler's bed. Once beside it, the figure stood and watched the sleeping woman. The sheets were shoved to the side and the comforter lay on the floor.

Tayler tossed and turned, mumbling inaudible words and whimpering softly. In the light from the hall she looked like a child—a child running away from a terrible, deadly monster.

"I know who wants you dead," Erica whispered.

In the dim light Tayler turned over and Erica could see the scar on Tayler's neck. Erica bent down to get a closer look. She wanted to touch Tayler's soft, blond hair with her fingertips and kiss her lips but something stopped her.

From her memory came the words on the yellowed paper.

> "A crown of Light, a sea of Blue —
> a Lightning mark, a darker Hue;
> A brush of Air, lips of Fire —
> A fragile heart, flame Desire."

eight

The next morning, Tayler was sitting at the breakfast table when Erica came through the back door into the kitchen. She was dressed in a pair of tight-fitting, black jeans and a hunter green, twill shirt. Her hands were covered in large garden gloves and her boots were caked with mud. Her hair was pulled back into a ponytail.

"Out for a morning stroll?" Tayler asked, amused by Erica's outdoor image.

"Good morning. I didn't think you'd be up yet." Erica sat down at the table, took off her gloves, removed the clip in her hair and shook her head. Her wavy black hair fell over her shoulders in smooth ripples. "You know the old saying."

"Which one?" Tayler took a sip from her coffee mug.

"Late to bed, late to rise makes you sluggish and despised."

Tayler grimaced. "Great. It's just my luck to be having breakfast with a poet."

Erica poured herself a cup of coffee and bit into a lemon poppy seed muffin. The strange expression on Erica's face unnerved Tayler.

"What on earth are you up to?"

With a strained grin, Erica walked to the door, stepped outside, and came back in with a black charred can.

"If you're looking for a donation, I gave at the office," Tayler folded her hands together.

Erica smiled, not accustomed to this lightheartedness in the morning. "I found this about a hundred yards from the house." She placed it on the counter. "It used to be a five gallon can of gasoline."

Tayler's eyes widened. Dread and apprehension pounded on her chest. "So it wasn't lightning after all."

"I'm on my way to call Steffan. I get the feeling he won't be surprised when he hears about this," she waited for Tayler to say something, but when she didn't, Erica added, "I'm running out of time."

"What?" Tayler's knuckles turned white. "What do you mean you're running out of time?"

Erica ran her hand through her hair. The words were forced. "We're not dealing with a novice here. Whoever wants to see you dead is getting impatient. I'm convinced there will be another attempt."

"Those aren't comforting words." Tayler said in a hushed voice. Her sleep had been wracked by nightmares and when she awoke denial had set in. She desperately tried to convince herself that it was all coincidence. "I can't believe a woman would do this." Tayler said trying to make sense out of the sudden chaos in her life. Within twelve hours, the death threat had taken on a very real and dangerous meaning. A gift of Black, to kill the Fool, she searched her memory, but couldn't recall the exact wording of the next line. Locked in her safe at the office, Tayler knew she needed to look at it closer for clues.

"Tayler," Erica said slowly, "evil comes in all shapes, sizes and sexes. If you let your assailant play on your emotions, she'll win. Caution is still your best weapon."

Tayler hung her head. She could feel a headache forming in her temples. Through the stabs of pain came a sudden realization. She raised her head and looked directly into Erica's eyes.

"Do you know who's trying to kill me?"

"No." The word echoed in the silent kitchen. Erica got up and walked to the door.

"Wait!" Tayler sprang from her chair. It hit the floor with a heavy thud. "Erica? Erica, damn it, what the hell's going on?"

Erica avoided Tayler's eyes. "I don't know."

"And I don't believe you," Tayler said when she was alone.

In her room, Erica heard a door slam across the hall. She stood next to her own door and listened. From the muffled sounds, she knew Tayler was crying. Her heart sank.

"What am I doing?" Erica groaned and turned away. She walked to her balcony doors and watched the wind whisk away a clump of leaves. At the restaurant the previous night, the air had sparkled with passion and obsession. Against her better judgment, she had nearly kissed Tayler. The fire had stopped her.

"You are the woman mentioned in the curse," Erica looked at the black remains of Tayler's house. "Will you save me or will I kill you?"

Erica shivered. She wanted to feel hopeful but she could only imagine the evil that awaited them. She pressed her fingers to the window.

Time was running out.

"Come in," Erica called out in response to the knock on her bedroom door. Tayler entered, dressed in the deep purple running suit Erica had given her to wear. "I'm sorry, I didn't mean to yell."

Erica could feel Tayler's eyes following her. "I know you didn't. With what's happened, it's perfectly within your rights."

"Someone's trying to kill me and I have no idea why." Tayler sat on the edge of the bed. She stared at Erica without blinking. "I'd say that puts me at a distinct disadvantage."

Tayler's blue eyes darkened, reminding Erica of impenetrable steel. Her insides churned. "Tayler, I want you to come with me to southern Mexico."

"Isn't it a bad time to take a vacation?" Tayler retorted.

"It's not for a vacation," Erica said holding up her hand to deflect Tayler's anger. "I have a friend there who can offer you protection. I don't want anything to happen to you."

Disarmed by Erica's concern, Tayler asked, "Is it safe to travel right now?"

"I don't think you have a choice, but we can talk about it some more in the car. I'll drop you off at your office. I'll be ready in a minute." She disappeared into the bathroom.

Tayler sat down on a chair and surveyed Erica's massive bedroom. A sunken sitting area with a fireplace on one end opened up to the balcony doors on the adjoining wall. She got up and walked down the three steps to the sliding glass doors. She glanced back at the room decorated in shades of blue. It was all very luxurious, mysterious and dark.

She knows who it is, but isn't saying, Tayler thought to herself. This is crazy. Those attempts were meant to kill. Tayler's mind raced over the facts. A woman; two attempts involving fire, water and a knife; the attempts happened a month apart; and both took place immediately following Erica's return from Spain and Greece. Tayler sighed. But it couldn't be Erica — she was injured in the first attempt, and it was her house that went up in flames last night. A thought hid in the shadows of her subconscious. Erica's concerned about me. Do I believe her? Tayler asked herself. She turned toward the doors. Yes, yes I do believe she's sincere.

The view from the balcony was serene, unlike the fear enveloping her. She closed her eyes against the memories of the attack, the moments before the fire, the fire and Erica's disappearance. With two seeds of violence planted in her consciousness, and the possibility of future attempts, panic grew insidiously into her thoughts. Her emotional intrigue and physical desire for Erica threatened to fog her natural instincts for answers —

answers that could explain what was happening. Tayler felt torn. Someone destroyed her home and sense of security. Before her was an invitation to go to southern Mexico with a woman she desired — a woman she barely knew. With her head down, Tayler turned slowly from the balcony.

Erica watched Tayler from the top step.

Tayler's gaze wandered deliberately up Erica's body, her fear momentarily overcome by fascination. Erica was dressed in a black, pin-striped suit that emphasized her narrow waist and long, slender legs.

"You're staring."

"Nice suit." Tayler climbed the steps and stood next to Erica, but grew light-headed as she took in Erica's perfume. She walked over to the side of Erica's bed and sat down — before she fell down. Her heart raced, she felt out of breath, and her body throbbed. She tried to restrain her raging emotions, but the sweet sensation felt more enticing than the fear she had so recently come to know.

Erica sat down on the bed next to Tayler. "You're hot. Are you okay?" Erica's nearness only made Tayler feel more faint. No one had ever made her feel this weak. Erica's brown eyes drew Tayler into her and Tayler found she could not look away. The skin on Erica's face looked so alluring. She wanted to touch Erica and she wanted Erica to touch her.

The phone rang startling them both.

Erica reached across Tayler and picked it up. "Hello."

Tayler felt Erica's body tighten.

"Christina, what can I do for you?"

Hearing her mother's name, Tayler got up from the bed and readjusted her suit. She took several deep breaths.

"Yes, she's fine." Erica's eyes followed Tayler across the room.

Tayler didn't want to eavesdrop, but she knew her mother was asking Erica about the fire. She was plagued with guilt for not having called her mother before Christina read about it in the newspaper. The guilt deepened when Tayler wondered what her mother would say if she knew what her call just interrupted.

"Tayler?" Erica walked over and handed the cordless phone to Tayler.

"Hi, mom," Tayler's voice cracked. Her body was still tingling from Erica's fragrance and nearness. "Yes, I'm going into the office today. I need a sense of normality. I also need some clothes." As she spoke, Tayler watched Erica stop in front of a low dresser. She picked up a long silver necklace, swung her hair off her shoulders and placed it around her neck. When she put on her earrings, Tayler caught Erica's gaze in the mirror. Her voice squeaked. "I'm sorry I forgot to call you. No, really, I'm okay. My throat's pretty scratchy from yelling and inhaling smoke," Tayler paused. "Can you meet me for lunch today? Great."

Erica turned toward Tayler, leaned against the drawers, and smiled.

Tayler boldly met Erica's eyes, but then shyly looked away. "Erica's on her way out the door and she's giving me a lift to work. I'll see you at noon. Yes, I promise I'll be careful. Bye."

On the way to her office, Tayler sat next to Erica full of confusion and uncertainty. Was Erica feeling what she was feeling? Was she scared? Tayler looked over at Erica but could find no emotion on her face. Tayler wanted to grab the wheel and pull the car over to the side of the road. She wanted to talk about what was happening—her fears and confusion. But more than anything, Tayler wanted to talk about what was happening between them.

The two attempts on her life brought excitement into her life, but it wasn't the type of excitement she wanted. The sparks and intensity Tayler felt were even stronger than those she had experienced years ago with Gabrielle, but Gabrielle had been her father's lover and Tayler had kept her feelings to herself. She wasn't sure she could keep her feelings for Erica a secret.

The thought of being attracted to women—being a lesbian—didn't frighten Tayler. As a writer, she knew the public's opinion of gays was changing, yet she also was very aware of the hatred. Ted, one of the photographers she worked with, had been badly beaten solely because he was gay. She cringed at the memory of his broken nose, black eyes and bleeding ear. His attackers had ripped his earring through his ear lobe. The violent image made her flinch.

Erica reached over and squeezed Tayler's hand. "I'm making all the arrangements for our trip. Would you be ready to leave first thing tomorrow morning?"

"Tomorrow morning?" Tayler coughed. "I've got to get money, my passport, clothes, luggage — "

"It's best we leave before something else happens," Erica's mouth tightened into a thin line.

Tayler watched the downtown shoppers along the street. "I'll see what I can do."

When Tayler opened the door Erica leaned over and caught her by the sleeve. "Tayler, be careful today."

"I will," Tayler stepped out and shut the door.

"I'll pick you up at eight tonight, okay?" Erica said through the open window. "I'll help you with your errands."

"Great," Tayler paused not wanting to say good-bye. "Um, thanks for the lift." She watched Erica pull away from the curb. The hunter green Jeep took a left and was soon lost in the morning traffic.

Wrapped in confusion, Tayler stepped inside the revolving door unaware of the eyes that followed her across the sidewalk and through the door.

nine

The early October weather was the warmest in years. An earlier chill had caused the fall colors to splash vibrantly across the city. People hurried to the city's lakes to take advantage of the last warm days before winter. Crisp leaves cluttered the sidewalks.

Tayler stood at the window perturbed she couldn't enjoy the sound of crunching leaves under her feet or the honking of geese flying overhead on their way south. She wanted to lie on the grass and take a nap in the sun, but she had so many phone calls to make. She didn't dare take a chance of losing herself in the warmth and fragrance of autumn — her favorite time of year.

"Tayler, your mother's here," the receptionist said through the intercom.

Tayler walked to the door and opened it. As her mother entered, Tayler slipped her arm through Christina's. "Hi. Thanks for being so flexible. I ordered out. Lunch should be here in a minute."

"Tayler, my god, this is serious." Christina searched her daughter's eyes. "I'm canceling our trip to Europe. Catherine agrees."

"Mom, please don't. I know how much you and Catherine have been looking forward to this trip." Tayler smiled. "I don't want to cause marital mayhem between Christina Windquest and Lady Catherine Winthrop Sullivan because some weirdo has a grudge against me."

Christina folded her arms across her chest.

"Mother, I want you to go." Tayler protested.

"Darling, your safety is more important than any trip. We'll just go when things quiet down." Christina sighed. "How do you know you're not being watched right now?" Christina looked around the office. Her yellow sweater was draped over her shoulders and she wore a pair of jeans, a white polo shirt and deck shoes.

"What type of life would I have if I were too afraid to walk out my front door? I can't live in fear, Mother, and neither should you."

"I just wish they'd catch this guy." Christina sighed.

"He'll be caught. It's only a matter of time." Tayler winced. She wanted to tell her mother that it was a woman who had attacked her, but Christina would not believe a woman could be so evil—just like she hadn't at first.

"What happened to Erica's security system the night of the fire? I'd have thought it would have prevented an arsonist from getting near your house?"

"It malfunctioned. The camera, however, did catch a glimpse of something," Tayler paused.

"What was it?"

"A large black cat. It ran away from the house right before the first explosion."

Christina shook her head. "I should've known."

"Known what?"

"If Erica's involved—and she has been in both attempts— it won't be a male in his early twenties, muscular build and a mustache. It means witches, black cats, fires, curses and things like that."

"Mother, you're starting to sound like some New Age fanatic."

"Tayler, this is serious." Christina stopped talking, while she scooped some fried rice and chicken almond ding on her plate. "I think these attempts have something to do with Erica."

"What?"

"I'm talking witchcraft, Tayler."

"Oh, Mother, please, I—"

"She's dangerous," Christina eyes silently pleaded for her daughter's understanding.

"Well, I'm not scared," Tayler retorted. She drummed her fingers on the table unable to eat her lunch.

"Darling, why don't you come with us to Europe? You'd love it and you could relax. I've never seen you so edgy. There's so much to see and so many opportunities to be seen. I'm sure we could find someone to help you relax."

"Male or female?"

"Whatever you prefer," Christina squeezed Tayler's hand. She took a bite of her chicken.

"Mom?" Tayler began slowly. "When did you realize you preferred women over men—I mean physically?"

Christina chuckled. "Do I have your promise that this won't appear in *The Narrator*?"

"I promise," Tayler raised her right hand. "Cross my heart and—" she let the rest of the saying go.

Christina's breathed a heavy sigh. "When you were born I thought my life was complete. I was married and had a beautiful baby girl. Life as a new mother was busy and I had you to fill my days, but I began to feel an emptiness deep down inside. At first I thought I was going through postpartum, but then I stopped my charity work, gained fifty pounds and had no interest in sex. Doctors in California told me that I was going through a normal stage and that I would snap out of it. But I didn't. Your father sent me to a clinic in France for treatment."

"And?"

"And that's where I admitted my attraction to women. I'd

always been interested in women, but it scared me. When I 'came out' I experienced such deep excitement, passion and fear."

"Fear?" The word surprised Tayler. "Why fear?"

"Because I had to come back and face your father."

"I've read the transcripts from the custody case. He was pretty angry with you."

"Pretty angry?" Christina winced. "He was vicious."

"Why?" Tayler looked at her mother, puzzled.

"Because I was his cover."

"I'm not sure I understand," Tayler squinted her eyes in the bright sunlight.

"He had a wife, a little girl who adored him and a beautiful home. He was the top publisher in the country, he was wealthy, good-looking and had a string of mistresses. I blew his world apart by admitting that I preferred women. I threatened his masculinity and his life was suddenly filled with chaos."

"He never told me any of this." Tayler stopped talking. A memory wavered on the brink. "Whenever my birthday or Christmas came and I didn't receive a card or a present from you, he'd use that to demonstrate how awful you were."

"But I did send you cards and gifts," Christina's voice rose. "You have some of the gifts, I've seen them."

"After Dad died I went through his belongings. In a storage closet I found the things you had sent. I think I cried for weeks when I realized how I had let his feelings for you poison my own. That's when I decided to find you. I had been such a fool."

"No, not a fool. Your father loved you and wanted to make you happy. Hopefully, you've come to realize that I did too." Christina's eyes brimmed with tears.

"What's the hardest thing for you about being a lesbian, the religious condemnation or the public hatred?" Tayler had so many questions to ask.

"Society's unwillingness to acknowledge the bond two women or two men can make to one another is rough. Then there's the attitude that homosexuality is a sickness. But the hardest part of all is," Christina stopped and squeezed Tayler's hand, "is wondering if your child will someday have to face the same hatred and prejudice that you face."

Tayler coughed. "Assuming your child is gay."

"Assuming your daughter is spending a lot of time on the fence deciding," Christina smiled knowingly. "Be careful, Tayler. You're a very powerful and attractive woman. There are a lot of sharks out there. And believe me I know — I've slept with some of them." Christina laughed.

"You really love Catherine, don't you?"

"Yes, I really do. She hates the mosquitoes and 'Minnesota nice,' but then she's English, what can I say?" Christina's eyes took in her daughter's facial features. "I love it here but I also love Paris."

"Then go." Tayler stood. "Your flight leaves in five hours and Catherine is probably in hysterics because you're not home yet."

"I'm already packed." Christina took Tayler in her arms. "I really am worried. Are you sure you'll be okay?"

"Absolutely. I'll let you know if something happens," Tayler promised.

"Sure you will," Christina replied sarcastically. "Just like I found out about the fire in the morning paper."

Tayler held up her hands. "How many times do I have to apologize for that one?"

"Just be careful — please." She dug around in her purse. "Here's the number. Call me no matter what, okay?"

"Don't worry, Mom, I've got my crystals handy." Tayler laughed when she saw Christina frown. She opened her mouth to say something but Tayler cut her off, "I've got to get back to work. Have a good time and give Catherine a hug for me."

"I love you, Tayler." Christina tightened her arms around her daughter.

"I love you, too, Mom."

ten

The night was uncommonly dark and a fierce wind rattled the windows. The warmth of summer had finally surrendered to the chill of winter. Standing in front of the view, Tayler wrapped her arms around herself though it was warm in her office.

Jane knocked on the open door. "Hey, Tayler, look what just arrived for you." She walked in carrying an ornately wrapped package.

Tayler, however, continued to look out the window. "Jane, when I get back I have to find a place to live."

"Oh no, it sounds like there's trouble in paradise." Jane set the package on Tayler's desk. "Did something happen?"

Tayler shook her head, shivering in the prevailing eeriness of the late hour. She turned around eyeing the expensively wrapped package.

Jane looked at Tayler, "I've never seen such exquisite wrapping before. It's really unusual." The 'paper' was black velvet. Silver stars and crescent moons danced across the its surface.

The bow and ribbon were silver and sparkled in the evening light. "Should we guess who it's from?"

"No," Tayler ran her fingers through her hair.

Jane lifted a ribbon and ran it through her fingers. "If you ask me I think you've fallen in love."

"I didn't ask." Tayler stared at Jane and then looked away.

"Tayler, I've been your friend for twenty-five years and your editor for fifteen. I've seen you conquer the hula hoop and city hall. Don't you think I've noticed your behavior these past weeks? You rush out of meetings to find out if you have any messages, you cancel lunch engagements right and left, and you bounce from one topic to the next without a thought."

"That obvious, huh?" Tayler coughed. Her voice ebbed and flowed like the tide. It was still strained with occasional instances of clarity.

"I bet this is from her," Jane pointed to the gift box. "I think she's both attracted to and afraid of you."

"Why would she be afraid of me?"

"Because you're a writer and you work for a magazine. Everyone knows how much she dislikes publicity."

Tayler thought about Jane's theory. "I know. I haven't written a word about her, yet because of me, one of her houses was burned to the ground and her arm was sliced. I don't think she appreciates the attention." Tayler shook her head. "I seriously doubt she's happy with me for shining a spotlight on her private life."

"From what you've told me I think she's mad about you. So open the box and see if it's from her," Jane coaxed.

"Wasn't there a card with it?" Tayler asked.

"Elite gift shops place the card inside the box," Jane winked at Tayler and walked to the door.

"Don't you want to stay and see what it is?"

Jane shook her head. "I've got a few errands to do tonight and I'm already behind."

"Okay. I'll see you tomorrow," Tayler eyed the package closely.

She had never received such a magnificently wrapped gift before. Tayler slowly untied the bow and removed the paper from the box.

"Tayler!"

"God, Jane, you scared me half to death," Tayler pulled herself away from the package. "What are you—"

"I've got a bad feeling about this." Jane warned, "Get away from the box,"

Tayler looked down and saw the cover move. "Shit!"

Jane's voice was low but urgent. "Back up slowly. Don't make any sudden moves."

"What is it?" Tayler whispered, her nerves straining against the sudden surprise. She felt her way from the desk with her hands, her eyes never leaving the box.

"Tayler, stay where you are, don't move," Jane inched her way out of the office. "I'm going to call security. Just don't make any sudden moves."

A three foot black snake with blue and white stripes slithered out of the box. It slipped its way down the desk and on to the floor.

Hurry, Jane, Tayler's mind screamed.

The snake moved silently closer, its tongue darting in and out. The sound of hissing filled the quiet office. Tayler could hear Jane's high-pitched voice calling for help.

The snake was now two feet from Tayler. She held her breath and forced herself to look past the snake. She knew that staring at a dog made them feel threatened, but she didn't know if the same logic applied to snakes.

Inches from Tayler the snake coiled, its body swaying in the heaviness of the air.

A large shadow flew past Tayler's shoulder and landed squarely on the snake.

Tayler felt herself yanked from behind.

"Get out, Tayler—" Jane screamed.

In her car on the way to Tayler's office, Erica was grateful for the silence. The past months had been filled with too many questions and no answers. Now it seemed signs were appearing. Though she sensed a quiver of hope, her growing desire for Tayler terrified her. She knew too well that if she acted on her feelings Tayler would die. She tried to stay away from Tayler, afraid that she would succumb to Tayler's beauty and energy, but tonight she needed to take Tayler home and try to explain the curse.

When she arrived at Tayler's office she was shocked to see six police cars with lights flashing parked in front of the building. She jumped out of her car and ran to the entrance.

"I'm sorry, miss, but you can't go in. This building is off limits." A police officer stopped Erica.

"It's okay, officer, you can let her through," Detective Steffan emerged from a crowd of police officers. "Why don't we go in and have a chat, Ms. Laird?"

The officer raised the yellow tape for Erica. Steffan took her by the arm and led her to an empty conference room on the first floor. The table was filled with used Styrofoam cups and smelled of cigarette smoke. Steffan sat down across the table from Erica. His eyes moved slowly across her face.

"Detective, what's going on here?" Erica's eyes rapidly shifted from Steffan's face to the door.

"There's been another attempt on Ms. Windquest's life," he said watching her reaction.

"Oh no," Erica cried.

Steffan motioned for her to sit down.

"Is she okay?"

"She's fine. Shaken up, but fine." He lit a cigarette.

"What happened?" Erica's eyes darted around the room and back to Steffan's face.

"Before I let you go up I'd like to ask you a few questions."

Steffan sat back and blew smoke in the air. He straightened. "Have you ever had any business dealings in India?"

"No, never," she replied quickly. She wanted to see that Tayler was okay with her own eyes.

"In any Asian countries?"

"No."

"You're sure?" Steffan rolled the cigarette between his fingers.

"Yes, I'm certain." Erica clenched her fist. "Detective, what does this have to do with Tayler?"

Steffan sat up and blew a line of smoke. "Someone sent Miss Windquest a rather dangerous gift."

"A gift? What kind of a gift?" Erica drummed her fingers on the table.

"Earlier this evening Miss Windquest received a member of the Indian Krait family." Detective Steffan consulted his notes.

"A snake?" Erica's eyes widened.

"Yes, a Blue Krait to be exact."

Erica rubbed her eyes. "Oh no —"

He referred to his notes again. "The lethal dose for a human is only a few milligrams. The majority of bites are fatal even with the anti-venom."

"But snakes don't bite unless they're provoked," Erica countered. "Was someone bitten?"

"No, luckily. Miss Windquest's editor threw a book at it and pulled her out before it struck. We called a herpetologist from the Minnesota Zoo and he's already been here. Amazingly he caught the damn thing and checked it out."

Erica got up from her chair and stared out the window. All afternoon she had felt uneasy and upset. Now she understood why.

"The person we're dealing with is no amateur." Steffan rose from his chair.

Erica already knew this.

"Whoever sent Miss Windquest this snake knew two things.

First of all he knew that Miss Windquest was working late. And second, he knew that Kraits — Blue Kraits in particular — are only active at night. I guess it's kind of a curious thing for snakes." He waved his hand. "The herpetologists at the zoo would've liked to have studied this particular specimen."

"It got away?"

Steffan nodded.

"But I thought you said it was caught," Erica shivered.

"It was. When the guy opened the container at the zoo it was gone." The detective scratched his bald head. "Poof. Just like the apparition who tried to slit Ms. Windquest's throat. No trace of a damned thing."

Erica stared at the large man. "So, what about the fire? Any clues there?"

"Apparently our killer mistook the housekeeper for Miss Windquest. When we talked to Maria we found that she had borrowed Miss Windquest's car that day. While she was out that evening the arsonist spread gasoline around the house. When the car returned, we assume he thought the driver was Miss Windquest and torched the house." Steffan's cheeks reddened. "The report's been sent to your insurance company."

She turned to go but stopped at the door. "Detective, where is Tayler's mother?"

"On her way to Paris." Steffan lit a second cigarette. "Miss Windquest and her editor are with one of our officers upstairs."

"Detective, I want to take Ms. Windquest out of the country for awhile, for her safety, and while you find who's behind these attempts. She's in too much danger here."

"What makes you think she'll be safe anywhere she goes?"

"I don't, but don't you think it's better than waiting around here for something else to happen? Her assailant apparently seems to know her every move. Her only hope is to go into hiding."

Steffan nodded. "Where would you take her?"

"To a remote spot in southern Mexico."

"Lemme think about it. I'll let you know tonight if it can be arranged." Steffan made several notes in his notepad.

Erica hurried to the elevator and got in. As the door closed, she leaned her forehead against the fabric on the wall. She was certain Raven was behind the attempts. The curse was beginning to make sense.

When Erica reached the top floor she saw a female police officer talking with Tayler in her office. The room looked as if a tornado had stripped it of its elegance. Tayler sat on a sofa with the officer's jacket draped around her shoulders. Her hair was disheveled and her hands were shaking. Erica knocked softly on the door not wanting to alarm her.

"Erica—" Tayler rose unsteadily and collapsed in Erica's outstretched arms. "It was so horrible," she said between sobs.

Shortly after they reached Erica's house, Detective Steffan called with the arrangements to get them to the airport in the morning. As Erica relayed the message to Tayler, tears streamed down Tayler's cheeks. Erica's heart sank seeing the fear in Tayler's beautiful blue pools.

"Tayler, Detective Steffan has the house surrounded by officers. You'll be okay tonight. We'll get on the plane tomorrow and leave what's happened behind." Erica looked into Tayler's tear-streaked face.

"Jane was so brave," she whispered reeling from the tranquilizer the paramedics had given her.

"And so were you," Erica held Tayler's hand. It felt cold.

"Where are we going?"

"We're going into hiding. Luckily, it's to one of the most beautiful places in the universe," Erica smiled. "Let's get you upstairs."

In Erica's room, Tayler sat on a chair and watched Erica turn down the sheets on the bed. She went into the bathroom and started a hot shower for Tayler. She came back into the room and went to one of the closets and pulled out a silk night shirt. "This should fit you," Erica handed the midnight blue shirt to Tayler. It smelled like its owner.

The water felt good as it rushed over Tayler's aching body. She tried to wash away the memories of the attempts but couldn't. She turned off the water and stepped out of the shower. In the mirror Tayler noticed the red scar on her neck. It didn't seem to be fading like Dr. Evans had said it would. She felt the scar tissue and winced. It was smooth to the touch, but ugly. Her physical appearance and her voice had both suffered from the attacks. She silently grieved for her losses.

She buttoned the night shirt and walked back into the bedroom where she found Erica putting away some of her things. "Your favorite color is dark blue, isn't it?"

"It is." Erica threw her robe on the bed. "Make yourself comfortable. I'll be back in a minute."

Tayler eased her body between the cool sheets. The tranquilizer the paramedics had given her was still having an effect. Her thoughts came in fragments. Snug in Erica's king-size bed, Tayler felt safe, but her mind repeatedly returned to the snake.

With her eyes closed, Tayler sighed, but bloodied, burned images slithered across her mind. She jerked and quickly sat up. Too afraid to sleep, she looked around for something to do while she waited for Erica. An issue of *Minnesota Monthly* lay on the night stand. Still crisp and new, Tayler flipped it open to the table of contents. Her eyes ran down the list of article titles. She stopped at the featured story. The title read, "Return to Enchantment: Local Architect Weaves Her Spell." The accompanying photo showed Erica at a construction site. The wind had caught her black hair and tossed it over her shoulders. Her eyes were dark and mysterious looking. It was one of the most stunning pictures Tayler had ever seen of Erica. Mesmerized, she recalled a statement Christina had made to her.

"Erica is a typical Scorpio. Scorpios are the most complex and mysterious personality in the Zodiac." Christina's facial expression was one of awe. "You've known the compelling mystery of a lovely witch who brews a pretty good cup of tea — when the cup is empty, let her read the tea leaves for you. She can, if she wants to."

If she wants to. Tayler put the magazine in her lap and looked around the room. Everything seemed to be in its place. "Maybe that's it," Tayler whispered. "Maybe everything appears ordinary to hide the extraordinary." She picked up the magazine again and peered intently at Erica's picture. "There was no way you could've escaped the fire alive...unless...unless you're a witch. And what was so important that you risked your life for in the fire?" Drowsy and unable to think straight, Tayler shrugged off the questions and began reading the article.

The clock in the hall ticked away the hour.

"It must be an interesting article," Erica walked over to the bed drying her hair with a towel, "or you're the world's slowest reader, which I'm not sure is a good trait for a writer. You've been on that same page for ages."

"Actually, I'm too sleepy to read it." Tayler glanced at Erica and then at the photo and then back at Erica. "But it's one I should read."

"What's it about?"

"It's about architects who hate the media," Tayler watched Erica frown.

"Would you like something hot to drink? It might help you relax." Erica sat next to Tayler on the bed. She picked up the magazine and scanned the article. "You shouldn't be looking at this stuff before going to sleep. It'll give you nightmares."

"Or some pretty stimulating dreams," Tayler slurred.

"I think you're still feeling the effects of the tranquilizer,"

Erica smoothed the hair on Tayler's forehead.

"When I was in college my father dated a wonderful woman. She would bring me tea each night before I went to bed. It became almost a ritual."

"Did it help you relax?"

"I don't really remember. I do remember that it got me up in the middle of the night," Tayler laughed at the memory. "I wonder whatever happened to Gabrielle."

Erica opened her mouth, but then closed it. She shook her head.

"Is something wrong?" Tayler asked.

"No," Erica replied and then quickly added, "Would you like some tea?"

"I don't know." She felt suddenly reckless. "How do I know you won't lace it with an aphrodisiac?"

"What a marvelous idea." Erica leaned over and brought her face close to Tayler's. "But I don't think you need an aphrodisiac."

"I don't?" She slowly raised her eyes and smiled. Her breath came in shallow waves of air. "Erica?"

"Hm?"

Tayler's fingertips touched Erica's face and slid over her cheekbones to her lips. Her fingers stopped. "Would you...will you...kiss me?"

"With pleasure," Erica murmured.

Their kiss, at first, was timid. Tayler marveled at how soft Erica's lips were. She raised her face to meet the melting tenderness Erica offered. Her lips parted to the warm moisture of Erica's sensuous, demanding tongue. It felt as if silk fabric was being tugged playfully across Tayler's lips. She savored the aroused, intoxicating feeling that trickled over her nerves and coursed through her body. She returned Erica's kisses with a passion that frightened her, but despite the fear, Tayler could not stop herself from wanting more. She cried out when Erica pulled back.

"Shhh," Erica pressed her fingertips lightly on Tayler's lips.

Tayler's eyelids grew heavy and her speech slurred. "Did I

tell you...my mother...my mother thinks...you're a...a witch?"

Erica laughed.

"I'm beginning...I'm beginning...to think...you...are—" Tayler's voice trailed off.

eleven

Erica sat next to Tayler on the plane pretending to be absorbed in the blueprints in front of her. Unable to concentrate, her mind drifted to the night before and the kiss they had shared. She was still reeling from its effects when she awoke but, luckily, packing and getting to the airport for their flight had occupied her mind. Now, seated for the long journey to southern Mexico, Erica found herself returning again and again to their kiss.

Only ten days were left before Halloween—Hallow's Eve— the day that would determine her future. For the first time in twelve years, Erica's spirits were raised realizing Tayler was the woman mentioned in Raven's curse. A flicker of hope mingled with the constant feeling of dread, for the attempts on Tayler's life were becoming more and more deadly. She feared for Tayler's safety and for her own. The return to Puerto Arista not only marked the end of the first part of the curse, but, perhaps, the end of her life.

Raven's curse involved three equal parts. In each part, "good" was pitted against "evil" in a contest of illusion, deception and desire. If Erica could not destroy this first part by Halloween, she knew Raven would claim even more lives. Tayler, unknowingly, was Erica's only hope for survival. Guilt consumed her, for she knew Tayler had no idea what was about to happen once they reached Ana's.

Erica's mind screamed for Tayler's love while her body craved for the intimate touch of lovemaking. But she knew if she gave in to her desires, Tayler would die. When Patricia Locksley was murdered, Erica vowed to herself to remove all temptation. Now, however, the greatest temptation of all was seated quietly next to her reading a book.

Tayler glanced at Erica. "The flight attendant is going to take your pencil away if you keep drumming it on your blueprints."

"I'm sorry. Was it bothering you?" Erica put her pencil down.

"No, but I couldn't quite figure out what tune you were playing," Tayler smiled. She closed the book.

Erica noticed the name on the cover. "Do you enjoy her novels?"

"Sterling Navarre's?"

Erica nodded.

"Immensely." Tayler sighed and looked out the window at the clouds below them. "She's an excellent writer. I'm not surprised she's the country's best-selling author. If I wrote novels, I'd like to write like her. I'd love to meet her someday."

"She is an incredible woman," Erica's voice cut into Tayler's thoughts.

"You know her?" Tayler sat up in her seat.

"She's a close friend. In fact, these are the blueprints for the house I'm designing for her."

"Wow. I'd love to do an interview with her, but she's impossible to reach." Tayler sat back in her seat. "It's a funny thing about Sterling. None of her books carry her photo and I've never seen her on talk shows. No one I know, in fact, has ever seen her—except you." A thought suddenly crossed Tayler's mind. "She wasn't at the luncheon was she?"

"No," Erica laughed. "She's been out of the country."

"If you tell me you were in Greece with her I'll die of envy,"

Tayler squirmed.

"Okay, I won't."

Silence fell over the two woman like a blanket. Tinges of jealousy prickled Erica's consciousness. Tayler had seemed unimpressed with celebrities but her comments and questions about Sterling threatened Erica. An elegant beauty surrounded by poise, a quick wit and charm, Erica suddenly feared the possibility that Tayler might fall for another woman before Erica could make her own feelings known. The thought haunted her like a predator.

When they reached Oaxaca, Mexico, and disembarked, it seemed like hours before they made their way through customs. A five minute drive brought them to a private airstrip where they boarded a small plane.

"Where are we going?" Tayler sighed .

"Aeropuerto de Arriga," came Erica's reply. "It's only an hour to Arriga. Once we're there we'll drive the rest of the way to Puerto Arista. Have you ever been to southern Mexico?"

"I spent two weeks in Acapulco last year, but that's as far south as I've gone." Tayler shrugged her shoulders. "Where are we staying?"

"At a hacienda located several miles outside of Puerto Arista. The ranch belongs to Ana Ariani. A friend of mine."

Tayler nodded. The image of a stocky, dark featured woman with the crude manners of a ranch owner came to mind.

"I think you're going to find Ana a very interesting woman." Erica smiled to herself.

The October sun beat down on the two women as they emerged from the plane and walked to a car waiting for them in Arriga. Tayler took in the terrain from behind her sunglasses.

"Southern Mexico is part of the neotropics that span Central and South America and the West Indies. The neotropics include everything from lowlands to mountains." Erica explained. "Below the volcanic belt just south of Mexico City, there are jumbled masses of mountains known as the Sierra Madre del Sur."

"I heard one of the flight attendants say that the volcanoes were 17,000 feet above sea level," Tayler added.

Erica nodded. "The Sierra Madre del Sur mountain range makes southern Mexico one of the most inaccessible, picturesque and undeveloped sections of the country." Erica pointed out the mountain range on one side of them and the Pacific Ocean on the other.

"Wow! It has something for everyone."

"Puerto Arista is also one of the last matriarchal societies in the world." Erica smiled as the car slowed down to allow a woman to cross the road. "It's been said that the two main attractions in this area are the women and the Pacific beaches."

Tayler sat back in her seat, her cheeks hot from embarrassment. She wasn't aware that she had been staring until Erica commented on the beauty of the place and its people.

As they drove toward Puerto Arista, Erica pointed out the neat, short, stone walls that bordered Ana's property. The stones dipped and curved with the land and disappeared into the horizon. Ana's property stretched for miles.

"Is Ana from this area?"

"Not originally. She was born in Spain. Though she went to school in France, you'll probably notice that she's very, very Spanish."

"Why did she come to Mexico?"

"Ana inherited this land from her grandmother. I'm sure she'd love to give you a tour. She's fiercely protective of her land and her community. The people here adore her." Erica stopped herself from going on. "You can just barely see the hacienda from here."

Tayler followed Erica's outstretched arm. She whistled. "That's not a ranch, that's a palace."

The white stucco structure had giant pillars that supported a red tiled roof. Tropical vegetation including palm trees gave the house a great deal of privacy and protection from the intense sun. Pink bougainvillea spilled over the windowsills and cascaded over balconies. Beyond the house stood several small cottages. Past the deep green lushness, the blue Pacific Ocean glittered in the background.

"It's absolutely breathtaking," Tayler whispered, "and I've only seen the outside. I can just imagine what it looks like inside."

Erica chuckled, but when their eyes met, Ana's hacienda was momentarily forgotten. She reached for Tayler. Her fingertips burned against Tayler's cool skin, increasing the heat from the late afternoon sun. When their lips met, Tayler's excitement splashed wildly through Erica's senses.

"Welcome to paradise," she said, her voice low and breathy. She hungrily sought Tayler's lips until the limousine stopped in front of the hacienda.

"Señorita Erica," a short, stocky woman squealed as she opened the car door.

"¡Hola! Buenas tardes!" Erica emerged from the car with Tayler behind her looking flushed. "Tayler, this is Marina," Erica winked at the woman, amused at Tayler's visible mistake. "She's responsible for running this ranch."

Tayler smiled and nodded. Her cheeks were red with embarrassment.

"¡Bienvenido! Señorita. We are so happy you've come to stay with us." Marina's smile was warm. She turned to Erica. "Señora Ana sends you her greeting. She's disappointed she couldn't be here when you arrived. The Señora was called away earlier this morning."

"Trouble?" Erica asked, her eyes moving rapidly across Marina's face.

"No, but you know the Señora. She must investigate everything. The people here are so reluctant to make decisions without first consulting her. She should be returning soon. Let's get you inside where it's cooler. You look like you could use a drink and, maybe, a swim, no?"

"Sounds tempting," Erica slid her hand around Tayler's waist.

Surprised by the obvious show of affection, Tayler allowed

herself to be led into the house.

Once inside Tayler stood transfixed. The hacienda had a multitude of open, panoramic views of the ocean. The shaded openness allowed the ocean air to breeze through and cool the interior areas. Brightly colored woven rugs were scattered on the gray-streaked, white onyx floors. Marina led them through the rooms located around a large reflecting pool. Situated in the middle of the pool, amid several fountains, was a three-foot crystal pyramid.

"It's magnificent!" Tayler released the breath of air she had been holding.

"Ana's ancestors found this crystal in a nearby cave. The original house was leveled by an earthquake—this crystal was all that remained. When Ana asked me to design this house, I put the crystal in a prominent location to protect all those who live here." Erica turned toward Tayler and grinned. "I also combined Mayan architecture into the design, though the Mayans never made it this far west."

Tayler stared at the crystal, absorbed in its beauty. "Do they have earthquakes a lot?"

"No, but this house has survived one major earthquake." Erica said watching Tayler's expression change from fascination to concern. "Ana strongly believes that the casa protected by a crystal will come to no harm."

"Can they protect you from things other than earthquakes?"

"They have mucho powers," Marina led Tayler and Erica up the stairs to their rooms. They first stopped in Tayler's.

The huge, square bedroom had a contoured ceiling and the walls were textured. Tayler's eye was immediately drawn to her left where the bed stood on a raised platform. Its wood frame and posts were elegantly handcrafted from mahogany, while the comforter blazed with the colors of the rainbow. The predominant color in the room was a deep purple. Like the first floor, matching woven rugs were scattered on the onyx floors. Opposite the bed, next to the balcony doors, was a small sitting area with a love seat, chair and an intricately hand-carved writing desk.

Erica watched Tayler move around the room. When she came

to a medium-sized wooden stand in the corner, Tayler stopped. On top of the tall mahogany stand was a large, hollow quartz rock with a crystal dangling inside. Midnight blue candles were placed on each side. The crystal began to turn slowly.

You'll be safe here, Erica thought to herself, at least for a while. She wanted to take Tayler in her arms and reassure her, but she couldn't. Erica cringed knowing that even the crystals in the house could not protect Tayler — or her — from the curse.

The cool water enveloped Tayler's tired body. After a few refreshing laps she swam to the edge of the pool and sat with her legs dangling in the water. Her royal blue swimming suit matched her eyes and its daring French-cut added a provocative look to her figure. She could feel Erica's eyes on her.

"The water's great," Tayler hoarsely yelled out.

Erica tested the water with her toe and then dove gracefully into the pool. Tayler watched her swim and marveled at how strong and sensuous her movements were. Her Greek tan, emphasized by the black, one-piece suit she wore, revealed her curves and her muscles. Tayler could not take her eyes off the daring cuts in the suit, which accentuated Erica's full breasts and long, shapely legs. Drops of water delightfully rolled off her bronze skin each time she emerged from the pool and stepped up to the diving board. Her swan dive was executed with perfection. Tayler whistled to herself. It occurred to her she had never seen Erica use her pool at home — but then Erica was never home. It amazed Tayler how little she actually knew about Erica.

Tayler stood and walked to her lounge chair under a large, leafy palm tree. As she tried to relax, troubled images of the first attack crashed into her thoughts. She roughly adjusted the angle of the chair and leaned back. Sounds from the ocean filtered through the chaos in her head. Though the openness of the hacienda was impressive, it also made Tayler feel extremely vulnerable. The only thing familiar to her was Erica, and she'd only started to get to know Erica in the past few days.

Her mother's words echoed in her memory. "...if Erica's involved...it means witches, black cats, fires and curses..."

The gate opened, interrupting her thoughts.

Tayler turned her head and saw a tall, slender woman enter. She had very dark features and wore a black sombrero, which she threw on a nearby chair as she passed. She untied the bun at the nape of her neck and walked to the shallow end of the pool. With a quick shake of her head, the shiny black mass of hair cascaded down her back. She wore a loose fitting white blouse and black leather pants. Black boots came up to her knees and she lightly tapped a crop against her right thigh. Slowly, she stepped into the water, descending two steps before leaning against the handrail.

"Ana!" Erica yelled and waved from the other end of the pool. She dove into the water, swam to the shallow end and walked up the steps. She paused for a brief moment before speaking. "Oh, Ana, I've missed you."

"Ricah," Ana opened her arms to the drenched woman.

Their embrace on the steps of the pool was long and tender. Ana held Erica's face between her two hands and kissed the tip of Erica's nose. It was difficult to see who was taller since Erica was barefoot and Ana was wearing boots. They spoke in subdued voices before breaking their embrace.

"Tayler," Erica called.

As she neared, Tayler realized why Erica hadn't described Ana to her earlier on their trip. She would have been intimidated by the immense beauty and power Ana possessed. Her pulse quickened. When Ana smiled at her, Tayler felt her legs go weak, but she neither took her eyes off Ana nor looked to Erica for reassurance. Out of the corner of her eye Tayler saw Erica smile.

"Tayler Windquest, this is Señora Ana Catalina Galeano Ariani," Erica began the introductions.

"It's a pleasure to meet you."

"Señorita Windquest, the pleasure is truly mine," Ana said kissing Tayler on both cheeks. "Welcome to my casa. ¿Le gusta aqui?"

"Forgive me, Señora Ariani, my Spanish is very poor," Tayler couldn't help but stare at the color of Ana's eyes. Though she was extremely dark featured, Ana's eyes were a very light brown and appeared almost transparent. They were the eyes of seers and mystics. Tayler turned to Erica for help.

"Ana asked if you like it here."

"Mucho gusto," Tayler spread her hands wide. "Please call me Tayler." Ana took her hand and lightly kissed it. "As you wish." When she straightened, Ana's gaze took in the scar on Tayler's neck. Her eyes darkened. Tayler wanted to cover the imperfection with her hand. It's so ugly and visible, she thought. I'll go through life wearing turtlenecks if this damned thing doesn't fade.

"Ricah has told me about the attempts on your life. I am glad you are here. I will do everything possible to keep you safe. If you tire of Ricah's company, I would be delighted to entertain you. There is much to see here."

"Gracias," Tayler smiled wondering if she could get away with calling Erica 'Ricah.'

"Can you ride a horse?"

"Yes, I mean, sí." Tayler saw Ana wink at Erica.

"Mucho bien. I'll see that we find a horse to match your spirit."

Through the entire discussion, Ana remained standing in the water. Her boots were soaking wet. Tayler saw Erica slide her hand around Ana's waist. She smiled at Tayler, tightened her grip around Ana, and suddenly jerked backwards into the water taking Ana with her.

"Ricah," Ana cried. The two women fell into the water. Ana broke the surface sputtering, "I'll get you for that."

"Is that a promise?" Erica taunted.

Erica dove into the water and tried to swim out of Ana's reach but she wasn't quick enough. Ana caught Erica by the foot and pulled the laughing woman to her. Ana cradled Erica in her arms.

"I've prayed for this moment, Ricah."

"I have, too, mi amor."

Stunned by their words, Tayler realized she had made another mistake since arriving in Mexico. Ana was Erica's lover. Even from where she stood, Tayler could see the intense gaze in Erica's eyes.

"Ricah, I've never seen you in a suit. You gringos are so shy," Ana taunted.

Tayler walked to her chair and gathered up her things. Before she opened the gate, she turned and saw the two women still in the pool. Ana and Erica clung to each other hugging and laughing. "What am I doing here?" Tayler mumbled under her breath. She abruptly turned away from the scene. Before anyone noticed, she silently closed the gate behind her.

twelve

The morning sun bounced off the fluid surface of the ocean creating millions of sparkling diamonds. It was a hot, tropical October day. From where she stood, Ana was surprised to see Erica sitting alone drinking coffee, but the creases in her forehead told Ana why she was up so early.

Ana joined Erica at the table. She poured herself a cup of coffee and refilled Erica's cup. The morning breeze played with Erica's hair. Her eyes, however, were swollen and tinted with crimson. They had talked late into the night, but their discussion revealed minimal clues about the curse.

Ana searched her friend's eyes. "You didn't sleep?"

"No," Erica looked away. "With nine days left, how can I?"

"But this is exactly what Raven wants," Ana took Erica's hand. "You stop eating and sleeping and you become weak. Then slowly she tears you apart. Raven is a master at turning your own mind against you."

"I can't beat her. She's too powerful," Erica clenched her fists.

"She may be powerful but now we have the young one."

"But she knows nothing of the curse and I don't want to see her hurt." Erica dropped her head to the side.

"You're in love with her?" Ana let go of Erica's hand.

Erica nodded, her eyes spilling over with tears of pain and longing.

"She's a beautiful woman—" Ana looked directly into Erica's eyes. "So young and filled with fire. I'm sure with proper instruction she could become an adequate lover for you." She waved her hand in dismissal.

Erica sat up in her chair. "Ana, you're jealous!"

"I don't know what you're talking about," Ana said between sips of coffee.

"I never thought I'd see the day!" Erica's laugh was edged with disbelief. "What are you jealous of?"

"I'm not jealous." Ana's enunciation was precise. "I know you and I know when you've lost your heart."

Erica shook her head trying to understand Ana's reaction to Tayler. "You know more than anyone that Tayler and I can't be lovers."

"You can be in love with someone, Ricah, without making love."

"It isn't the same," Erica groaned. "It's pointless to talk about this. I don't have time to deal with your jealousy or even to think about making love."

"Maybe you should. It might give you added strength," Ana's words came out slowly. "Unexpressed passion is deadly. Look what it did to me—and to us—" Ana closed her eyes.

"Guilt is as deadly as unexpressed passion." Erica replied.

"Sí, but I cannot forgive myself for what I did to us." Ana squared her shoulders. "You'll never capture what we had together—with her."

Erica raked her hands through her damp hair. "You mean what you threw away?" Seeing Ana's face go pale Erica softened her tone. "Ana, Tayler is my only hope. I want so badly to believe that she possesses the power to beat Raven. She's survived three attempts so far." Erica took a deep breath. "Yes, I've fallen in love with her, and I want all of us to survive this ordeal. And when Halloween passes and if I'm still alive, I just want to love her."

"I've brought you such sadness." Ana traced the veins in Erica's hand. "I will burn in hell for what I've done."

Erica got down on her knees and wrapped her arms around Ana. "I won't ever forget what we had."

"I am a fool—" Ana sighed her eyes filling with tears. "How I wish our love could set you free, but Raven gave us no choice. She should have claimed my heart like she did Patricia Locksley's."

The breeze stopped blowing while a cloud passed over the sun. The ocean suddenly looked angry to Erica. "Time is running out," Erica bit her lip. "We need to concentrate on what we're going to do."

Ana took Erica in her arms and kissed her forehead. The cloud passed. The sun reappeared restoring the morning's warmth.

"We'll find a way, Ricah, I promise." Ana raised Erica's face and stared into Erica's eyes for a long time before speaking. "Hallow's Eve will come and go, but the love I hold for you in my heart is forever. Forever."

Erica's tears dripped on to Ana's white blouse. "I hated what you did, but love is stronger than hate. Ana, I've never stopped loving you. I want you to believe that."

"I do." Out of the corner of her eye, Ana caught a glimpse of Tayler moving back into the shadows. She let go of Erica and gestured in the direction of the corridor.

Erica returned to her chair and wiped her eyes with her sleeve.

"Good morning, Tayler, come sit down. Are you ready for breakfast?" Ana tried to ease the awkwardness.

Tayler sat down across from Erica and next to Ana. She looked briefly toward Erica, then looked down quickly, choosing to stare in the coffee cup Ana had placed before her. "I, um, didn't mean to interrupt."

"You didn't," Ana offered.

Erica stood. "If the two of you will excuse me, I think I'll go lie down and try and get some sleep."

"Won't you at least try to eat something?" Ana's coaxing had little effect. "You need your strength."

"I'll join you for lunch." Erica's voice softened. She turned toward Tayler. "Would you like to go for a swim in the ocean this afternoon?"

"I'd love to," Tayler replied. When Erica disappeared down the corridor she looked at Ana. "Is she okay?"

"Sí," Ana removed the silver chain from around her neck. On it hung a small pyramid-shaped crystal with a midnight blue dagger in the center. She handed it to Tayler. "While you're here I'd like you to wear this. Whatever you do, please don't take it off."

"What is it for?" Tayler peered at the crystal with fascination.

"It's for your protection," Ana quickly replied. Her voice was a whisper.

"Protection from—"

"Erica."

Tayler's hand shook as she tried to clasp the chain.

thirteen

Tayler dug her fingernails into the seat fabric in the open Jeep. The long, rutted road was made from old tire tracks leading to the ocean in a choppy, zigzag pattern. With her seatbelt securely fastened, she held on to the safety bar, trying to take in the sights, but the bouncing Jeep made her view fuzzy.

It seemed strange to Tayler that Ana would warn her about Erica and then allow them to go to the beach alone. But then, Ana seemed to be a woman of polar behaviors. Her love for Erica was obvious, but to Tayler, it bordered on a possessiveness she didn't care for. Ana was an enigma. Her wealth and charm were mixed with a strong undercurrent of arrogance. Her beauty was undeniable, but it was her sensuality that took Tayler's breath away. Tayler found herself contemplating what it would be like to be Ana's lover.

She closed her eyes.

"I love this drive," Erica's voice cut into Tayler's thoughts. "The view is so spectacular."

Tayler opened her eyes and struggled to raise her voice over the wind in the open Jeep. "I'm glad Ana hasn't sold out to greedy developers looking to turn this oasis into condominium heaven."

Erica leaned toward Tayler. "This land means too much to Ana," she glanced at Tayler, smiled and turned her gaze back to the winding dirt road before them.

"Are we almost there?"

"Just over this sand dune," Erica shouted. "Hang on."

The Jeep flew over the sand.

Tayler held on to the safety bar while she watched Erica expertly maneuver the Jeep. Erica's appearance was wild. Her shoulder length, black hair whipped around in the wind, her expression one of bound determination.

When the Jeep finally came to a halt, Tayler jumped out and raced to the edge of the water. The waves created ripples of fine, two-toned sand, a pattern that reminded her of pine trees in Minnesota. The beach was devoid of stones and shells but was occasionally dotted with tracks left by sand crabs. The turquoise waters of the Pacific sucked at her feet, pulling her in deeper.

Tayler spread her arms out wide. "Ana owns all this?"

"Sí, twenty miles of private shoreline." Erica stood near the Jeep and watched Tayler absorb the peaceful surroundings. She unloaded two lounge chairs and a bag.

"Wow, this is great! And to think we don't have to fight the crowd for a place in the sand." Tayler walked back to the Jeep and helped Erica with the chairs. "You were right, this is paradise."

Tayler sought the water again. The waves engulfed her ankles and the sand rushed between her toes. Again, she could feel the ocean's mighty force pulling her into the water. Such potent strength amazed and humbled Tayler. The power of nature was something she respected. In all its natural splendor and violence, Tayler found a simple truth—beauty and harm have always existed together.

She turned toward Erica wanting to share her thoughts, but her breath stopped in her throat. From the water's edge, Tayler watched Erica slowly remove the top of her bikini.

Here lies the beauty, she thought, but if her simple insight held, harm was certainly not far behind. Tayler looked up and down the shoreline but saw no signs of danger. The sun took the wind's breath away causing the temperature to sit at a humid 95°.

Erica's body seemed to have been painted and brought to life by an artist's hand. Her breasts were full with nipples the same reddish-brown color of her lips. In the sunlight, against the vibrant color of her teal bikini bottom, her skin shimmered. The silver bracelet on her forearm sparkled in the sun and her eyes were hidden behind dark sunglasses. Tayler wondered if the silver bracelet was Erica's attempt to hide the knife's gash from the first attempt.

Tayler walked back to her things and began to unfold her chair. Satisfied with the arrangement, she bent over and pulled her beach cover-up over her head. The pendant and silver necklace Ana had given her caught on the material and ended up behind her neck. Just as she was about to turn it to the front, she heard Erica ask,

"Would you mind putting some lotion on my back, please?" Erica turned over on to her stomach.

"Sure—" Tayler dropped her hands to her side. She sat down on the edge of Erica's chair and placed a generous amount of lotion in her hands. Tayler hesitated, biting her bottom lip.

"I promise not to bite," Erica said in a teasing tone. Then she growled. "At least not yet."

With rapid strokes, Tayler spread the lotion on Erica's skin, but as it began to soak in, and her awkwardness turned to confidence, Tayler slowed her movements. She slid her hands over Erica's shoulder blades and down her back. She touched every curve and muscle, working in the lotion. An intense heat radiated off Erica's skin sending chills down Tayler's spine.

Unexpectedly, Erica turned over. Surprised by her sudden predicament, Tayler hands foolishly hovered above Erica's chest.

Erica picked up the bottle and poured lotion into Tayler's hands. She then brought them to her breasts. Slowly and gently, she guided Tayler's palms and fingers. The clean fragrance flowed through Tayler's senses.

Tayler looked down at Erica, but with her eyes hidden behind sunglasses, all Tayler could see was her own reflection. She averted her eyes to the mountains off in the distance, feeling like an inept teenager.

Erica raised her chair up a notch. "You have very strong fingers. Do you play an instrument?"

"Piano—" Tayler's voice cracked. *God, I sound like I'm going through puberty*, she thought.

Erica removed her glasses. Her eyes were a light brown in the sunlight. "Will you play for me sometime?"

"It would be my pleasure—" Tayler held her breath when she felt Erica's fingers gently roll over her own breasts. She closed her eyes, feeling herself being pulled down.

Their kiss was timid at first, like two dolphins playfully dancing in the waves. But the softness of Erica's lips washed over Tayler like the tide. A force as great as the ocean's current pulled her deeper and deeper into Erica. Tayler sunk to her knees kissing Erica's smile and then the dimple on each side of her mouth. Lightly, so very lightly, Tayler bit Erica's bottom lip.

"I never said I wouldn't bite," Tayler whispered in Erica's ear. When she heard a growl deep in Erica's throat she laughed. Tayler bent her head and kissed Erica's neck down to the hollow and ran her tongue over the spot, tasting the salt on Erica's hot skin. Light-headed and dazed, Tayler returned to Erica's mouth. Her body sank with a desire that didn't have a need for air.

She marveled at the strength in Erica's hands as they caressed her shoulders and back. She couldn't believe the sensations the tides of passion brought as they crested over her. Her hands gripped the steel frame of the lounge chair wanting so badly to dive in and feel the rush of pent-up fervor.

Erica's fingers circled around Tayler's shoulders and up to her neck. Deftly she untangled Tayler's necklace and brought the pendant to the front. Her hands dropped to her side. She sat up, pushing Tayler away.

"From Ana?" In the intense sunlight Erica's voice was ice cold.

Tayler tried to catch her breath. "Yes."

"You don't need to be afraid, Tayler, I won't touch you anymore." Erica stood and threw on a matching teal cover-up.

"But I want you to touch me," Tayler sat back on her heels trembling. Arousal and fear crashed against her heart. When Erica didn't respond, Tayler whispered, "I've no reason to be afraid of you, and no one has told me why I need to be protected from you."

"Ana has her reasons," Erica looked at Tayler. Her eyes were dark.

"I don't understand."

"Let's go for a swim," Erica began walking toward the water.

Tayler continued to kneel in the sand trying to hold back the tears. She closed her eyes tight wanting her body to cease its shaking from pure arousal and naked abandonment.

I have no right, kissing Erica. She is Ana's lover. Tears stung her eyes and her lips trembled. Guilt ebbed into a sudden wave of anger. *How did I get myself into this?* Tears dripped to the corner of her lips. She could taste only salt. Loneliness shrouded over her like a dark cloud.

A noise nearby made Tayler open her eyes. She found Erica standing before her. Drops of water slipped off her body and made a pool in the sand. Her nose and eyes were red.

"I'm sorry, Tayler, it's nothing you've done…" Erica's voice broke. "I'm so sorry."

Tayler shook her head and sat on the vacated lounge chair.

"Tayler?"

She looked up and gazed at Erica for a long moment. "I don't understand you, Erica. You touch me and then you push me away. You give me answers only to create more questions. You disappear without a word and reappear without a sound. I look for clarification, but find only confusion. One minute you kiss me and hold me and the next you slap me and let me go. Ana warns me about you and then lets me come to the beach with you—alone. And you won't tell me why you brought me here even though I'm somehow involved in this mysterious caper," Tayler took a breath, holding back on the questions she really wanted to ask. Instead, she resisted the urge to attack and said,

"If wearing this necklace is so offensive to you, then I'll just take it off." She began to unclasp the chain.

"Tayler, no," Erica stopped Tayler's hands. She knelt next to the chair. "Please keep it on."

"Why? Does it have magical powers?" Tayler's face was red. "Will it keep the danger away? Will it help me understand the situation I'm in?"

"Yes," Erica said, crying. "It will protect you."

"But I'm not afraid of you, Erica. I'm not afraid of weirdoes or the threatening letters they send."

Erica's eyes were wide with horror. "What threatening letters? Did you receive threatening letters?"

Tayler waved her hand. "I'm exaggerating. There was only one."

"When did you receive it?"

Tayler could see the vein pulsating in Erica's neck. "The day of the luncheon."

"What did it say?"

"Oh, it just said something about the flames being hot and a gift of black to kill the fool." Tayler felt like she had sand in her throat. "It was just nonsense. Someone's poor attempt at poetry."

Erica shook her head. "Why didn't you tell me about it?"

"Because I didn't think it was important. Don't forget that I periodically get threats when I write about topics that don't fall in sync with some reader's opinion."

"We'd better tell Ana," Erica stood and began gathering their belongings.

"Erica," Tayler reached for her, "you promised me we were going to spend the afternoon at the beach. Can't we stay?" Tayler removed the towel from Erica's hand. "We can tell Ana at dinner."

"Will you promise me you'll keep the necklace on?" Erica searched Tayler's eyes.

"I promise." Tayler stood. "Now, can we go for a swim?"

Erica nodded and led Tayler to the ocean.

They played in the tepid water for thirty minutes under the blazing sun. Tired, Erica excused herself and went to relax on her lounge chair. A half hour later, Tayler came out of the water to show Erica her collected ocean treasures. When she drew closer, she noticed Erica was sound asleep. Too restless to sit, Tayler decided to take a walk along the beach.

Still reeling from Erica's extreme moods, Tayler's thoughts were confused. She wanted answers and she wanted Erica to explain. *What did Erica and Ana know about the attempts? Did they know who was behind them? What was Ana really protecting her from? And, while she was at it,* Tayler thought, *why was she brought to Puerto Arista?*

"I guess I'll just have to take Ana aside after dinner and ask her for an explanation," Tayler stated to the ocean.

The cry of a seagull brought her back to her surroundings. She stopped and looked back, but could see neither the Jeep nor Erica. The curving of the shoreline blocked her view, and the sound of waves crashing against the rocks filled her ears. She peered at the terrain on her right and glimpsed a large opening to a cave. She walked toward it.

As a child, Tayler and her father explored many caves. He had an obsession with them. She remembered the cave she had seen on an island off the shore of Mazatlán. The tour guide had called it "Pirate's Cove" because it had been used to store stolen treasure.

"Be very cautious when approaching a cave," her father had warned her. "Search for tracks and listen for the sounds of possible inhabitants."

She remembered asking him why.

"Caves are places that offer both refuge and entrapment." When he realized she wasn't following him, he explained. "If an animal or reptile needs a place to rest, caves provide the shelter. But, if that same animal or reptile feels trapped in the cave, they will strike out at the intruder."

Heeding his advice, Tayler cautiously walked to the entrance and peered into the cave. It took several minutes for her eyes to adjust to the dark interior. An opening in the ceiling of the cave provided a ray of natural light. The cave was large enough to comfortably shelter a dozen people. She stepped inside and followed the stream of light to the floor.

From inside the cave she could hear the muffled sounds of waves hitting the rocks. An iguana the size of a large rat scurried by her. Tayler jumped back smacking her head on a low boulder.

Light-headed, she sat down and leaned against the wall. The cave swirled around in her dizziness and nausea. She held her head in her hands to stop the spinning. She tried to take in several deep breaths of air to calm her nerves and stomach. Minutes passed before Tayler could finally close her eyes. The spinning and nausea gradually ceased. She opened her eyes.

The dark figure of a woman stood in the opening of the cave.

"Erica!" Tayler whispered, her voice gone. "Erica!"

The woman did not move but continued to stand in the shadows near the entrance. She was taller and broader than Erica. The light behind the woman made it impossible to identify her.

Tayler's heart raced with rising panic. "Who are you?"

There was no reply.

The woman bent down and picked up a handful of dirt and started walking slowly toward Tayler. Tayler inched her way along the wall going deeper into the cave's depths. When the woman reached the spot where the light streamed in from the opening in the cave, she stopped. The blade of a knife glimmered in the light. The woman's green eyes glowed eerily in the shadows. In a moment of clarity, Tayler knew she was face-to-face with the woman who had attacked her at her pool.

"Who are you and what do you want?" Tayler gasped.

Her questions were answered with the sound of laughter. Tayler covered her ears in response to the shrieking. The woman snapped her wrist back catching the light on the nine inch blade.

"Tayler, Tayler, where are you?" The sound of Erica's voice stopped the woman and she turned toward the opening. Erica's voice came from somewhere nearby. "Tayler, where are you?"

"In here," Tayler squeaked.

The woman turned back toward Tayler. Raising her arm high above her head, she sent the knife flying. It whizzed through the air with a hissing sound.

Tayler ducked, but the knife was overthrown and harmlessly hit a rock two feet away. She collapsed on the floor of the cave too stunned to get up.

"Tayler, where are you?" Erica called. She stood at the entrance out of breath. Guided by the light in the cave, she rushed to Tayler's side. "Are you hurt?" Erica knelt down and helped Tayler sit up.

"Did you see her," Tayler's choked. Her hands shook uncontrollably.

"Who?"

"The...woman...it was her," she repeated, "the...woman..."

"What woman, Tayler?"

"The one who...attacked...me—"

"Let's get you out of here," Erica helped Tayler stand. "Can you make it?"

Tayler nodded.

Clothes flew haphazardly into suitcases. Viewing the chaos, Tayler realized she'd never get all of her belongings packed, so she slowed down and began to methodically fold her things. Nearly finished, she glanced up at the little crystal shrine in her room. She walked over to it lost in thought. Tears fell down her sunburned cheeks.

A knock on the door was followed by Ana's voice. "Tayler, may I come in?"

"It's open."

Ana walked in, eyeing the suitcases. "Marina told me you're

not having dinner with us, but it appears you are leaving. No?"

"You're a wonderful hostess, Ana," Tayler said without turning, "but I've got to get out of here."

Ana placed her hand on Tayler's shoulder and turned her around. "I don't want you to leave," Ana spoke softly. When the sobs came, Ana took Tayler in her arms.

"I don't understand what's happening. Someone's trying to kill me and I know it has something to do with Erica. But she won't talk to me about it." Tayler said between sobs. "I thought I wanted to know what was going on, but now I think I'm better off away from here and her."

Ana led Tayler to the bed and they sat down. "But what about your love for her?"

Tayler threw Ana a glance, then quickly looked away. Her lips quivered.

"True emotions are difficult to hide."

"But you and Erica are together—"

"No," Ana took Tayler's hand. "Erica and I were once lovers—years and years ago. Now she is my dearest friend."

Tayler looked at Ana, opened her mouth to respond, but was stopped by the depth of sadness she saw in Ana's eyes.

"She needs you."

"Oh, Ana, she needs you, she doesn't need me."

Ana arched her eyebrow, her gaze never leaving Tayler's eyes.

Tayler looked down at her hands. "I don't know what to think, Ana. I've never encountered anyone like Erica before. And I've never been good with people who withhold information. She's driving me crazy."

"Tayler, listen. We are all caught in a horrible and deadly situation. Unknowingly, you are involved in this situation, too. To make things more complicated, you've fallen in love with a woman who could kill you."

"What?" Tayler's eyes widened.

"You've had a difficult day, amiga. I think it best that you rest. Tomorrow I will explain."

"No, wait, I—"

"Please, Tayler." Ana held up her hand. "Try to get some sleep. Things will be clearer once your mind and body have had time to relax."

"But I—"

"Tayler, you've got to trust me." Ana stood.

"Ana, wait." Tayler stood up. "Did Erica tell you about the woman in the cave?"

"Sí, she said you saw someone—a woman."

"I know she's the same person who attacked me in Minneapolis." Tayler searched Ana's face. "Luckily, she's not very good with a knife."

Ana paused. "On the contrary, she's very deadly with a knife—and with fire and snakes." She turned her head toward the crystal shrine. "If she missed, it's because she was trying to scare you."

"Oh, god," Tayler sat down in a chair. "Well, she did a damned good job."

"Where is the knife?"

"In the cave. We didn't think to get it," Tayler's eyes were wide with fear. "Ana, you know who this woman is, don't you?"

"Sí." The crystal began to spin furiously. Ana waved her hand and the spinning stopped. "Her name is Raven."

"What's her issue with me? I don't even know her!" Tayler cheeks burned. She swallowed hard.

Ana leaned against the foot board, perspiration dotting her forehead. She walked to the door.

"Tayler, I know you don't understand what's going on, but I'll explain everything to you tomorrow. In the meantime, I'll have a tray brought up for you." Before closing the door, Ana added, "Rest, Tayler. Raven will not try anything more tonight."

The cave was dark and musty. Waves outside crashed against the rocks creating a constant thunder in the decayed interior. With her fingertips, Tayler gently guided herself along the dim passage. She lit a small candle and used its tiny light to find her way, but despite its help, she wandered aimlessly down long, curving tunnels.

The cold damp air in the cave made her shiver and her eyes burned with fatigue. When she came upon a lit passage, she blew out the candle and followed along until it spilled into a large cavern. The floor was littered with sparkling crystal pieces. A current of cold air snaked through the cavern and Tayler wrapped her arms around her body for warmth. Her hands were like ice.

Pieces of crystal clinked under her bare feet. The jagged points poked into her skin and the ground began to tremble. Tayler lost her balance. Exhausted, she laid her body on the dirt floor and surrendered.

"Go back, Tayler," Ana called out. "You must get out."

Tayler looked around and saw Erica standing at the opening in her teal bikini bottoms. "You can't touch me, Tayler, if you do you'll die."

"But I want to touch you. Please Erica," Tayler cried but Erica vanished into the shadows.

A strange light appeared at the opening. Fog drifted in and swirled around the cavern. Tayler shivered from the sudden blast of cold air. Out of the fog came a darkly clothed woman. Her skin was very pale.

"Tayler," the woman's voice was just above a whisper. "Tayler."

"Are you the Raven?" Tayler backed up against the wall.

"Raven, Raven, Raven," the name echoed in the cave.

"What do you want from me?" Tayler was shaking.

The woman stood directly in front of her. Her eyes were green and her eyeteeth were white and pointed — like fangs.

"I want you," came the reply.

The strange woman picked up a handful of dirt and began

to throw it over Tayler.

"Ana," Tayler screamed.

"You have no choice."

Tayler tried to brush the dirt away, but it wouldn't come off. "No!" Tayler yelled.

"Kiss me, Tayler. Kiss me and the world is yours." Raven's laughter resonated in the hollowness.

"No!"

Raven's face contorted with anger. "You will kiss me and then I will destroy you." Her cold hands grabbed Tayler by the shoulders and fiercely shook her.

"No, no—" Tayler struggled against the cold hands.

"Tayler," Erica's voice rang through the fog. "Tayler, wake up. You're dreaming."

"Help me." Tayler sobbed.

"It's only a dream, darling, open your eyes," Erica coaxed.

Tayler's eyes fluttered open. Upon seeing Erica she sat up quickly and clung to her. Through her tears she saw Ana standing next to the bed. Ana's forehead was creased and her lips were drawn into a line.

"What time is it?" Tayler shivered.

"It's midnight," Ana replied. She walked across the room to shut the balcony doors, which had been blown open by the wind.

"Are you all right?" Erica asked. She smoothed the damp hair away from Tayler's eyes.

"She was in my dream—Raven."

Erica stared at Tayler and then looked at Ana.

"It wasn't a dream, was it?" Tayler demanded.

"No, not really." Ana turned and looked at the crystals. They were spinning.

"She was going to kill me," Tayler whispered.

"How? Did she say?" Erica asked.

"Dirt. She picked up some dirt from the floor of the cave, like she did this afternoon. But in the dream she sprinkled it over me. I tried to brush it off, but I couldn't."

"The fourth element." Ana said. She looked directly at Tayler. "Tayler, this is important. What did she say exactly?"

"I just want to forget this, please don't make me— "

"Tayler, it's important. What did Raven say to you?"

Tayler cringed trying to remember. "She said I had no choice."

"No choice in what?"

"She wanted me to kiss her. She said if I kissed her the world would be mine." Tayler shut her eyes. "But then she said she would destroy me." She leaned against Erica's shoulder and hoarsely pleaded, "Please don't leave me alone tonight."

⁓⁓

The waxing moon lit the bedroom and cast shadows on the walls. Tayler laid on her side studying Erica's long dark eyelashes, listening to her breathing, soft and steady. The impulse to touch the velvety skin was strong. Instead, Tayler resigned herself to a visual caress of Erica's body.

Her eyes wandered over Erica's face. Dark half-moons attached themselves below the sleeping woman's eyes. Tayler could see the lines of worry stretched across the surface of Erica's face. Tayler gently lifted her hand to touch Erica, but stopped. She didn't want to disturb the sleeping woman.

"Why the hesitation?" Erica's voice was as soft and lush as the sheets that enclosed them.

Tayler looked into two black pools. "Did I wake you?"

"I wasn't asleep," Erica took Tayler's hand and guided it to her face.

The feeling of her dry hand on the smooth, moist skin pierced Tayler's composure.

"You've fallen in love with a woman who could kill you." Ana's earlier warning stopped Tayler's hand. She looked away.

Erica brought Tayler's head up so she could look into the

younger woman's eyes. "I frighten you."

"No—well, maybe a little," Tayler confessed.

"Why?" Erica leaned on her elbow so she could look into Tayler's eyes.

Tayler looked away. "I'm not sure how long I can be near you without making a fool of myself."

Erica again lifted Tayler's face. "I can't imagine that happening," Erica's voice was soothing.

Tayler laughed. "I come from a long line of fools. Look at my mother."

"Your mother's not a fool."

"She let you go," Tayler countered. "I think that was pretty foolish."

Erica sighed. "No, it wasn't foolish. I was too young to understand what was happening. Christina wanted an explorer, an adventurer. I was still learning how to put one foot in front of the other."

"You've done very well for yourself," Tayler felt her cheeks grow warm.

The room was quiet. "Professionally, yes, I have. My personal affairs, however, have been far from ideal."

In the moonlight, Tayler saw Erica frown. "Because of Raven?"

"Yes."

"How long has she been affecting your life?" Tayler ran her fingers along the blanket's satin border.

"It seems like an eternity," Erica closed her eyes. "Twelve years."

"Why haven't you stopped her?"

"I've been trying to find a way. I've traveled everywhere for help, but it's not so simple. The pieces are only now falling into place."

"And I'm one of those pieces?"

"Yes," Erica's reply came in a whisper, "you're the key."

"The key?" Tayler asked surprised. "But I also could get

killed?"

"Only if we make love," Erica sat up.

"Is it just with me or with anyone?" Tayler propped her pillows and faced Erica.

"Anyone."

"Including Ana?" Tayler held her breath.

"Yes."

Tayler grew quiet, weighing this new information. "I don't mean any disrespect, but this sounds like some gothic tale — an evil sorceress, a beautiful lady in distress, an uneducated key person."

"I wouldn't describe you as uneducated," Erica tried to smile.

"But I have no idea what's going on or how I'm involved."

"You will after Ana explains everything."

"Why can't you tell me?" Tayler asked reaching for Erica's hand.

Tears fell down Erica's face and dropped on the blanket. "Because she's the reason I'm in this predicament." She leaned into Tayler's shoulder and breathed deeply.

Tayler wrapped her arms securely around Erica. Her mind flew from one question to the next. From fatigue and the late hour, she simply asked, "Does another piece of this puzzle happen to be that this key person falls madly in love with the beautiful lady in distress?"

Erica chuckled and rubbed her eyes with her fingers. For a long moment, she peered at Tayler. "It would appear so, but I just don't know if they'll live happily ever after."

Their eyes met.

Tayler pulled Erica down on to the bed. "I want to make love to you, Erica, so they better." Silence blew in through the open balcony doors. "Good night, beautiful lady in distress."

"Good night," Erica whispered.

A willowy shadow with green eyes stood on the balcony and watched the sleeping women. The crystal in the room began to spin furiously, but when the sun peeked over the horizon the shadow vanished. The crystal stopped its spinning.

fourteen

When Tayler awoke the next morning she found herself alone in the queen-size bed. Her thoughts were muddled, she could not tell fact from fiction, and her fantasies and nightmares were becoming more and more mixed. All of this greatly unnerved her. The only thing clear was the need to learn why she would die if she and Erica made love.

She showered and threw on a pair of white shorts and a sleeveless denim shirt. As she picked up her watch from the nightstand, she noticed a long stem red rose in a porcelain vase. Surprised, Tayler bent down and smelled its sweet fragrance. A light sleeper, she was amazed that she hadn't heard Erica get up or bring in the rose. She shook her head in an attempt to dislodge her mixed emotions. She needed some physical exercise to control her thoughts and calm her fears.

When Tayler walked through the library doors she found

Ana and Erica hunched over a table. They were intensely studying some papers. Unnoticed, Tayler coughed.

"Good morning," Ana looked up and smiled. She walked over and kissed Tayler on the cheek. "You look wonderful."

Tayler blushed. She avoided looking at Erica and spoke directly to Ana. "You look like you've been out riding already this morning."

"I went to the cave to see if I could find the knife," Ana picked up a rock that easily weighed ten pounds and handed it to Tayler. The blade of the knife was deeply embedded in the rock.

"From lady in distress to Excaliber," Tayler mumbled. She caught a glimpse of a grin on Erica's lips.

Tayler peered at the knife. Its handle was made of black onyx and she could see a partial image of a snake etched in the blade just above the rock. She wrinkled her nose. Knives, fires, snakes and god knows what else, Tayler thought.

"This piece of paper was attached to the knife." Ana handed Tayler the note.

She immediately recognized the paper. It was the same as the note she had received at her office. She held her breath, opened it and read the contents.

"Erica told me you received a similar note a month ago. Do you have it?"

Tayler nodded. "I was going to throw it away, but didn't. The way things were disappearing, I thought I'd hang on to it. If anything, I thought it might offer some clues."

"Did you bring it with you?" Ana raised her eyebrows.

"Yes, it's upstairs."

"Would you get it for me?" Ana asked.

Tayler looked briefly at Erica and then left the room.

When she returned, Ana placed the two notes together along with a document Tayler had never seen before. The paper was yellowed, its edges were torn and the corners were curled. As Tayler read the document her hands began to shake. The written images began to take on a realistic, visual significance.

Beware the Kiss

"A Lover's touch, a soft Caress –
the Dance of Lust becomes possessed.
Sighs fuel passion, a deep Embrace –
Twelve hours lost, a Life erased.

A crown of Light, a sea of Blue –
a Lightning mark, a darker Hue;
A brush of Air, lips of Fire –
a fragile heart, flame Desire.

The Mist betrays, and hides the Fool –
the Curse begins, adhere the Rule;
Beware the Kiss, Beware the Time –
on Hallow's Eve, your Soul is Mine.

The Flames are hot, and fuel the Fear –
a Storm at bay, clouds disappear;
A gift of Black, to kill the Fool –
a frightened Soul, a Game so cruel.

The Cave is dark, the Air is thin –
the Night is long, your Life will Dim;
Beware the Kiss, Beware the Time –
on Hallow's Eve, your Love is Mine."

The last note read,

"The Time has come, for You to die –
my Hunger burns, for your goodbye.
You cannot run, no longer free –
surrender now, come honor Me.

The Raven calls, you must obey –
Flames lick your Lips, your Bones decay.
Beware the Kiss, Beware the Time –
On Hallow's Eve, your Life is Mine."

"What does it mean?" Tayler sat down, her knees too weak to support her body.

"It's referred to as the 'Curse of Five Elements.'" Ana stated.

"Five attempts, of which three have already taken place,"

Erica peered at Tayler.

"Sí. We can expect two more before Hallow's Eve. This is one of the few clues we have that relates directly to Raven's plan," Ana said absorbed in the documents.

"We do know that if she succeeds in either of these attempts, she may not need to do anything on Hallow's Eve except—" Erica's words drifted across the room and sank at the door.

"Sí, but we have five days to figure out what she's going to do. The others will be arriving tomorrow." Ana's tone was strained. She gathered the papers and placed them in a file. She turned to Tayler. "I need to discuss these stanzas with Luis again. We can talk tomorrow."

Tayler's impatience spilled over. "No, Ana, I can't wait until tomorrow. There are only five days left. If I'm such a key person in all of this, don't you think it's crucial we talk right now?"

Ana and Tayler locked eyes. After several tense seconds, Ana looked away. She tied a string around the documents and placed them under her arm. "Ricah, I want you to take Tayler to Luis Joseito. Explain to him what we know about the stanzas." Ana looked at Tayler. "First thing tomorrow morning, I'll tell you how the curse began. I give you my word. I ask only for your patience, Tayler. It's not a story that is easy to tell."

Tayler watched the color drain from Ana's face.

"Before this is over," Ana hesitated, "Raven will see to it that we all walk through the flames of hell."

fifteen

Luis Joseito's house was small and cramped. Located in the center of the small town of Puerto Arista, his wife and four children lived in simple accommodations with a one-eyed dog named Gus.

"¡Buenas tardes! Señoritas," Luis greeted Erica and Tayler. He was a short man with large brown eyes, jet black hair and a crooked smile. His mustache was dusted with gray, making him seem older than his fifty years. Tayler noticed the clean, but faded and patched, shirt and pants he wore.

"¡Hola! Luis," Erica embraced the man accepting his kisses and welcome. She introduced Tayler.

"Come in, come in," he ushered them through the house to the back patio. "¿Habla español?"

Tayler shook her head. "I'm sorry, I don't."

He waved his hand. "No problem. Ana taught me Inglés, she's bien, no?"

Erica chuckled. "Luis is Ana's brother-in-law."

The patio was covered by a trellis filled with pink and white flowers. From where they sat, they could look out onto the mountains. In the shade of the afternoon, Luis and Erica talked about the weather and his health, Tayler ran her gaze over Luis's features. He smiled frequently revealing a large gap between his front teeth.

"You have a copy of the curse?" Luis asked Erica.

"Sí," she replied pulling her copy from a canvas bag. She looked from Luis to Tayler and smiled.

The look in Erica's eyes made Tayler melt. In the sunlight, Erica's white jeans and peach-colored polo shirt emphasized her tan. Her jewelry sparkled in the bright light. Tayler looked down at her own clothes, feeling overdressed. She shifted in her chair and quietly removed her gold bracelet and ring.

"Is something wrong?" Erica moved closer and placed her hand on Tayler's arm.

In the gentle breeze Tayler caught a whiff of Erica's perfume. It was light and sensual.

"No," Tayler pulled out her sunglasses, "I'm just not accustomed to this air." Or your presence, she thought.

One of Luis's children appeared. "This is my oldest daughter, Vania." Luis smiled proudly.

Vania hugged Erica and said in broken English, "Your señorita she es mucho hermoso."

"Sí," Erica replied and glanced over at Tayler. Vania approached the table staring at Tayler's blond hair. Tayler removed her sunglasses and smiled. The girl blushed.

"Quisiéramos tomar algo," Luis's voice cut through the air in crisp Spanish. "Sangría." The girl looked at her father for a brief moment and then turned her gaze back to Tayler.

"Pronto," Luis snapped. The girl jumped and quickly disappeared. "Now, for this curse." He put on thick glasses. His lips moved as he passed his eyes over the words. "We know that the first lines deal directly with the beginning of the curse and Señorita Locksley's death."

Tayler's gaze flew to Erica's face. She saw Erica recoil. She wanted to ask who Señorita Locksley was, but Luis continued.

"These lines describe Señorita Windquest," he looked up and ran his eyes over the scar on Tayler's neck. "Sí, the mark of lightning. The following lines describe the beginning of the final years."

"The next stanza talks about the fire and the snake," Erica added. "But we're unsure of the meaning of the next one."

"The Cave is dark, the Air is thin/the Night is long, your life will dim." Luis sat back in his chair and hooked his thumbs on his belt loops. "You found Señorita Windquest in a cave yesterday, no?" Erica nodded.

"Raven threw a knife." He saw Erica nod again. "And Raven appeared in a dream?"

"Sí," Erica replied. "It made for a very long night," she added referring back to the stanza. Tayler reached out and grasped Erica's hand. For a long moment she searched Erica's eyes for answers. A cauldron of emotions bubbled to the surface, but she held back the swell of fear she felt inside.

"Your life will dim," Luis murmured to himself. "I am not sure I understand this. The act of dimming something often implies—" he sat rigid in his chair.

"Luis?" Erica shook his arm. "Luis, what is it?"

He shook his head. "I'm sorry to have to tell you this." He cleared his throat. "Dimming a life, in this curse, could mean Raven is planning a slow death for one of you."

Tayler gasped.

Erica pulled Tayler toward her. "Are you sure, Luis?"

"It is a guess," Luis shrugged his shoulders, "only a guess." He stammered. "Lo siento mucho, Erica, Señorita Windquest," He apologized again to the two women, wringing his hands. Tayler stood and walked to the edge of the patio wanting to scream from the tension. The thought of a slow death for Erica, or herself, was too dark for her to imagine. Erica gathered up the papers, shattering the paralysis that held them in their places. "We'd better leave."

Tayler nodded, unable to speak.

Luis held up his hands in an excited gesture. "Señorita Windquest, the curse describes you—"

"Luis, we've been through this," Erica interrupted.

"Sí, Erica," Luis said gently, "but if she's mentioned in the curse it is because she possesses special powers—powers that threaten Raven." He continued before Erica could interrupt again. "The curse has revealed things line by line. Therefore, the Señorita's powers will be revealed event by event."

sixteen

The morning mist clung to the base of the mountains overlooking the ocean. On the pale pink horizon, the ocean flowed with waves of silver. Just beyond the breakers, four dolphins surfaced, searching for an early meal. Ana and Tayler cantered along the beach on two black Arabian horses, absorbed in the morning calm.

"You ride very well," Ana brought her horse next to Tayler's. "Who taught you?"

"My father," Tayler smiled as she recalled the man who had filled her life with wonder. "He felt that learning to ride a horse was as important as learning to read."

"A smart man." Ana looked at the sky and then returned her gaze to Tayler. "You miss him."

Tayler bit her bottom lip. "He was such a big part of my life."

"What was he like?"

Memories began to seep into Tayler's consciousness. She cleared her throat. "He was a very complex man. He was kind and gentle with me, but to his business associates, he was ruthless. He made a lot of money—and a lot of enemies." Tayler rolled her eyes. "Including my mother."

Ana's lips curved into a wicked smile. "Ah, Christina Windquest. I recall her sizzling reputation."

"You know my mother?" Tayler looked at Ana in surprise.

"I only know of her. Ricah and I met several years after their relationship ended. Ricah was still mending from that wound."

"That's my mother," Tayler added.

"Or to be more correct, that's human nature." Ana sat upright in her saddle. Her white blouse accented her dark skin and her riding boots emphasized the long, slender legs that flowed seamlessly into them. Her eyes, at times, were hidden in the shadow of her straw sombrero.

On the horizon, the sun rose over the silver surface spilling rich reds and oranges across the fluid expanse.

"The one thing I can say about my father is that he met some fascinating people. It didn't usually bother me, but I remember one night I needed to talk to him." Tayler removed her feet from the stirrups. "We met at a restaurant in downtown St. Paul. I thought we'd be able to talk without the usual interruptions. I can't even remember now what had been so important."

"How long ago was this?" Ana asked.

"I was twenty-three. I had just finished college and was working on my master's degree. I guess that would make it a little under ten years ago. Anyway, we were sitting at the bar waiting for our table when a woman approached us. I was completely enthralled." Tayler smiled.

"Why?"

"It seems they knew each other through the mutual love of book collecting. She was so fascinating, I was surprised that Dad had never mentioned her before. He invited her to join us." The sun felt warm on Tayler's face. "Gabrielle seemed to know something about everything." Tayler added quietly patting her horse's neck. "Looking back over the months she and I spent together, I've come to the realization that I had a real crush on her."

"What did your father think of her?" Ana sat with her hands

placed comfortably on the saddle horn.

"I know he enjoyed her, but he seemed so spaced out that night. I blew it off. By then Gabrielle and I had scheduled dates to go to the science museum, lunch at the arboretum, concerts, plays, you name it." Tayler dropped the reins. She pinched the bridge of her nose. "I eventually found out that Dad had received his first death threat that day."

"What happened?"

Tayler sighed heavily. "The detective on the case told me that Dad had received a total of five threats. On the morning Dad was killed, he had received the final note, but he was meeting my mother for lunch and had to hurry." Tayler took a deep breath. "He got in his car and it blew —"

"I'm sorry, Tayler," Ana said. "So, what became of Gabrielle?"

"She just vanished. I think there's still a warrant out for her arrest."

"You don't believe she did it?" Ana watched Tayler closely. Ana slid down from her horse and walked along the sand with her horse trailing.

"She was more interested in me than my father. No, she didn't do it."

They walked their horses to a flat outcropping of rocks. While they rested, their horses stood in the shade of a large boulder.

"What happened between you and Erica?" Tayler asked.

Ana twirled the crystal pyramid she wore around her neck. It was similar to the one she had given Tayler, except it did not have a midnight blue dagger in its center. The image of Raven's dagger wedged in a rock suddenly pierced her thoughts. The coincidence was unsettling. Ana removed her sombrero and placed it on the ground next to her. "When Ricah and I met, I thought our relationship would last forever, even though our backgrounds were so diverse and our interests so varied. I had my place here." She gestured to the land with her right hand. "This land has been in my family for hundreds of years. I knew I couldn't leave. And Ricah couldn't leave the place she loved."

"Why is Erica so rooted to Minnesota?"

"Her house stands on the site where she was born. It's her

only connection to her parents. The house you rented, in fact, was the house Erica built for her aging grandparents."

"That explains their close proximity," Tayler interjected.

"Exactly. Ricah is very proud of her heritage." Ana squinted her eyes. "As I am."

"Erica is so private about her personal life. I know of at least fifty editors around the country who'd love to publish her story."

Ana sighed heavily. "She's private because she's been badly hurt. I'm sure your editors would love to get their hands on some of the things in her background. They would destroy her."

Ana's vehemence registered in Tayler's conscience like a streak of lightning. She chose to ignore it and instead said, "So the two of you decided on a long distance relationship."

"Sí."

"Did it last very long?"

"No. Unfortunately, Raven brought our relationship to an abrupt end."

Tayler's memory recalled the green-eyed woman. "What did she do?"

Ana removed a bandanna from around her neck and wiped her forehead. The sun was growing hotter. "She placed a curse on us."

"The one you spoke of the other night?"

"Sí. It is a very ancient curse. Not many people have heard of it. We're not sure where she found it, but Raven possessed a book of black magic."

"You mean a book of curses and spells?"

Ana nodded. "She did her research very thoroughly. It took many of us to gather information on the curse. There are still areas of the curse we are not sure we comprehend. As we near Hallow's Eve, I can only hope that Raven will shed some insight as to what she has planned—for all of us."

"That's cutting it close," Tayler shook her head again. "Okay, so we have this curse, but I'm confused why Raven chose to use it on you and Erica. I mean, what was her reason?"

"Love," came Ana's reply.

Tayler cocked her head to the side, but said nothing.

"Unrequited love to be exact." Ana threw a pebble into the sea.

"I don't understand," Tayler blinked.

Ana took a deep breath before speaking. She let the air out of her lungs very slowly. "I had not seen Ricah for two months and I was lonely. It was a beautiful Mexican evening, the type of evening artists try vainly to capture with their paintbrushes. The sun was descending into the ocean in a rainbow of vivid shades of reds, purples, blues and golds. Ricah was in Minnesota. I craved her presence. The emptiness I felt tormented my soul. I needed to feel her in my arms, smell her hair and hear the sound of her laughter."

Tayler watched Ana turn pale.

"I called her, hoping that the sound of her voice would lessen my loneliness and desire, but all I got was her answering service." Ana twisted the bandanna with her fingers. "My body was so thirsty for her I thought I was going insane."

Tayler nodded. "I think I can understand. I've had a few of those moments in the past two months myself."

Ana wiped her forehead. "My emptiness fueled my fears. As the hours passed I had convinced myself that Ricah no longer loved me. The thought drove me crazy. I longed for her touch, her voice, for anything. I got in my Jeep and drove to the beach and went into a cave." Ana's gaze took in the rocky landscape in the distance. She looked down at her clenched hands. Her voice lost its strength. "I sat in the darkness for hours. I was tired and cold. I wanted someone to fill my emptiness and take away my need."

Tayler sat in silence, never having seen someone in such despair.

Ana shivered in the heat. "Raven found me in the cave and built a fire. She had a flask of something and offered it to me. All I remember is that it was warm and soothing. In the firelight, she began to look so alluring. I could not look away."

Tayler's nerves strained against the visual picture Ana created.

"It grew very warm in the cave, so Raven took off her coat. Her body was covered with scarves. She started to dance, tormenting me with her seductive, deliberate movements. I took another drink from the flask. She removed layer after layer until I could see the outline of her naked body through the last remaining scarf. I tried to get up but couldn't. Much too late, I realized I had been drugged. The vibrations and cadence of her dance made my body ache. I wanted her so badly."

Tayler saw Ana pick up her sombrero and run her fingers around the brim. Tears ran down her cheeks. "Ana?"

"I don't know what poison Raven gave me. What I do know is that it made me face the hidden side of my personality, and I enjoyed it."

"I don't understand," Tayler said. "What do you mean?"

"Through the drug, Raven unleashed the behavior I would have never shown to anyone. It's a powerful side, very animalistic—seduce and conquer. I thought I could do anything, be everything. I wanted it all, including Raven. I felt I was invincible. I demanded that she take away my hunger, but she continued to taunt me with her body. Finally, I asked her what she wanted from me."

"Give yourself to me," Raven had said.

Ana hung her head. "And I did."

Tayler watched Ana's tears blot her white shirt. She wanted to say something, but Ana was not finished.

"In the light of morning, when the drug had worn off, I knew I had made a terrible mistake. My hands and feet were bound to the floor. Raven stood over me, gloating in her pleasure at my surrender. I told her to release me, but she only laughed. I asked her why she was doing this. I can still recall her answer."

"I have loved you, Ana, since we were children, but you never cared for me. I was too poor, too homely for you, but I needed and wanted your love. I thought you, Sterling and Devin were my friends, but it was all an illusion—you just kept me around for laughs. I was nothing to any of you. Only when I tricked you, you allowed me to touch you—love you."

Ana placed her head in her hands.

Tayler laid her hand gently on Ana's shoulder. "Then what happened?"

"After our tryst, she took out a small black book. She opened it and began reading something. I didn't understand the whole thing at first because I hadn't kept up with my Latin. I was able, however, to translate several words." Ana took a breath. "I couldn't believe it. Raven had placed a curse on me."

Tayler peered at Ana for some indication that this was all a myth, but she found only misery.

"This must all be very strange to you, Tayler, but please believe me — you must believe me."

"My god, Ana, we're in the twenty-first century. Things like this aren't supposed to happen." Tayler looked perplexed. "You keep talking about this curse, but the attempts on my life could've been orchestrated by a psychopath." Tayler lowered her voice. "Do you have proof that it exists?"

Ana kneeled in front of Tayler and began unbuttoning her blouse.

"Ana, what are you doing?"

When Ana opened her blouse and unhooked the front of her bra, Tayler gasped. Ana's right breast looked like it had been gouged repeatedly with a sharp object. "Oh, my god — "

"It was an ingredient for the curse to work." Ana grew silent for a moment. "Raven clawed me with her nails."

Tayler sat stunned holding her breath. Finding her voice she asked, "And the curse?"

Ana's voice was cold and distant. "That morning in the cave, Raven tried to kill me, but couldn't. I was the only person in the universe she loved. So, she altered the curse, redirected it away from me and focused it on Ricah instead." Ana inhaled the ocean air. "Raven knew that if I was cursed she'd never be able to touch me again. By cursing the woman I loved, Raven knew Ricah would be out of the way. Raven thought I'd grow to love her, but I didn't."

Tayler felt the guilt and betrayal that consumed Ana. Now she understood why Ana was responsible for Erica's solitary life. She waited in the heavy shroud of silence, not knowing what to say.

Ana's voice was barely audible, "The curse affects only the women Ricah becomes involved with."

"Like me?"

"Sí. If Ricah makes love to you, you will die within twelve hours." Ana's fiercely cold warning sounded acerbic in the tropical setting.

"What does that mean exactly?" Tayler's eyes grew wide.

"She can kiss and caress you, but she can't make love to you."

Tayler got up and started to pace. "What proof do you have that this curse actually exists? Surely, that old document proves nothing."

"There's more."

Tayler ran her fingers through her hair. "I'm listening."

"When I didn't return home the next evening, Marina called my sister and brother-in-law. They found me in the cave. The wound was infected and I was hallucinating. It took them two days to calm me down enough to find out what happened. My sister called Ricah to explain, but when Ricah learned that I had sex with Raven, she was devastated. She hung up on Carmen. We did everything we could to reach her and warn her about the curse, but Ricah wouldn't talk to me. I finally got through to Susan Evans and found out that Ricah had flown to Los Angeles. While she was there she had dinner with a woman named Patricia Locksley. The two got drunk and went back to Ricah's hotel room."

In her files at the office, Tayler remembered coming across an article on a charity Erica had established in Los Angeles. It was called the Patricia Locksley Foundation. At the time she had read the article, Tayler had assumed that Patricia had become an icon for violence against women, and that Erica had not really known her.

"When the police arrived at Ricah's hotel room the next morning they questioned her about Patricia. Ricah told them that she had dinner with her the night before and that they had come back to the hotel for a drink. She couldn't remember when

Patricia left, but figured that it had been earlier that morning. The police informed Ricah that Patricia Locksley had been found a mile from Ricah's hotel — dead."

Tayler turned and stared at Ana. "What did Erica do?"

"By that time, I had finally gotten through to Ricah and explained the curse. When she got off the phone she went to the police and tried to confess to the murder. The police laughed at her and sent her away."

"But you both believe it was Raven?"

"Sí," Ana stood and took Tayler's hand. "In one of Raven's notes you'll remember that she refers to a 'fragile heart'."

Tayler nodded.

"Raven cut Patricia's heart out of her body."

Tayler staggered. She sought the support of a rock and leaned against it. Drops of sweat rolled down her face. She felt feverish, nauseated and light-headed.

Ana took her canteen and poured water into her bandanna. She lifted Tayler's hair and placed the wet cloth on Tayler's neck. Tayler took the canteen and swallowed the cold liquid.

Tayler's voice was strained. "Am I destined to die that way, too?"

"Unlike Patricia Locksley, you have the power to put an end to this curse."

"What power? Ana, I'm a writer. On most days I'm lucky to have enough power to get out of bed and meet my deadlines. I use a computer, not a magic wand. Sure, I know a thing or two about a lot of things, but I don't know this kind of power. I don't possess this kind of power." Tayler paused. "And if I never make love to Erica, I won't be killed."

"It's not as easy as that," Ana looked away to avoid Tayler's eyes.

"Why?" Tayler demanded.

"If you choose not to help Ricah she will die."

Tears flooded Tayler's eyes. "How?"

"At the stroke of midnight on Hallow's Eve, if Raven has not been stopped, she will claim Ricah's soul." The wind suddenly picked up. "Her heart will be ripped out like Patricia's..."

"Stop, Ana, please, please stop," Tayler's groan cut through the wind. "How can I help her? Us?"

"By destroying the curse." Ana watched Tayler. "You have already survived three attempts."

"But you said the curse has five elements. What will the other two involve?"

"The most common elements in curses are earth, water, air and fire. If you look at the attempts, so far, the elements have included water and fire."

"But what about the snake?"

"That's the fifth element. The fifth element identifies the person who cast the spell. Raven has a personal affiliation with snakes."

"But couldn't the attempts have been made by some crazy weirdo who's out to get me for some far-out obsession or religious belief?" Tayler wanted to run away. The more she knew the less she wanted to hear.

"When your house was destroyed by fire, Ricah knew Raven was behind the attempts. Piecing the two attempts together, she realized you were the person referred to in the second stanza."

"So you're saying that there will be two more attempts on my life—one using air and one using earth?" Tayler shuddered.

"I don't know." Ana shrugged her shoulders.

"What do you mean you don't know? Today is October 26—we have only four days until Halloween."

"Raven found you in the cave the second day you were here. She threw a knife, but it missed you. I met with my sister yesterday, but even though she knows Raven, she is not sure this was an attempt. We don't know where to go from here."

"Did Erica tell you what Luis said about the curse?"

Ana nodded. "She told me."

Tayler looked down the beach, her eyes focusing on the mountainous terrain. "I want you to take me to the cave where Raven entrapped you. Maybe we'll find a clue to help us."

seventeen

Tourists filed off the plane as Erica anxiously waited in the small terminal. She stared past the faces of new arrivals looking for the two faces so dear to her. Dr. Susan Evans and Elizabeth Barrett had always been compassionate and devoted friends and Erica often looked to them for support. Their arrival in Puerto Arista marked the annual Mexican Day of the Dead celebration and, hopefully, the end of the curse for Erica. For the millionth time since she found out about the curse, Erica wondered if she had a future beyond Hallow's Eve.

"Hey, lady, you wanna buy something for your amigas?" arms went around Erica.

"Beth, Ev, hi. Am I glad to see you two." Erica embraced the two women. "I'm sorry I wasn't paying attention."

"It's okay, Erica, you were easy to locate." Susan Evans kissed Erica on the cheek. "You're the only one in the airport not wearing three-inch heels."

"Hey, was that a cultural slam?" Beth looked at Ev in disbelief.

"No, not at all. My observation on Mexican culture is due to my concern for increased breaks, strains and varicose veins. All I'm saying is that women in Mexico wear higher heels more frequently than we stodgy Midwesterners."

"But what about New York and—" Beth was just getting started.

"I'm glad you're finally here," Erica's tone brought the conversation to a halt.

"Things must be getting tense," Ev breathed. Her physician-trained eyes examined Erica. Despite her tan, Ev could tell that Erica wasn't sleeping. She also noticed that Erica had developed a nervous habit of clenching and unclenching her right hand, as if she were preparing for a fight. Ev was glad she brought sedatives, but doubted that Erica would use them. For the first time since the curse began, Ev wondered if Erica had the strength to win.

"I thought I was finally going to meet Tayler, but it looks like Ana coerced her into doing something other than hanging out at the airport," Beth tried to ease the seriousness of the conversation.

"They went riding early this morning. Ana is giving her the grand tour."

"And the grand story, I would imagine," Ev stated matter-of-factly. The women began to walk toward the exit.

"Ana needs to explain the curse. It wasn't my place to tell Tayler," Erica looked momentarily helpless.

"When are the others arriving?" Ev asked.

"Later this afternoon. Marina will be here to pick them up, but I wanted to get the two of you."

"We're honored," Ev smiled.

"Let's get you to the hacienda. I'm sure you'd like a chance to relax before everyone arrives." Erica saw Ev throw Beth a seductive glance. The exchange made Erica sad. She wondered if the day would ever come when she would be free to love again.

"It's not much further," Ana called to Tayler. The rain began shortly after Ana and Tayler set out for the cave.

The black clouds in the sky made the day seem dark for one o'clock in the afternoon. Absorbed in Ana's story, Tayler hadn't realized how hungry and tired she was. Her wet clothes didn't help her disheartened spirit.

"Storms here are brief, but heavy," Ana had said. "They are known to pass very quickly."

"Not quickly enough," Tayler muttered to herself.

A streak of lightning broke through the clouds. The horses reared from the thunder that followed. Tayler held on tighter and encouraged her horse to keep going. Finally, when Tayler felt she could hang on no longer, she saw Ana dismount. Through the rain, Tayler could see the opening of a cave.

Ana waved to her and yelled. "Bring your saddle with you."

When she entered the cave, Tayler was greeted by the glow of a lantern. She looked around the cave for iguanas, but saw no signs of life. The hollow cavern was slightly smaller than the cave Tayler had explored two days before, but she was surprised by its barren interior. The ceiling was slightly higher but there was no opening in the top to let light through. Inside the cave, Tayler turned back to the opening. Rain was still falling, but it started to sound like the storm was lessening. She shivered in her wet clothes.

"I brought a lantern to give us more light, and we could use its heat right now to dry our clothes," Ana's voice sounded strained in the confines of the cave. She stood rigid against a boulder still clutching her saddle.

"Is this the first time you've been back here?" Tayler asked taking the saddle and placing it on the ground near the opening.

"Sí."

With her arrogance stifled and the exposure of her vulnerability, Tayler saw Ana go from a self-possessed, demanding woman to a frightened victim. In the light of the lantern, against the rough edges of the boulders, Tayler saw a softer side of Ana, a side that was very appealing. Remembering the reason they had come to the cave, Tayler said quickly, "I'll just take a short look around, okay?"

Ana nodded but said nothing.

"Where were you tied down?" Tayler asked as gently as she could.

Ana pointed to a spot. It was located in an alcove.

Tayler walked over to the spot and looked around. She noticed she could not see the entrance from this location. The cave seemed to be deadly still. There were no tracks of any kind, making it clear that the cave was uninhabited. She walked over to the spot and both looked and felt with her hands. Finding nothing, Tayler took a deep breath of air and let it out slowly.

Love, Ana had said, was the reason for the curse.

Tayler grimaced imagining the loneliness Ana must have felt from Erica's absence. Only love would drive someone to such extremes. It was difficult for her to think of Ana making love in such a desolate place. Being violated, she corrected herself. Her heart pounded against her chest.

A small tremor jilted the cave.

Tayler grabbed Ana's arm. "What was that?"

"The valley is sometimes shaken by tremors, but they are never very serious," Ana stated without emotion. "We should leave."

"Just a minute," Tayler studied the cave again. The tremor stopped, but the shaking caused some of the cave floor to shift. A dark object was visible now where Tayler had previously searched.

"We should leave now," Ana repeated. This time her voice was laced with urgency.

"Wait, I just want to check this out," Tayler said as she reached down into the dirt. The cave shook again.

Ana saw what Tayler had found and looked away, the memory searing her nerves.

Tayler pulled a five-foot leather strap and a stake from the loose dirt. It was one of the straps used to bind Ana to the ground. "Ana, tell me again why Raven didn't kill you?"

"She wants me alive." Ana's eyes moved anxiously around

the cave. "She's hoping I'll learn to love her — someday."

In the lantern light, Tayler could see Ana's plea for help in her eyes.

The cave shook again.

Ana looked at the entrance. "We should leave."

"Ana, wait." Tayler caught Ana by the arm. "Why am I the one who must destroy Raven?"

"You're the only one who has the skills to beat her," Ana called over the increasing noise. Thunder sounded beyond the cave.

"I don't have any skills," Tayler protested.

"You have always possessed the skills, Tayler, but you must learn how to use them."

The sound of crashing rocks could be heard somewhere behind the cavern.

"Come, we must go," Ana grabbed Tayler's arm as the cave floor began to buckle.

Tayler reached out to the wall for support, but the dust was so heavy she couldn't tell if they were moving toward or away from the opening. Pieces of ancient rock broke loose from the walls and ceiling, obstructing their way out. The sound in the cave became so deafening that Tayler's voice couldn't be heard above the thunderous clamor. She tried to call out to Ana, but the chaos of moving earth made it impossible. A small rock hit Tayler in the head and she stumbled. Ana reached for her and helped her up. She said something, but Tayler couldn't hear her. The whole cave appeared to be crashing down around them.

Tayler's arms and head ached and her ears hurt from the noise. The dust swirling around made it difficult to breathe. She coughed and tried to wipe the dirt from her eyes. When she opened them she caught a glimpse of light at the opening. Only five feet from the entrance, the cave was again thrown into total darkness.

"Ana, where are you?" Tayler screamed. "Ana!" she screamed again.

As a large boulder fell, a hand came out of the blackness and grabbed Tayler's arm. The force of the boulder knocked Tayler off her feet. Still unable to see, Tayler blindly stood and began to search for Ana. The earth heaved, smashing Tayler against the rock. As she lost consciousness, Tayler heard Ana scream.

"They should have been back hours ago, Ev," Erica paced back and forth, clenching and unclenching her fists. The storm had passed, but brilliant flashes of lightning still pierced the sky.

"My guess is Tayler wanted to see the cave where the curse began. They could have waited out the storm there." Ev got up from her chair and put her arms around Erica.

Erica shuddered. "Look, I can't wait here any longer. I'm going to get the keys for the Jeep. Do you two want to come with me?"

"We're right behind you." Ev and Beth stood.

Erica rushed down the open corridor.

"Tayler," the voice was weak and barely audible.

Dazed, Tayler sat up feeling dizzy and nauseous. She wasn't sure if she was alive or in the midst of a bad nightmare, but the pain in her shoulder told her the earthquake at least had been real.

"Tayler," the voice called out again.

Tayler knew from the weak, desperate tone that Ana was hurt. She reached out to find the wall. The quiet seemed eerie. "Ana, where are you?"

"Over here," came the weak reply.

"It's so dark in here. Keep talking while I try to find you."

Ana coughed. "I'll try," she said with a voice heavily laced with pain. "I'm right here."

It took a few seconds for Tayler to gain her bearings, but when she did she quickly located Ana. She knelt down and oriented herself to Ana's body by running her hands around Ana. She was laying on her back, a large boulder pinned her legs to the ground. Her breathing was sporadic.

"My legs are broken," Ana groaned.

"Oh god, Ana, I wish I could see you," Tayler cried.

"Tayler—"

Tayler felt Ana's fingers. They were ice cold and shook violently. "What is it?"

"I think...the lantern is...behind me. I dropped it...when I fell," Ana's body convulsed with coughing.

"Okay," Tayler said crawling along the floor cluttered with rocks and clumps of dirt. "Ana, I found it." She made her way back to Ana. "But I don't have matches to light it."

"You don't need a match."

"But, Ana, how am I suppose to light the lantern?" Panic spilled over into Tayler's voice.

"Use your mind, Tayler," Ana coughed again. "Hold the lantern in front of you and visualize the flame."

Tayler shook her head.

"Try and relax. Slow down your breathing," Ana wheezed. "Concentrate...visualize the wick...imagine what the flame looks like—blue in the center and orange, yellow and red surrounding the blue. Feel the heat building."

Ana's words seeped into Tayler's being. She saw the wick and the flame. The heat grew stronger.

"Breathe deeply. Feel the flame—"

When Tayler slowly opened her eyes she saw the glow of the lantern. For a moment she was astonished by what she had done, but her accomplishment was lost when she saw the rock on Ana's legs. Dark liquid stained the fine dirt on the ground near her.

"Oh god, Ana." Tayler knew it was impossible for her to move the rock on her own. Ana was very pale. "What can I do?"

Ana feebly raised her hand to Tayler. "I need to rest. Don't panic. Remember…you have the power…to get us out of here."

Tayler sat next to Ana and took her hand. She watched helplessly as Ana slipped into oblivion.

The curse had now destroyed Ana's freedom — just as it had Erica's. Tayler clenched her fist as anger turned to rage. "I'll get us out of here, Ana," she whispered. Without really thinking, she removed the crystal from around her neck and placed it between her hands. She breathed deeply. "Erica — "

As she pulled the keys to the Jeep off the hook Erica saw two horses come charging past the hacienda, heading for the stables. "Marina!" she yelled.

Marina, out of breath, quickly appeared in the hacienda.

"Marina, look, two horses have gotten out of the stable. It must have happened during the tremor — "

"No!" Marina screeched. "Those were the horses Ana and Tayler took. "

"What?" The new information registered and Erica stopped. "Marina, get the ranch hands. I'll have Ev bring her bag. We'll meet you at the cave where Ana was hurt. Do you remember where it is?"

"Sí." Marina grabbed the phone. "I'll call Luis and ask him to get as much help as he can."

Erica ran to the Jeep, jumped in and started the engine. In the rearview mirror she saw Ev and Beth climb in. "Did you bring your bag?" But Erica saw it before Ev could answer. She floored the gas pedal and they drove off in the direction of the ocean.

"Tayler."

Startled by the low, weak voice, Tayler opened her eyes. She knelt beside Ana. "I am so sorry, Ana. This is all my fault. We should've left when you warned me the first time."

Ana said nothing.

Tayler's eyes searched her face. "You knew this was going to happen?"

"Sí."

"Why didn't you tell me? We didn't have to stay."

"I misjudged Raven's power," the flame in the lantern flickered.

Tayler watched it closely. In the small space they were trapped in, she knew they didn't have much time or oxygen left. "What do you mean?"

"Raven combined two elements of the curse in this attempt."

"Earth," Tayler let dirt fall through her fingers and then gestured toward the lantern. "And air—or should I say the lack of." She shook her head. "You weren't convinced the other episode in the cave was a real attempt."

"No," Ana groaned.

Tayler watched the flame flicker.

Ana looked at Tayler and tried to smile. "You have special skills."

"No," Tayler shook her head. "Survival training taught me about caves and air—it has nothing to do with special powers."

"Aren't they the same thing, amiga?"

Tayler crawled to the wall searching for the opening. She looked at Ana refusing to answer her question. A moment passed. "You have more faith in me, Ana, than I do in myself. Teach me—show me how to get us out of here."

~~~

"We're almost there," Erica yelled, driving the Jeep at high speed along the beach.

Ev and Beth hung on tightly knowing that their requests for a slower speed would be futile.

"We're going to need all the help we can get. I only hope we can get to them in time," Erica pushed the pedal farther into the floor.

Moments later, Erica slammed on the brakes and the Jeep came to an abrupt halt at the entrance of the cave — or what formerly was an entrance. Several pick-ups arrived with a dozen ranch hands. "If you've got shovels, bring them with you." Erica yelled. Someone handed her a shovel and she ran toward the cave.

"Tayler, Ana, can you hear me?" Erica yelled. She waited for a reply. "Tayler, Ana can you hear me?" Erica pounded her shovel on the rock and waited. Only silence answered.

Marina and Luis appeared at Erica's side.

Luis shook his head. "The whole village is coming out here to help Ana."

"Great. Let's divide into two groups and remove the rubble. Marina, your team's responsible for getting the larger rocks cleared, okay?"

Marina nodded.

"Luis come with me. Ana and Tayler may need to hear a calm voice to get them through. Everybody, work as quickly as you can. They've got to be running out of air in there."

"Ana, hang on," Tayler said in the darkness. The lantern had gone out. She wasn't sure whether it ran out of fuel, air or both.

While the lantern was still lit, and she could see, Tayler had used the leather strap she found as a tourniquet on one of Ana's legs. The other leg was completely buried under the rock.

It was becoming more and more difficult to breathe. Ana coughed frequently. From the sound, Tayler guessed that Ana's lungs were filling up with fluid. She cried out, but her words were engulfed in a fit of coughing.

Tayler could feel the earth moving, but it wasn't shaking like it had been. Her lungs hurt from gasping for air as she clawed at the dirt searching for the fresh, ocean air just beyond the cave. Her fingers suddenly hit something. She felt the object and realized it was the necklace Ana had given her. When did I drop it? Tayler asked herself. She grabbed it and felt a strong surge of energy flow through her body. Without thinking, Tayler found Ana's limp hand and wrapped the necklace and pendant around Ana's fingers.

"I won't let you die—" Tayler vowed, feeling herself grow suddenly weak.

The frantic pounding of pick axes, shovels and gunning truck engines sounded like the construction sites Erica worked at. One large boulder impeded their progress.

"Okay, try it Marina," Erica yelled as Marina pressed the pedal and the pick-up truck dug its tires into the sand.

The boulder moved only a few inches before Marina let up on the gas and it settled back into its previous space. "We need another truck to help pull. I'll burn this engine out if we don't," she called to Luis.

Luis spoke quickly to one of the ranch hands. Another pick-up truck appeared and more ropes were attached to the boulder. When they were secured on the second truck, Luis gave the signal to the drivers. The combined engines roared, edging the boulder from the front of the opening.

"I see saddles," Erica yelled, running toward the gap in the rocks. There they are, Ev," Erica called out over the noise of the shovels. Erica pointed to two lifeless forms on the ground. Ev knelt down and placed her hand on Tayler's and then Ana's neck.

"They're alive, Erica, but we've got to get them out."

Erica saw Ev's confused expression in the light. "What's wrong?"

"Ana's legs are pinned under the rock, but her pulse is strong. Tayler, on the other hand, has superficial wounds to her head and face, but her pulse is dangerously weak. I don't know what happened in here, but we've got to get them out."

A stretcher was brought in and Tayler was carefully lifted out of the cave while the others went in to help Ana. It surprised the villagers to find Ana so alert and calm. They moved rapidly trying to remove Ana's leg from underneath the rock. Several ranchers pushed against the rock while Erica, Marina and Ev carefully freed Ana's mangled leg. Ana groaned, but did not scream. Her bones were splintered and her skin was torn and bloodied. They carried Ana out on another stretcher and placed it next to Tayler.

The late afternoon was hot and humid. The ocean waves sluggishly slapped against the rocks. The scent of seaweed and dead fish permeated the air. The women and men from the town and the hacienda gathered around the two injured women. With Beth at her side, Ev administered what medical attention she could to Tayler and Ana. Tayler's face was deathly pale. Ev summoned Erica. She lowered her voice so that only Beth and Erica could hear.

"We need to fly Ana to Oaxaca. She needs surgery right away."

"And Tayler?" Erica's eyes searched Ev's face.

"Erica, her breathing is shallow, her lips are blue and her pulse is almost too weak to feel. I don't know if she's going to make it." Ev took Erica's hand.

Erica ran over to Tayler and knelt down beside her. She took Tayler's cold, limp hand in hers. Her chest barely rose from each shallow breath. The scar on Tayler's neck caught Erica's attention. It was a dark red hue against her pale skin. Exhaustion and relief from finding the two twisted into absolute rage. She seethed with bitterness at Raven's curse and Ana's betrayal of their love. Tayler's life was now ebbing with the evening tide. Tears flooded and stung her eyes. She wiped them away and looked at Ana.

"Ana," Erica tried to control her breathing. "Ana, do you have the necklace?"

Ana opened her hand.

Erica reached down and took the necklace from Ana. The sudden surge of power rocked her body. She leaned over and placed the necklace around Tayler's neck. She stood, peered into the sky, breathed in the ocean air and whispered, "Tayler, you saved Ana's life—now you must save your own." Erica closed her eyes.

Ev was the first to notice the blue tint of Tayler's lips turning a deep red color. She watched as Tayler's fingers twitched. Her eyelids fluttered open. Ev smiled when Tayler sat up and looked at her.

Though she was weak and unsteady, Tayler was helped to her feet with Erica's assistance. She noticed Erica's face and clothes were caked in dirt and sweat, but it was the sweetest picture she had ever seen.

"What happened?" Tayler asked Erica. She saw Ana laying on the ground with her legs snapped like twigs.

"We need to get Ana to the hospital," Ev said. She was a healer, but her skills and abilities could not give Ana her legs back.

"Wait, Ev." Tayler knelt unsteadily next to Ana. "Isn't there something I can do?"

Beth walked over and knelt beside Tayler. "There is, Tayler. You have to have a lot faith in your abilities to do this. Okay?"

Tayler nodded and closed her eyes. Then she raised her eyes to the heavens and whispered, "Show me how to heal her."

A powerful, unseen force took Tayler by the hand. She drew the pendant and necklace over each of Ana's legs. Still breathing deeply, she closed her eyes and pleaded to the heavens for help. She opened her eyes, looked at Ev and Beth, then nodded.

Ev carefully removed the cloth from Ana's legs. A collective gasp rippled through the gathered crowd. Ana's legs bore no markings of injury. Beth and Ev helped Ana stand.

Carefully, Ana tested her legs and then walked toward the others. They met her with cheers, hugs and kisses. She blew Tayler a kiss and mouthed, "¡Gracias, mi amor!"

Erica saw the exchange and walked away.

eighteen

As she slipped beneath the surface, the water in the sunken tub enveloped Tayler into its warm, fluid arms. The oil Ana had added filled the air with a pleasant almond scent that made Tayler's skin tingle. Voices drifted in and out through the closed bathroom door. She tried to relax, but her concentration was gone. Tayler ached from horseback riding and being tossed and thrown in the cave.

With so many strange things happening, Tayler found it difficult to believe that she was still the same Tayler Windquest that left the ranch that morning. Since meeting Erica, more than two months ago, her life had become so strange and she felt even stranger. Piece by piece the puzzle was beginning to fall into place, but she vacillated between total awe and absolute fright. She possessed abilities she didn't know she had, and to make things worse, she understood less how to use them.

Tayler sank further into the water. She didn't want the power and she certainly didn't want to deal with Raven. What she did want she couldn't have. After she and Ana were rescued from the cave, Tayler noticed Erica increasingly distancing herself.

Tayler released the air in her lungs with a rugged sigh.

The warm Mexican breeze blew in through the open glass doors, subtly pulling her from her reverie. She took another deep breath and closed her eyes. After the close call in the cave and the dwindling lack of air, Tayler knew she would never again take fresh air for granted.

The night was near perfect — a warm evening breeze, almond-scented water and burning candles. Now if only Erica would walk through the door, slowly undress and join her in the bath, everything would be perfect. The thought of Erica undressing made her body throb. The longer Tayler waited, however, the more she doubted that Erica would come on her own initiative.

"I wonder if I can summon her," Tayler murmured to herself. It's certainly worth a shot.

She unclasped the necklace and held it in her hands. Tayler closed her eyes and took several deep breaths and made her summons. She waited a moment, listening for footsteps. When she didn't hear anything, Tayler tried again. Still there was no response. Disappointed, she opened her eyes.

"Maybe I just need to wait."

Tayler put the necklace down on the marble rim and slid deeper into the water. She closed her eyes and tried to visualize Erica's dark naked body descending the steps into the bath. The water seemed to grow warmer with the visualization. Minutes leisurely moved along with tranquil abandon. When she finally felt a presence in the room, Tayler smiled to herself. She was beginning to like this crystal pendant business.

Tayler opened her eyes.

The woman who stood before Tayler had flawless, alabaster skin framed by thick, black hair that draped over her broad shoulders. She was dressed in a red silk blouse, which partially revealed two full, firm breasts. A silver belt emphasized her slender waist and a short, black leather skirt displayed two shapely legs. Her black boots had three-inch spiked heels. Her eyes were as green as emeralds and as piercing as daggers. Around the woman's neck, hanging from a silver chain, was a snake made from white gold. The eyes appeared to be diamonds. Her fingers were long and elegant, but her nails were filed into sharp points.

Tayler sat up quickly and tried to calm her beating heart. Her fingers went up to her neck but she remembered she had removed her necklace. *"My god, I summoned the wrong woman!"* Tayler thought to herself. Outloud she said flatly, "Raven, how nice of you to drop by."

"You've been so clever. I thought I had you in the cave today," Raven's voice was silky. On any other woman the same voice would have been intoxicating. "Did you summon me to join you in your bath?" Raven ran the nail of her index finger across her bottom lip. Her smile was seductive.

Even without the dance, Tayler understood why Ana had let Raven in. Raven's beauty and presence was undeniably scintillating. "I want you to stop this madness."

Raven took a few steps forward and stopped. "Madness? I see it more as foreplay." Raven stood with her legs apart.

From her vantage point in the tub, Tayler could see that Raven had nothing on underneath her skirt. Tayler looked down into the clear water and became fiercely aware of her own nakedness. She wished herself out of the tub and fully clothed.

"I've survived the five elements, Raven," Tayler tried to sound tough but her body tingled.

"Ah, Tayler, you are so naive. Or is it your lust for Erica that clouds your thinking?" Raven smiled and slowly gyrated her hips. "I could make you forget her."

Tayler's eyes followed Raven's hips.

She knelt down alongside the tub and swirled her hand around in the warm water. "The only way to stop the curse is to destroy me. But you won't. Especially since I can offer you so much," Raven cooed. The clear water turned to blood.

"But I will destroy you, Raven," Tayler retorted, unaware of what Raven had done.

"I have until Hallow's Eve — when the past and present meet — when everything of yours becomes mine." Raven's reference to the midnight hour on Halloween was only four days away. She ran her tongue over her upper lip. "I know you want me, but you'll have to wait for Hallow's Eve." Raven's devilish laughter filled the bathroom. "You're so tempting lounging there in such a creamy red sauce."

Tayler looked down into the tub. The sight and smell of the thick, red liquid was appalling. She quickly stood, stepped out of the tub and reached for her necklace. Tayler held the crystal pendant out in front, her hand perfectly still.

Upon seeing the pendant, Raven retreated several steps.

"You're sick, Raven. When the clock chimes midnight on Hallow's Eve—I'll destroy you," Tayler's face was flushed.

"I'm soooo frightened," Raven mocked. Her teeth were a brilliant white and perfectly straight.

"Four days, Raven, that's all you have," Tayler warned.

"I look forward to our time together, Tayler Windquest. I'll have so much pleasure watching you grovel at my feet." Raven walked over to the tub, bent down and dipped her index finger into the blood. She swirled it around and brought her finger to her lips. She smiled and stood. "Tell your friends to be careful."

"Raven," Tayler called out. "Why are you doing this? What have they done to you?"

Raven's eyes narrowed. "You'd never understand, you who have women falling at your feet. You don't know what it feels like to be betrayed." Raven sneered.

"Who betrayed you?"

"I don't have time to share my list with you," Raven spat.

Tayler slowly closed her hand on the pendant. "Why these women?"

Raven stared at Tayler's closed fist feeling an intense pressure at her temples. "One wouldn't love me. Another wouldn't translate a very precious book for me. And the third? She warned the others to stay away from me." Raven's voice was hushed. "They will pay."

The lights suddenly went out in the bathroom. Disoriented, Tayler twirled around trying to find the door. Before she could reach it the lights came back on and Raven was gone.

Tayler hurried over to the toilet and threw up. For the next hour, she sat next to the toilet with her head in her hands, her body shaking uncontrollably.

nineteen

An untouched lunch tray sat on the table in Tayler's room. Twelve hours after her blood bath, she was still too nauseated to think about food. She walked across the room drying her hair with a towel. It was the third shower she had taken that morning. Though she tried, Tayler could not forget the rancid feeling and putrid smell of the blood. Anger raged through her each time she thought about Raven's grotesque humor.

What angered Tayler more than Raven's power and evil ways was the realization that she could easily have succumbed to Raven's beauty. The more she thought about Raven, the more she understood why Ana had become a victim of Raven's curse.

Raven's timing was superb. She appeared at the most vulnerable moments and gave her victims exactly what they desired. In Ana's case, Raven had taken on Erica's appearance and given the illusion that she was real. Deception, Tayler guessed, was Raven's magic. She shivered.

Tayler pulled on a pair of dark blue, cotton pants and an oversized T-shirt. Her hair was combed but still wet. When she passed the floor-length mirror, she stopped and looked at herself. She still looked the same but she felt so different. She lightly touched the scar on her neck.

As she opened the door and walked out into the deserted hallway, Tayler knew the curse had changed her view of life. In her mind she now could visualize the very thin lines that separated good from evil—and life from death.

They were lines she didn't want to cross, but knew she had to.

"But how can I destroy her?" Tayler expelled an anxious stream of air. "Raven has lived with her powers for a long time. She's schooled on how much and how far she can go. We're not evenly matched," Tayler drummed her fingers on the sofa cushion. "I play with words—she plays with death."

Ana sat at her desk listening intently. The afternoon sun fell across her papers and on to the floor. "For every evil deed Raven performs, you counter with something good. She destroys, you build; she takes lives, you help people live; she hurts, you heal; she takes away, you give back." She put her glasses on.

From across the room, Tayler thought Ana looked sophisticated and wise but, in the sunlight, she could clearly see that Ana was pale and exhausted.

"I thought that if I survived the attempts it would be the end of the curse. But it's not." Tayler stood and walked toward the desk. When she reached Ana, she placed both of her hands on the wooden surface. "There's more, isn't there?"

"Sí," Ana replied. She picked up the phone.

Tayler turned away and walked to the patio doors. In the background she could hear Ana speaking to someone. After several minutes of silence, she heard Ana replace the receiver. The door to the den opened and Erica, Ev and Beth walked in.

Tayler turned and faced the women. Ev and Beth sat together on the sofa, Ana resumed her place at the desk, and Erica stood near the door. With her arms folded she demanded, "I want you to tell me everything you know about Raven's curse."

The air in the room grew heavy. Finally, Ana spoke. "There are three parts to the curse," she glanced at Erica. "This is only the first part."

"What? I thought you said—"

"Tayler, please," Ana stood, walked over to Tayler and placed her hands on Tayler's arms. "I will explain."

"I want everything this time, Ana," Tayler whispered so the others wouldn't hear.

Ana turned. "Ricah, do you have it?"

Erica reached in her pocket and pulled out a small, black velvet box. She handed it to Ana.

"Several months after Ricah and I became lovers, she had two matching gifts made—two very precious gifts." Ana opened the black case. "They looked like this."

Tayler peered down into the box. Surrounded by black velvet, seated in the center, was a white gold ring. A large midnight blue sapphire sat in the center while six waves, on each side of the stone, fell away in diminishing brilliance. From every angle, the ring caught the ebb and flow of light. Like the tide, the white gold waves crested with every movement. The gemstone was the deepest blue Tayler had ever seen. She closed her eyes. In her heart she understood the significance of the stone. "Love deeper than the deep blue sea," she whispered. She glanced at Erica but Erica was staring intently out the window. "What happened to your ring?" she asked Ana.

Ana took off her glasses. "The night in the cave—with Raven—Raven removed my ring while I slept. The next morning, before she did this," Ana gestured to her right breast, "Raven gave me my ring back. It was in three pieces."

The room was still. Tayler leaned against a wall hoping its coolness would bring her some relief from the heat. "What did she do?"

"Before she ground each piece into the sand, Raven picked up each part of the ring and cursed it. She vowed revenge in three stages. The first part of the curse would end at the twelve year mark, the second part the following year, and finally, the last a year after that." Ana sat alone at her desk. "In the next three years, Raven will return, in some form, to first destroy Erica—and then two other women who, so far, Raven has not yet identified."

Ana picked up the paper and read the remaining stanzas.

"Rejection mocks Love —
Beware the Kiss.
Pain a constant shadow —
Beware the Serpent.
Grief to shatter the Soul —
Beware the Cry at Night.

Darkness calls you,
and enthralls you,
I await you with delight."

Ana placed the paper back on the desk.

Tayler slid down the wall to the floor. "Why didn't you share those stanzas with me the other day?" She asked looking around the room, but no one answered. "And were you cursed, Erica, because you loved Ana?"

Erica nodded her head very slowly, never looking at Tayler— or at Ana.

"So, on Hallow's Eve I can only try and stop the first part of the curse?" Tayler asked.

"Sí. In order to end the curse each of the three parts must be destroyed." Ana wrung her hands. "If Raven is successful in any of the parts, the curse will claim you and Erica—and two others."

Beth reached for Ev's hand.

"And you don't know who the two others are?"

"No," Ana shook her head, "but in the next to last stanza love, pain and grief are specifically mentioned."

Tayler pinched the bridge of her nose and closed her eyes. Without opening them, she said, "You told me yesterday that the reason for the curse was love—unrequited love—love Raven had for you, but you didn't feel." She grew quiet. A cough broke her silence. "Could pain have something to do with the second part?"

"And grief with the third," Ev added following Tayler's logic. "We never thought of that."

"Ana, what were the two names Raven mentioned — you told me them yesterday?" Tayler got to her feet.

"Sterling and Devin," Ana cried. "We all attended the same boarding school."

"Who?" Tayler asked gently taking Ana's hand in hers.

"Sterling Navarre, Devin St. Ives, Raven Delaire and I," Ana groaned remembering their shared past.

"Where are Sterling and Devin?" Tayler coaxed.

"They should be here tonight," Ana's response was solemn.

Tayler squinted trying to recall the evening's event. "For the annual Day of the Dead festival?"

"It is a tradition here at the hacienda I cannot break. If I did so, the people in the valley would be concerned. There are only a few who know about the curse. If this were to get out, they would hunt Raven down. I'm afraid there'd be more bloodshed."

Tayler walked over to where Raven's dagger was still lodged in the rock. She wanted to touch it but couldn't. She looked closely at the women in the room. "Ana, you told me the book of black magic was written in Latin. Did Raven study Latin with you?"

"Only the first semester. She was asked to leave the school after she took a knife to one of our instructors." Ana ran her fingers nervously along the desk.

"Who translated the book for Raven?" Tayler asked.

"I don't know," Ana looked puzzled. "She asked Sterling, but Sterling refused."

"What did the instructor teach, the one Raven took the knife to?"

The room grew tense.

"Latin," Ana's eyes filled with horror.

"Did the instructor live?" Tayler asked persistently.

"Yes, but after the incident the instructor was institutional-ized. Rumors at school said she went insane." Ana looked at Tayler. "Oh, no—"

"And Devin?" Tayler whispered.

"She and this teacher were lovers." Past memories crashed into the present. "Devin warned us to stay away from Raven, saying she was evil. Sterling and I thought Raven acted peculiar and felt Devin needed someone to blame for her lover's malady. Devin and Raven never got along, so, we figured she was Devin's natural choice for someone to hate. That was until the curse."

The women stared at Tayler.

"Say nothing to Sterling and Devin until we are sure. I could be very, very mistaken."

twenty

Tayler stood on the balcony outside her room watching the moon. In two nights it would be full, and in two nights either she would destroy the first part of the curse or the curse would destroy her. She gripped the iron railing.

Moonlight illuminated the patio below her balcony and wispy clouds created eerie shadows on the adjacent buildings. Tayler rolled her head from side to side feeling emotionally and physically exhausted. Even the cool evening temperature had little effect. She took several steps into the room and sat at her desk. She took out a piece of paper and a pen.

"Okay, what do we have so far?" Tayler bit the end of the pen. "We've got a curse that breaks down into three parts. We think we also have Raven's three reasons for the curse—love, pain and grief. We have three potential victims of which we know only one for sure. We have the outcome and we have—me," Tayler leaned back in her chair. "And I'm the only one who can stop Raven. That leaves me as the antidote—"

Tayler got up and began pacing. Downstairs she could hear the guests arriving. Ana wanted to formally introduce Tayler to the people of Puerto Arista. With an anxious sigh, she knew she must hurry.

Her robe collapsed on the bed and she walked to where her dress was hanging. The mirror reflected her anxiousness. She made a face at herself. "Wait! I'm only the antidote for the first part. That's why Raven was in such a hurry to get rid of me." She cocked her head to the side. "There must exist an antidote for each part—I help Erica, someone helps Sterling and somebody else helps Devin."

Tayler took her dress off the hanger and put it on.

The strapless midnight blue silk dress revealed Tayler's tanned shoulders and neck. The waistline was nipped in and a silver belt was added to accent her narrow waist. The skirt was streamlined and had a long slit in the front. When Tayler moved or crossed her legs, the slit opened exposing her shapely legs. For accessories she wore a thin, white gold bracelet and the necklace Ana had given her. The crystal pendant sparkled in the light and hung just millimeters from her cleavage. She stood before the mirror examining her transformation. Although the features were familiar, Tayler stared at her reflection in disbelief. Before her stood a confident, sensual woman—but inside she felt differently. She nervously picked at nonexistent lint, smoothed unseen wrinkles, and readjusted the bodice.

She walked to her desk and saw the unfinished letter to her mother. Christina seemed worlds away—too far away. As Tayler pressed her fingers to the paper she felt the sting of tears. She picked up the letter. "Oh, Mother, I wish you were here," Tayler said softly to the night. "I really could use your advice and support right now." The curse was becoming less of a mystery for her, but she wondered if she would ever understand the mystery surrounding these women—Erica in particular.

Hours before in the library, Erica was withdrawn and aloof. She left the room as soon as the discussion had come to an end. Tayler hoped to steal her away for a few minutes, during the party, so they could talk. Tayler crossed her fingers.

Tayler's footsteps on the open, onyx floor were lost in the sounds of the marimba. Small mallets hitting hard wooden bars coursed the pulse of the party through the hacienda. Torches were lit around the grounds casting a heated ambiance over the authentic colorful costumes, Mexican blankets and sombreros. With each step Tayler took, the music eased the tension in her body. Her heart wanted to dance. At the end of the corridor she stopped behind a pillar and took several deep breaths. She told herself that she had nothing to fear. Without realizing it, Tayler reached up and touched the scar on her neck.

She walked around the pillar and stepped into the torchlight.

"She es beautiful—" Tayler heard someone say in broken English. She smiled in reaction to the unsolicited compliment.

Ana came forward and kissed her on both cheeks. "You look exquisite," her eyes twinkled with sensual delight. "You bring that dress alive. I'm not sure I want to share you with the others." Ana held out her hand.

"You flatter me," Tayler laughed, noticing how lovely Ana looked. Her black hair cascaded down her back in smooth, thick ripples. One strand on the left side was braided and finished with small beads. The simple peasant dress Ana wore took Tayler by surprise. She had become so accustomed to seeing Ana only in white shirts, black pants and boots. Ana's brown eyes sparkled and danced.

"Simple but elegant," Christina's familiar description floated through Tayler's thoughts. She smiled.

Ana led Tayler under a colorful banner, past several hanging animal-shaped piñatas, to the low wooden stage where the band was playing. When the music stopped, Ana took center stage. Her guests applauded enthusiastically.

"¡Buenas noches! Welcome. Me allegro mucho de verle. I'm delighted to see you all. From generation to generation, century through century, the history of our community has been richly preserved. This evening's celebration honors our hard work and the harvest of the endless hours and dedication we give to the land. Tonight, I also have the pleasure to introduce to you someone very special to me and to our people—Señorita Tayler

Acker

Windquest. Please welcome her to our land."

Ana turned and kissed Tayler on both cheeks. The crystal around Tayler's neck grew warm. She looked around for Erica, but could not find her. Disappointed, Tayler turned her attention back to Ana.

As Ana began to make introductions, Tayler saw a tall, neatly dressed woman with black onyx eyes approach. They embraced for a long time without speaking. The woman's facial features looked as though they had been carved by a sculptor.

"Tayler," Ana turned holding the woman's hand, "this is Sterling Navarre."

"The author?" The awe in Tayler's voice and her expression of shock made Sterling laugh.

"Yes," Sterling leaned forward and kissed Tayler on both cheeks.

"I've been a devoted fan since I picked up your first book. It's great to meet you. Hopefully, we can talk later."

"It would be my pleasure," Sterling replied in a low voice before moving on.

Tayler watched the illusive writer blend in with the crowd. Her growing excitement was difficult to contain.

Ana touched Tayler's arm and introduced her to the woman who stood before them. "Tayler, this is — "

"Devin St. Ives," Tayler smiled at the famous auburn hair and blue eyes. Looking into the woman's eyes, reality sent a jolt of pain through Tayler's nerves. So this is the third woman Raven felt betrayed her.

"You know each other?" Ana asked.

"We've never met," Tayler said, "but I know Ms. St. Ives' work very well."

In addition to her phenomenal success as a photographer, Devin also worked as a model. Her clean and classic looks were found in magazines and television commercials around the world.

"And I know of Ms. Windquest's work as the writer of many fine articles." Devin replied.

"Good," Ana said. "Then I'll let the two of you get better acquainted."

Marina approached and whispered something into Ana's ear. She nodded her head in response and smiled. "Marina told me that Ricah has just returned from the airport."

"Why was she at the airport?" Tayler asked.

"She went to pick up my partner. Unfortunately, her plane was delayed." Ana squeezed Tayler's hand.

She looked at Ana in surprise. "I didn't know—" Tayler said, but stopped abruptly when Erica and another woman appeared on the steps. Tayler's muscles tensed. Memories came flooding back in rapid succession. Her thoughts were thrown in several directions. She blinked trying to clear her vision, but the woman who stood next to Erica was not an apparition.

She was a tall woman with expressive facial features, and her shoulder length brown hair was heavily streaked with gray. Slightly taller than Erica, the woman's physical stature was overwhelming. She possessed a solid body that exuded strength and control.

Ana approached the woman, wrapped her arms around her lover's neck and kissed her. Ana laughed at something the woman said and then led her over to Tayler.

"Hello, Tayler."

"Gabrielle—" Tayler released the breath of air she had been holding since she saw Gabrielle on the steps.

Gabrielle opened her arms.

Tayler stepped into the long-ago, familiar embrace and enveloped herself in the past. "I've missed you."

"It's been a long time. Let me look at you." Gabrielle held Tayler at a short distance and took in the physical changes. She smiled and pulled Tayler back into her arms. Over Tayler's shoulder Gabrielle said to Ana, Devin and Erica, "I thought the Universe had its work cut out shaping a rough-and-ready tomboy into a woman. Now, all I can do is stand here awestruck."

Tayler's face blazed with embarrassment. "I can't believe you're really here." Tears tugged at the edge of memory. The last time she had seen Gabrielle was in the company of her father.

"Why don't we talk later when we've both satisfied our social responsibilities? We've got a lot to catch up on," Gabrielle said.

As the hours passed surrounded by new acquaintances and old friends, Tayler found it more and more difficult to concentrate. She made several attempts to talk to Erica, but each time she did, she was either summoned or Erica conveniently disappeared. Finally, when the evening began to wind down, Gabrielle took Tayler by the arm and led her from the crowd to the pool area.

The night was peaceful and serene with wispy clouds floating past the moon and the ocean shimmering in the distance. Despite their years of separation, Tayler and Gabrielle were soon deep in conversation.

"Tayler, I didn't kill your father. He was a good publisher and a wonderful father." Gabrielle turned away.

"Then why did you leave?"

"Because it wasn't safe." Gabrielle looked at Tayler.

"What do you mean?"

"Your father had been receiving death threats for months before his death. One night, he was showing me one of the rare books he had acquired. The letters fell out. I warned him, but he laughed and told me that they were idle threats. He no longer laughed when the last letter mentioned you." Gabrielle stopped.

"This is too weird," Tayler looked around.

"Your father asked me to take the letters to the police. It was the day before he died."

Tayler sat down on a bench as she tried to absorb everything. She placed her chin in her hands.

"He also made me promise that I'd get you out of town. He didn't want you hurt."

Tayler shivered in the cool night air. "The day before father died, I received a call from a woman saying she had damaging information about my father. We arranged to meet in Duluth, but she never showed. When I got back to the city, my father was dead." Tayler's eyes widened. "It was you?"

Gabrielle took Tayler's hands, helped her stand and snugly wrapped her arms around Tayler. "I promised your father. And now you're here saving Ana's life and Erica's future," she smiled.

Tayler placed her head on Gabrielle's chest, "No, I'm just trying to get—"

Gabrielle put her fingers on Tayler's lips. "You're bringing more and more pieces into place. I spoke with Ana yesterday. She told me you tied the loose ends of the curse together to create the larger picture." Her arms tightened around Tayler.

"I found out some more details," Tayler whispered. "Do you think we can slip away to my room so I can show you what I've got?"

"Yes," Gabrielle paused, "but let me at least tell Ana what we're up to."

"Okay, I'll meet you upstairs."

≈≈

At dawn, Erica found Tayler outside sitting under a palm tree. She could see that Tayler had not slept after the party. She tried to put her hand on Tayler's shoulder, but Tayler stood up and stepped away. Tayler turned toward her. The look in her eyes frightened Erica.

"I've had enough." Tayler stood leaning on the chair for support.

"I don't blame you. This is more than any of us could have imagined." Erica retreated several steps. "I'll arrange for your return to Minnea—"

"No, Erica! You don't understand," Tayler's anger and words only scratched the surface of the rage she felt inside. "I've had enough of Raven, her daggers and her snakes. And I've had

179

enough of your distance. You kiss me and then won't come near me for the next thirty-six hours. You assured me that I'd be safe here, but I'm more at risk here than anywhere in this universe. You treat me like a desired object, but then you push me away. Enough, Erica, I've had enough."

Erica flinched at Tayler's words. She had never seen Tayler so livid.

"We've been here for five days and I haven't once heard you talk about a plan to end this curse. Raven toys with you and the others like a cat playing with a mouse. Are you enjoying this game? What are we going to do, Erica?"

"I don't know," Erica said as the tears rolled down her cheeks.

"You don't know? In two days Raven's coming after you and you don't know?" Tayler's voice grew louder. "Time is running out and no one wants to answer my questions unless I get angry. Well, I'm damn angry. Who's going to tell me what to expect? You've refused to talk to me about any of this from the beginning. And yet, you want me to destroy her for you?" Tayler walked toward the hacienda. "Maybe the first thing you should do is decide whether you want to live or not, because—" Tayler stopped and looked Erica directly in the eyes, "from what I can tell, you died twelve years ago."

The gate closed with a slam.

twenty-one

Two hours after her explosive conversation with Erica, Tayler sat beside the pool. Tears slid down her cheeks and dropped into the water. Reality pushed aside her denial and splashed her in the face. It was October 30 — the day before Hallow's Eve. She put her head in her hands.

Without a plan, Raven would surely win. Though everyone around her pretended to be calm, Tayler could see the terror in their eyes. Everyone wanted this madness to end, but to Tayler, the price of freedom was the same price as death. From every angle of the curse, she was bound to lose Erica.

Murder — it had a hollow and empty sound. Tayler wondered if she were becoming immune to its lethal repercussions. Her father had been the one who had taught Tayler how to fight, but in the end even he lost. She did not want to follow his path.

Tayler stood up and dove angrily into the pool. She wanted to kill the man who had taken her father's life. She wanted to mangle Raven. She wanted revenge for Ana's injuries. She wanted Erica's freedom.

But most of all, she wanted to go home.

Tayler held her breath and swam to the deep end of the pool. She stayed under water until her lungs felt like they would burst. Unable to avoid the building pressure, she surfaced.

"Good morning."

Tayler turned in the direction of the voice. Gabrielle sat at the edge of the pool dangling her feet in the water. She wore a cream-colored bathrobe. Tayler swam over to her.

"Didn't sleep?"

Tayler shook her head, treading water.

"Didn't think so." Gabrielle's smile warmed Tayler's cold extremities and calmed her fear. "Do you want to talk?"

Tayler swam to the shallow end of the pool and grabbed her towel. She wiped her face and paused. "I yelled at Erica for not having a plan."

"I know. Ana and I heard."

"I should apologize, but I'm still so angry with her. She's been avoiding me since the cave-in. I wish someone would tell her that I'm on her side."

"I think you did this morning." Gabrielle took Tayler's hand. "Erica's an amazing woman. It's a miracle to see the things she's accomplished in these past twelve years. Many others would have completely shut down."

Tayler's cheeks grew red. She shrugged her shoulders and held out her hands. "Erica is a powerful woman."

"And so are you." The look in Gabrielle's eyes was sympathetic. "How do you feel about the power you possess?"

"I try not think about it."

"Why not?" Gabrielle looked puzzled.

"It's not for me." Tayler picked her words carefully. "I feel like the power comes from the crystal and that whoever possesses the crystal, possesses the power."

"But the crystal is only a tool." Gabrielle brought her legs up and hugged her knees. "Ana gave you the pendant to help you focus your powers."

"So," Tayler sat down on the edge of the pool. "I have the power to turn the water in this pool to blood?"

"Yes, if that's what you want."

Tayler's eyes widened. She gripped the edge of the pool.

"But only Raven would do something like that," Gabrielle added.

Tayler looked into her hands. "How did you know?"

"One of the housekeepers saw traces of the blood you tried to clean up. Marina alerted Ana because she thought you were hurt."

"Why didn't Ana say something to me about it?"

"Probably because you didn't say anything to her."

Tayler looked away, feeling ashamed. "She preys on my weaknesses."

"Raven preys on everyone's weaknesses, Tayler." Gabrielle looked at the blue sky above. "There are two women Raven can't kill."

"Ana and who?" Tayler watched Gabrielle intently.

"Her name is Carmen, Ana's sister." Gabrielle's answer surprised Tayler. "She'll be arriving this afternoon."

"What can she do?"

"She can help you better understand your power. Once you learn the extent of your abilities you'll be better able to fight Raven—on your own terms."

"So there is a plan?" Tayler's eyes grew wide.

Gabrielle nodded and helped Tayler to her feet.

"I'm so glad you're back in my life," Tayler's cheeks reddened. She looked away.

From the window in the library, Erica watched the embrace.

"Jealous?" Ana whispered.

"Yes, aren't you?" Erica question was filled with loss.

"No," Ana paused, "their friendship is bonded by the death

of Tayler's father. Tayler misses her father and, before last night, missed Gabrielle. Now that Gabrielle has returned, the sense of loss is deeper. They share an intimate bond—not a sexual one."

Erica sighed heavily. "She's very angry with me."

"She's angry with Raven." They watched Gabrielle and Tayler talking by the pool. "I believe she's frustrated with you."

"Me?" Erica pointed to herself quizzically. "Why?"

"You've been avoiding her since the cave-in. You still love her, but your actions make you seem indifferent."

"Indifferent—" Erica clenched and unclenched her fists. Her voice was bitter. "Absorbed, maybe, even preoccupied. Indifference is not telling us about Raven's visit the other night, and the blood bath."

"Tayler was frightened. We've known Raven longer. We expect bad things from her. To Tayler, Raven is intimidating and terrifying."

"She told me we needed a plan to destroy Raven." Erica searched Ana's eyes for answers.

"We have a plan." Ana faced Erica. "I've sent for Carmen."

Erica's eyes grew wide and she began to shake her head. "No."

Ana held up her hand. "Ricah, she is the only one who can help Tayler now. We have no other choice."

"Ana, her ways are basic and simple at best." Tears rolled down Erica's cheeks. "Just because she survived Raven's fury once doesn't mean she's an expert on how to destroy her."

"She's all we have, Ricah." Ana held Erica tight. Her voice reflected the dire consequence of the situation. "And whatever Carmen asks for we must give her." Ana turned when she heard the door open.

"Breakfast is ready," Gabrielle announced as she and Tayler strolled into the library. They stopped abruptly and stood in awkward silence.

Ana kissed Erica on the cheek and broke their embrace. "Join us when you're ready, Ricah," Ana walked past Tayler and took Gabrielle's arm.

At the door, Tayler stopped and turned back to look at Erica. As their eyes met, Tayler fought the urge to run to her and take Erica in her arms. Instead, she turned and quietly left the room.

twenty-two

As night approached, and Carmen's arrival loomed, the atmosphere in the hacienda became increasingly strained. At eight o'clock, Carmen appeared, sending Ana's household into chaos. A room had to be prepared according to Carmen's instructions. After the introductions, and before she met with Tayler, Carmen had a private conversation with Ana in the study.

Carmen returned the yellowed documents to Ana and chuckled. "She is a terrible poet, no?"

Ana closed her eyes. "It's what we have."

"It is enough." Carmen squeezed her large body out of the chair and walked to the window. "I live that evening in my dreams night after night."

"I would have died if you hadn't come."

"No, Raven wanted you alive. That was her first mistake." Carmen turned. Her eyes were dark and brooding. "Love is a weakness, a trap for the soul."

"Raven has no soul," Ana said through clenched teeth. "She sleeps with Satán."

Carmen slowly shook her head. "No, my dear, Ana, Raven does have a soul. That's why we are in this predicament. The good of her soul wanted someone to love, someone to believe in, someone to share life with. Her mistake was wanting all those things from you." Carmen lowered her voice. "She has always viewed you with such awe, an obsession perhaps. But the good of her soul wanted the love she saw you give so freely to others. To retain her sense of power and control, she turned to a book of black magic for the love she could not have. She had to drug you for you to love her."

"Are you trying to make me feel guilty?" Ana said through tight lips.

"No. We are human. We aren't attracted to everyone we meet. Unrequited love is a spark that ignites revenge on the dark side of the soul. Proof is in the records of civilization."

Ana nodded and stood abruptly. "We have little time. Will you help us?"

"Sí. But first we must discuss what I want you to do." Carmen returned to her chair.

In her fifties and dressed in bohemian garb, Carmen seemed more mountain than mortal. Even though she was eight sizes larger than Ana, Carmen was undeniably Ana's sister. Her light brown eyes, aristocratic nose and tender mouth were like Ana's, but unlike her sister's, Carmen's voice was deeper and her movements were exaggerated. The air swirling around her was filled with electricity. The scarf draped about her neck floated along with methodical jerks punctuated by her heavy footsteps. Unable to find something to say to break the silence, Tayler followed her down the hall.

Carmen led Tayler into a room and quickly dimmed the lights. She lit several candles. The room Ana had provided had no windows and was bare except for a few pillows on the floor and a low table placed between them. She lowered herself on one of the large pillows.

"I seek the security of the womb when dealing with the powers of evil. Everything human begins here."

"Raven is more animal than human," Tayler watched Carmen's lips tighten.

"She may be evil, but like you and I, Raven came from the womb." Carmen pointed to a pillow on the floor. "Sit."

Tayler adjusted the pillow beneath her.

For several minutes Carmen stared silently into the flame of one of the candles. "My purpose tonight is to enlighten you about the powers you possess. So far, you, Ana and I have escaped Raven's attempts to kill us. Ana survived because Raven is in love with her. I have survived because I mean nothing to Raven. But you, you have survived Raven because you are wise, kind and gentle." Carmen smiled at Tayler. "But!" Carmen's sharply raised voice caused Tayler to jump.

"Do not be fooled. Wise, kind and gentle women are only food for predators. Raven wants to succeed and she'll do anything, *anything* to win. Do you understand?"

Tayler nodded.

"So let us begin. We have much to do tonight." Carmen placed two unlit candles on the table. One was black, the other white. She lit the two candles and began to slow her breathing.

"Modern lie detectors were designed to capture the essence of these two candles," Carmen smiled. Her eyes danced.

Tayler silently wondered if Carmen had any theatrical training.

"It's all very natural," Carmen replied.

"What? How did you know that's what—"

"Be warned, Raven can read your thoughts even before you think them."

Tayler blinked nervously.

"I'm going to ask you a series of questions. These two candles will tell me if your answers are the truth or lies. Let me show you."

Tayler watched as Carmen held out her hands. The two small flames immediately stopped wavering. As Carmen raised her hands the flames grew in length, but when she dropped her hands the candles went out. Upon raising her hands again the flames returned.

"You are an only child?" Carmen asked.

"Yes," Tayler replied. The black candle went out. She smiled knowing it was the wrong candle.

Carmen raised her hand and the flame on the black candle returned. "You are troubled by your growing attraction for Ana?"

Tayler felt her face burning. "No."

The white candle went out.

"Your mother's partner is Lady Barbara Winthrop Sullivan?"

"Yes." The white candle again went out. Tayler drummed her fingers on her thigh. Her last two answers were false. She had told no one about her feelings for Ana, not even Gabrielle. And her mother's partner was Catherine not Barbara.

"Good, everything is working as planned. We can begin."

"Wait. The wrong candles went out when I answered your questions." Tayler cocked her head, her gaze flying from the black candle to the white.

"Ah, my dear, you are mistaken. We are dealing with the power of evil. We must reverse the images that we learned as children. Simply, black is white and white is black. When you told the truth the black candle went out, and when you told a lie the white candle did."

Tayler shook her head. It was going to be more difficult to work on Raven's level than she had imagined. She watched Carmen replace the candles with a dark blue one. Carmen lit this candle with a match.

"Hold your hand over the flame," Carmen commanded.

"But I'll burn my hand," Tayler protested.

Carmen raised her hand and held it over the flame without flinching. "Trust me."

Hesitantly, Tayler slowly brought her hand to the flame and held it. The heat seared her skin. "Ouch," she yelled shaking her hand in the air. "See, I told you I'd burn my hand." Tears welled up in her eyes.

"Trust no one—not me, Ana, Gabrielle, Erica—and least of all Raven. The moment you let your guard down you die. Understand?"

Tayler nodded. Her hand throbbed.

"Give me your hand."

"No." Tayler shook her head. "I may be slow, but I'm not stupid."

"Ah, but you are stupid. If you weren't I wouldn't be here tonight."

Tayler's back stiffened. Her nostrils flared.

Carmen reached across the table and grabbed Tayler's hands. The room filled with the sound of Carmen's heavy breathing. She rubbed Tayler's hands between her own.

The sharp pain from the burn slowly dissipated.

Carmen peered into Tayler's palms. "You hold a great deal of power in these hands. This frightens you." Carmen's eyes pierced Tayler's.

"No."

"Ah, you lie, but I'm pleased. You learn quickly. Very good." Carmen's smile was warm and inviting. Her voice softened. "Tell me why you are afraid."

"I'm beginning to understand the ways of evil, but what I don't understand is the power that I have. I don't know how to use it—" Tayler added softly, "appropriately."

"You feel inexperienced because you summoned the wrong woman to your bath?"

"I don't believe this," Tayler pulled her hands away. "Does everyone know about it?"

"It was a harmless mistake. Don't worry—your lines are pure. You'll neither misuse your gift, nor destroy anyone with it."

Tayler sat up. "But Ana and Gabrielle told me that I had to destroy Raven to end the curse. I have to—"

Carmen raised her hand to silence her. "You cannot destroy Raven."

"I was told that I—" Tayler felt her cheeks flush again. "They lied to me."

"They didn't lie to you." Carmen lowered her voice. "Tayler, you are so strong-willed. Listen carefully to me. You have misunderstood the meaning of the word 'destroy.' You can only destroy the curse by assisting Raven in destroying herself."

"Raven's too smart to destroy herself," Tayler argued.

"Absolute power corrupts absolutely. Raven has poisoned herself with the belief that she cannot be destroyed." Carmen's words were ominous. "She walks in her own poison, but she can still destroy you if you give her the chance."

"How do I protect myself from her?" Tayler looked distressed.

"It's very simple. You play the way she plays. Raven cloaks herself in deception. She gives her victims exactly what they desire and then she takes."

"Like Ana," Tayler whispered.

Carmen's eyes grew suddenly moist. "Sí." She blew her nose in a handkerchief and cleared her throat. "My sister lets her heart rule her actions sometimes."

"So, I must deceive Raven in some way," Tayler blinked.

"If that's what you choose to do," Carmen ran her tongue over her dry lips. "Remember, you are you. Let Raven use masks to shield her deeds. You stay in the light. She is not a fool. To be successful you must not only deceive Raven, but everyone in the hacienda as well."

"You mean Ana—"

"Yes, all of them." Carmen's smile was wicked.

"I have only until tomorrow at midnight. How can I deceive them? They know so much about me." Tayler rubbed her neck.

Carmen reached for Tayler's hands again and squeezed them. "They will believe you because they have no reason not to. There is one more thing." Carmen put a leather sheath on the table. From it, she extracted a nine-inch dagger with a black onyx handle. The image of a snake slithered around the grip.

Tayler bit her lip.

"Beware the kiss, Tayler. If you kiss Raven she'll penetrate your deepest desires. Your death will follow."

Tayler, wide-eyed, nodded.

"Now, lie down. I will teach you the art of deception." Carmen lit a stick of incense and began to chant.

As the room began to spin, Tayler felt her blouse being unbuttoned.

In the library, the clock ticked slowly as the hours dragged on for Ana, Erica, Gabrielle, Ev and Beth. Shortly before dinner, the women were joined by Sterling Navarre and Devin St. Ives.

When the door suddenly opened, and Carmen appeared, a collective sigh was heard. Carmen looked exhausted. Her clothes were disheveled and she had a wild look in her eyes. She stood in the doorway and searched the room for Ana. When she found her, Carmen bent her head and Ana got up and went into the hall.

Fifteen minutes passed before Carmen reappeared in the doorway. She motioned for Erica to follow her down the hall. When they entered the room, Carmen pointed to the floor. Tayler lay on the floor with her ripped clothes barely covering her body.

"Take her to her room," Carmen commanded Erica and walked away.

Green eyes watched from the balcony as Erica guided Tayler into Tayler's room. The crystal in the corner spun frantically but went unnoticed. Erica helped Tayler on to the bed and removed what was left of Tayler's shirt and pants.

Ana had given Erica a small bottle from Carmen and told her to generously apply the ointment to Tayler's body. Gently spreading the scented oil on Tayler's legs and arms, Erica stopped when she got to Tayler's breasts. They were spotted with red and purple bruises. Erica pulled her hands away and quickly sat on the edge of the bed to steady herself.

Erica poured a large amount of ointment into her hands and carefully applied it to the bruises. Tayler groaned from the pain. Carmen had the right to ask for any payment she deemed suitable for her work, but Erica recoiled from the thought that Carmen had touched Tayler where she, herself, was forbidden. She placed the bottle on the table. Carmen's parting words to Erica echoed in her head.

"Someday, Erica, you will thank me for what I did tonight."

When Tayler reached up and touched Erica's arm, Erica put aside her feelings about Carmen. Unable to hear what Tayler was saying, Erica leaned closer.

With her eyes closed, Tayler's words were breathy and seductive. "Stay with me tonight...let me show you what I've learned." Tayler paused. "I need you...want you — Ana."

Pain ripped through Erica's heart as she untangled herself from Tayler's fingers.

"Ana, don't leave—" Tayler called out as Erica raced from the room closing the door quickly behind her.

Outside in the hallway, Erica ran blindly to her room. She staggered to her bed and fell across it. Her pain and hopelessness came in sobs. In the late hour there was nothing she could do, but wait. She had lost everything — Tayler, Ana, her life. In twenty-four hours she would be Raven's.

twenty-three

Early in the morning of October 31, Hallow's Eve, the clouds rolled off the mountains in thick, gray blankets. The air was heavy with a bone-penetrating level of humidity and smelled of hay and manure. Out in the stables, the horses neighed and nervously kicked at their stalls, while the barn cats skittered under discarded containers. Around the pool, the leaves on the palm trees were thick with dew. The surface of the pool was perfectly still.

In the somber light of morning, Erica sat in a chair with an empty decanter tightly grasped in her left hand. The evening started out with it filled with Sangria, but as the night slowly dragged on, its liquid disappeared. She raised the black velvet case with her ring inside to eye-level. The white gold, sapphire ring radiated in the gloomy light. She dropped the empty decanter on the floor, threw the ring case on the table next to the chair and unsteadily got to her feet. Her hair hung in clumps and her clothes were wrinkled. It was barely six a.m., too early for breakfast and too late for miracles.

Sober and angry, Erica grabbed her jacket and left her room.

The kitchen was empty when Erica walked in and picked up the keys for the Jeep. Though the house seemed quiet, Erica knew that the others were beginning to stir from their sleep. She envied them and their ability to surrender to the night. Though her body screamed for sleep, Erica couldn't succumb. The image of smooth, warm sheets and the inviting body of a lover haunted her. She clutched the keys in her hand and turned to leave.

Soft voices coming from the dining area caused Erica to hesitate. She silently approached the doorway but did not go in. Instead she leaned against the wall and listened.

"You're driving me crazy," Ana's voice was low and husky.

Erica closed her eyes. The last thing she needed was to witness Ana's passion for Gabrielle.

"You are so sexually explosive." Ana drawled.

"Then let me explode in your arms."

Erica's eyes shot open. The second voice belonged not to Gabrielle but Tayler. She clenched her fists. Tears stung her eyes.

Ana laughed. "After breakfast, when the others are busy."

"I can't wait that long," Tayler's voice came in gasps.

Unable to hear more, Erica boldly stepped into the doorway. Her nerves shattered as she saw Tayler untie her robe. It fell open to Ana's eyes. Ana slid her fingers over the bare skin. Tayler moaned and closed her eyes in response to the caress.

"You could at least wait until I'm dead," Erica's frigid voice cut through the still room like a dagger.

Startled, the two women looked in Erica's direction. Ana withdrew her hands. Tayler backed away, tying her robe. The air in the room grew chilly. For a painful moment, the heavy silence of betrayal hung between the three women.

Erica hesitated and then turned abruptly. As she raced down the open corridor to the back of the hacienda she heard Ana call her name.

"Ricah, Ricah wait—"

"Let her go, Ana," Tayler commanded. "Let her go."

The smell of salt and seaweed permeated the air. Plate tectonics had pushed the shore into the mountains, making steep, jagged cliffs. The ocean waves below, a mix of shallow water and strong undercurrents, were deadly. With her heart in her shoes and tears streaming down her face, Erica leaned against the rocks.

Memory upon memory penetrated the veil of betrayal. Erica's body shook from a horde of tormenting faces—Tayler's, Ana's, Patricia Locksley's—and the one face she now despised—Carmen's.

"What have you done to her?" Erica sobbed. Her hands sought the wall for support.

No longer the fragile woman Erica had once held in her arms, Tayler was now a different woman—a powerful, demanding woman. Erica beat the rocks with her fists. No matter which way she went, she was destined to lose. Even if the curse were destroyed and she was released from her twelve-year hell, Erica knew that the only woman she wanted, needed and loved was lost. The dank October wind swirled around and rattled her spirit. Her gaze fell to the cliff.

"Go ahead—jump," the voice in the wind was unkind.

Erica shuddered and wiped her forehead.

"There's nothing to stop you," the voice coaxed.

Sweat marked Erica's collar and beneath her arms. "Give me the strength to live the next twelve hours. I have your deaths to avenge." The wind took her words and dispersed them into the sky.

A seagull cried.

"My, my, isn't this touching?"

Erica straightened her back but did not raise her eyes. "Fuck you, Raven."

"Tsk, tsk. Is someone becoming unglued?"

Erica turned to face the voice. Somewhere in the shadows of

the cliff stood her nemesis. "Come into the light, you coward, and face me."

"Why, I'd be delighted," Raven purred. She was dressed in black leather and held a whip in her hand. Her hair was swept to the side and the ends were caught in red and silver beads. Her leather vest strained against full breasts. "Don't you think it's a little late for this?"

"For someone like you—yes."

"Hm, I've never known you to be so spirited. Oh, how I love that in a woman," Raven smiled.

"You gutless snake."

The smile froze on Raven's face. She snapped her whip angrily, the sound of its hissing filled the air. "Enough. I didn't come here to trade insults. I came to make you an offer."

Erica threw her head back and laughed. She spread her feet apart and put her hands on her hips. "I can hardly wait to hear it."

"You're a stupid fool, Erica. You try my patience."

"And you try mine," Erica glared at Raven. "Either tell me what you want or leave."

Raven casually waved the whip in front of her. "All right, I'll come to the point. I want to try some new things and I need your help. With your beauty and my powers, we can leave Mexico and create an empire. You could do as you pleased and I would have new thrills for my—insatiable appetite."

"Thinking of taking over the world, are you?"

"Your so-called world leaders know nothing of control and domination." Raven ran her tongue along her upper lip.

"And you'd let me live until you were the wealthiest, most powerful woman in the world. Am I right?"

Raven nodded.

A slow smile spread across Erica's face. "With an offer like that how can I refuse?" Erica looked directly into Raven's eyes. "But I will."

Raven raised her hand and snapped her wrist. The whip came down and snagged Erica's cheek. Blood appeared in the wound and ran down her neck. "Bitch. Do I need to teach you how to obey as well?" Raven shrieked. Her voice echoed along the cliffs.

Erica wiped angrily at her cheek. "Apparently, you've overlooked a few details concerning tonight."

"Such as —"

"Such as you'll be destroyed."

"But I won't. It's as simple as that," Raven seethed.

"You're wrong, Raven. As midnight approaches, the door between the living and the dead will open. For one minute — from 11:59 to midnight — you'll be stripped of all your powers," Erica sneered.

"And so will Tayler." Raven's eyes darted from side to side.

"No, she has found a way to prevent that." Erica vehemently lashed out. She held the cuff of her denim shirt to her face. "While you've been out enjoying yourself, Tayler has claimed your most cherished possession."

The pounding waves roared against the rocks. Raven seemed stunned by Erica's revelation. "Ana?" Raven blinked.

"Sí."

Raven stamped her foot. "No! This is a trick. You're just saying this to get back at me."

"But I have proof. This morning before I left the hacienda, I saw Ana with her hands on Tayler's breasts."

"Nooo! You're lying —" fury and fire exploded in Raven's eyes.

"You think I'd lie about something like that? Raven, I saw it. Ana could hardly contain herself until after breakfast." Erica said gesturing in the direction of the hacienda. "I'm sure they've consummated their love by now."

"No. No, this isn't true. Ana is mine. *Ana is mine!*"

"We've both been betrayed," the wind took Erica's hair and threw it over her shoulders. "You couldn't kill Ana and you couldn't kill Tayler. They've overpowered you." Erica paused to let her words sink in.

"No. They are not together," Raven roared.

"Yes, Raven, they are. Bonds of love are the hardest to break—even your curse withers in the power of love."

"You—you are responsible for this," Raven spat. "Tayler was supposed to be your lover."

Raven's words stabbed Erica's heart. "You made it impossible, IMPOSSIBLE for Tayler to love me. The one element to your curse that you overlooked was the union—the love—between Ana and Tayler. You're too late, Raven, you're far too late."

"No. This is a trick, this is a trick," Raven stammered.

"It's happening right now, Raven," Erica taunted. "In less than twelve hours, at the stroke of midnight, Ana and Tayler will spread your ashes from one shore to the other."

Raven hissed, "If you are wrong...tonight, I'll take you apart piece by piece—"

"Never," Erica screamed as Raven vanished into the shadows.

twenty-four

The full moon cast its light through the open windows. A strong breeze came up and blew out several of the candles in the library. Gabrielle got up from her chair and closed the windows. Dark clouds began to overtake the moon. Within fifteen minutes the clouds had shut out its brilliance. Thunder could be heard in the distance. The clock in the room chimed the hour — it was eleven o'clock — one hour to Hallow's Eve.

It had been a long afternoon and the night was just as agonizing. Erica sat alone on the sofa with a cut and badly bruised cheek. Raven's whip had been savage. Ev had tried to administer some first-aid when Erica had returned to the hacienda, but she had pushed Ev's hand away.

The clock ticked loudly.

Underneath the pain, Erica vowed to fight Raven with all her soul. I have deaths to avenge. She discreetly ran her fingers over the dagger she had concealed in her belt. The plain ivory handle was smooth and the hidden blade had a razor-sharp edge.

The clock continued to tick.

Erica stood up and walked to the patio doors. The pool's surface was choppy. Between flashes of lightning, the darkness beyond the doors turned the glass into a giant mirror, reflecting the double-doors directly behind her and the figures trapped in the room. Ev and Beth looked haggard and held on to each other for support. Sterling watched as Devin read Tarot cards looking for clues to the future. Luis and Carmen sat quietly in the shadows, silent sentries waiting to fight a stalking enemy.

At 11:15, the clock chimed.

Erica saw Ana, Tayler and Gabrielle in the glass reflection. They were standing together near Ana's desk. Their voices were too low to be heard and their dark expressions too difficult to see. She could, however, see Ana's fingers laced through Tayler's. Feelings of abandonment frayed the remaining fragments of Erica's nerves. On the desk, both old and new pieces of the curse lay scattered near the rock that held Raven's dagger. The blade glinted in the lightning.

As she turned away from the images reflected in the glass doors, Erica heard the brass handle on the door rattle. When she turned back, nothing was there except the wind and her own reflection. She saw that her hair was in disarray and the clothes she had worn for the past forty-eight hours were caked in dirt and soaked with perspiration. In the past, she would never appear in the presence of others dressed this badly, but now she viewed her vanity only as a vulnerability. She no longer cared about what the others thought. She touched her injured cheek, the pain fueling her rage anew.

Erica pressed her face closer to the glass looking beyond the figures and into the night. The wind continued to growl as it sped around buildings and swirled the water in the pool like a cauldron. A white lawn chair skidded across the patio and landed in the pool. It sunk to the bottom. She sought Tayler's face in the reflection, but when their gaze met in the glass, Tayler looked away. The brief exchange revealed finally an absolute truth for Erica — she had fallen in love with Tayler on the night of the first attack. Her mind had cautioned her against this love, but her heart wouldn't let go. It was this love that Erica vowed to take to her grave.

The clock in the hall announced the half-hour.

The handle on the patio door rattled again. Another chair

zipped across the lawn. It teetered at the steps leading into the pool before it finally toppled in. Like the other chair, it quickly sank to the bottom. Lightning pierced the black sky, throwing the room into total darkness. As Erica turned toward the room, the lights flickered and came back on. The wind groaned and howled, ripping open one of the patio doors behind her. The sudden gust of air sent papers flying around the room. Erica tried to close the door, but was pushed back by the wind.

Somehow, Gabrielle managed to make her way to the door and leaned heavily into it. "Let me help!" she screamed at Erica.

The two women struggled with the door. When they finally got it partially shut, the lights went out and another blast of air sent the two women to the floor. Erica groped through the darkness and gripped the leg of a nearby chair.

"Hold on to me," Erica yelled to Gabrielle.

The noise was deafening. Suddenly the lights came back on, and the wind abruptly stopped. Erica and Gabrielle collided into one another on the floor. The door slid shut with a loud boom. Erica looked at Gabrielle, leaning against the chair out of breath. The noise in the room settled into near silence.

"¡Buenas noches! Good evening."

Erica turned toward the double-doors and the unmistakable voice. She clenched her fists.

Raven stood in the doorway in a hunter green velvet, floor-length cloak. The hood was pulled up around her head, but Erica could see Raven's luminous green eyes. Whether the glow came from within or was the result of an eerie reflection, Erica couldn't tell. Wrapped around Raven's fingers on her right hand was a brown leash. At the other end was a black panther. It, too, had green eyes.

"I see you found a date for tonight's gathering," Erica stood. The panther snarled and crouched.

"Dama, sentarse." The panther sat at Raven's feet. It's teeth looked like sharp white daggers. Raven's lip curled. "I should have killed you this morning."

She lowered her hood.

From where she stood, Erica surveyed the room. It was in

chaos. Papers and magazines carpeted the floor, furniture was askew and priceless Mexican vases lay in pieces. And it seemed as if everyone had stopped breathing, waiting for Raven's next move. Tayler appeared fragile in contrast to Raven's confidence and open sensuality.

Raven began to walk around the room, the panther following along at her side, its muscles bulging against its thin, shiny fur. "I'm happy to see everyone. Carmen, it's been a long time."

Carmen said nothing.

Raven stopped in front of Sterling and Devin. She towered over them in height and power. She abruptly reached out, wrapped Sterling's hair around her fingers and pulled Sterling's head back. "Sterling, my dear friend —"

"Raven —" Tayler interrupted.

"Silence," Raven barked. She looked at the clock. It was 11:40. "I have a lot to say and I don't have much time." She roughly released Sterling. "You should have translated my grandmother's book for me when I first asked. How dare you turn your back on me and refuse my request. Needless to say, I had to find someone else." Raven smiled wickedly. "Do you know what the pain of betrayal feels like, Sterling?"

Sterling hung her head.

"No, no you don't, do you?" With her index finger, Raven caressed Sterling's chin and then forced Sterling to look at her. "You will. Next year it will be your turn — Beware the Serpent."

Sterling turned her head away. Her jaw was set. "You won't live long enough to see it through."

Raven laughed. "How soon you forget. I need to succeed in only one of the curse's three parts. It matters little to me whether it's tonight or in a year or in two years. I WILL succeed. No one will ever deny me anything again. Ceaseless pleasures, unlimited riches, worldly control — will all be mine. You can join me now if you prefer." Raven looked around the room. "Anyone?" The panther yawned. "How about you Devin? Are you ready to join me?"

"I'd rather burn in hell, witch." Devin stood.

"Believe me, I'd enjoy that." Raven reached out and stroked

Devin's hair. "But, you're wrong, Devin, I'm not a witch. I have no belief in spiritual transcendence. I prefer the physical act of revenge." Raven stepped away. "Acts of betrayal can be reciprocated only with death—your death."

"What?" Devin's back stiffened.

"You turned my friends against me. You'll never know what it felt like to be alone all those years. I wanted friends and lovers, but you made me the enemy. I suffered endlessly because of you."

Devin shook her head. "No, Raven, your own actions made people turn away from you. You don't know what it means to love, you only know evil."

Raven's face burned bright red. "Enough. I know what I know. Beware the Cry at Night, Devin, in two years I'll be back to even the score."

Devin turned and threw herself at Raven.

Surprised by Devin's attack, Raven dropped the leash and tried to regain her balance, but Devin had her by the neck. Raven's face turned from a bright red to a deep crimson. Frantically, she kicked Devin in the shin with her right boot. Devin screamed. The panther crouched and bared its teeth.

"Dama, kill!"

Devin's scream exploded in the tense air. She fell on the floor. The panther took a swipe at Devin with its sharp claws. It ripped the arm of her shirt completely off. Blood spurted down her arm. She struggled to get up and get away, but the panther knocked Devin down again and pinned her to the floor.

"Raven, stop!" Ana screamed, her breath coming in gulps. "Take me instead!"

Raven whistled and the panther jumped off Devin. It quietly took up its post at Raven's side.

Ana ran to Devin and helped her up. "Are you okay?" she whispered. Devin nodded. Ev appeared at her side checking the wound.

At a quarter to the hour, the clock chimed once.

Raven leaned against a chair, rubbing her neck. Devin's fingers left red blotches on her throat. Her smile turned to scorn. "Take you instead? Oh, my dear Ana. What sweet words." Raven slowly approached Ana and walked behind her. She ran her hands over Ana's shoulders, down her back and around her waist. "I want to hear it again."

Ana's mumbled two words.

"Louder," Raven taunted, "I can't hear you."

"Take me."

"Again."

"Take me."

"Why should I?" Raven roughly turned Ana around.

"Because I—" Ana enunciated her words carefully. "Because I love you."

Raven slapped Ana hard across the face. "Liar! You don't love me. You never did. It was I who loved you. It was I who sought your kiss, your touch, your love." Raven took Ana's hand and placed it on her cheek. She closed her eyes. "I wanted you to hold me in your arms and make love to me. All I ever wanted since we were children was for you to love me."

The room grew quiet.

"But I do love you, Raven," Ana whispered.

Raven opened her eyes. A tear raced down her cheek, but she brusquely wiped it away. "No, you don't love me, Ana. You loved HER." Raven pointed to Erica. "And now you've got HER." Raven nodded toward Tayler. "Do you really think I would still take you after you spent the morning sharing a bed with Tayler?"

"I'll do whatever you ask."

"No! Go to your lover and let me take what I came here for." Raven pushed Ana toward Tayler and then faced Erica. "Come, Erica, we have only a few moments left." She walked to the patio door.

Ten minutes remained.

The dark clouds dispersed and the full moon returned, casting a soft light throughout the room. Raven stood in front of the glass and turned slowly toward the women. She untied the strings at her neck, unbuttoned her cloak and pushed it off her shoulders. It fell to the floor in a puff of air. The lights flickered and went out. When they came back on, a barely clothed Tayler stood in Raven's place.

Seeing her double, Tayler tried to move, but her body would not obey. Ten feet away from Raven and Erica, she frantically searched the room. Attempting to move, she realized that the light had somehow paralyzed her limbs and those of the people in the room. Horrified, she watched Erica take several steps toward Raven.

"Come to me, Erica," said the apparition. It held out its hands to Erica.

Erica took several steps.

"Yes, that's right. I want you, Erica," the breathtaking apparition beckoned Erica. "Come to me."

Erica took another step closer.

"Kiss me, Erica."

The words scorched Erica's mind. In a split second, she realized that they had all been misled. Raven had never planned on kissing Tayler, after all. It always was Erica who Raven was planning to kill. Tayler's nightmare of the cave, the one in which Raven had tried to kiss her, was nothing more than a trick.

Erica, don't, Tayler's mind was screaming. *It's a trick, Erica. Look at me.*

"Erica, come to me. I want you...I want you to kiss me," chanted the apparition in a soft, melodic voice.

Tayler watched as Erica took another step closer to Raven. She concentrated harder. *Erica, stop. That's Raven, not me. Look at her. It's Raven, not me. If you kiss her you will die.*

Erica turned her head and stopped. She looked at the real Tayler. Confused, she looked back at the illusion Raven had created.

"Erica, I love you. Come to me. I want to feel your hands on my body. I need you, I want to caress you, kiss you, make love to you." Raven chanted.

Two minutes remained.

Erica took another step. She was now only inches from Raven.

Carmen had told Tayler that, according to the curse, Raven could not draw Erica to her. Erica had to go to Raven of her own free will. Tayler searched her mind for any tidbit of information she could use. *Erica, that's not me, it's only an apparition. It's Raven. She's become what you desire. Take a good look, Erica.*

Tayler's words blazed through Erica's trance and lodged themselves in her brain. She stopped and took a step back.

The apparition's smile was beautiful. She spoke calmly. "Close your mind to her, Erica. She's really that evil Raven."

Raven's words struck Tayler like lightning. This was the key. Her eyes searched for the clock. Mere seconds remained. Tayler closed her eyes and rearranged her appearance. Her fingers began to twitch and tingle. She opened her eyes and felt the heavy fabric of the green velvet cloak. As Raven, the light had no numbing effect on her. When she looked back at Raven her heart froze. The long, silver blade of a dagger glimmered in the light.

"Come, Erica, it's time." The clock began to sound the hour.

Erica stepped into Raven's embrace. The dagger came down.

Dama, kill! Tayler's mind screeched at the crouched panther.

The panther leapt like lightning at the two women. A claw hit Erica in the side of her head. The force of the panther's body knocked her to the ground. The panther tore at Raven, its fangs sinking deep into her neck. In its grip, the panther shook Raven violently. The knife fell out of her hand. A garbled scream filled the room. Blood spurted from Raven's jugular and flew through the air.

Cries of agony and terror rifled through the room. The panther gave in to her instinctive fury, incensed by the smell of Raven's blood.

As the last chime rang out, Tayler grabbed Raven's dagger from the rock and plunged it into the panther's heart. It let out a long, terrifying groan before hitting the open door with a dull, loud thud. The glass shattered, spraying broken shards over the two motionless bodies.

A gust of wind whipped through the doorway and whirled around the room. Dust flew in every direction. When it stopped suddenly, both Raven's body and that of the panther's were gone.

Silence fell over the room.

twenty-five

By the patio door, Erica sat motionless in her chair, its fabric stained and still moist with blood.

Things had happened so quickly. Tayler looked at the bewildered expressions on Sterling's and Devin's faces. Carmen and Luis sat next to them talking in a hushed tone. While Beth finished wrapping a bandage on Devin's arm, Ev checked Erica's head.

"How many fingers," Ev asked Erica with her hand in the air.

Erica shook her head and blinked. "Four," she said, giving Ev the right answer.

Ev turned to Ana who knelt on the floor to one side of Erica's chair. "I want x-rays done of her head to make sure there's no internal swelling."

Ana nodded. "I'll drive her to the nearest hospital."

"I'm fine," Erica said as she stiffly got to her feet. "I would like to be driven to the airport."

"Erica, I don't think it's wise that you fly right now. Give yourself some time to heal," Ev pleaded.

"No, it's best I leave now." Erica closed her eyes holding back the tears.

Ana stood and reached for Erica's hand. "You haven't slept or eaten for days, Ricah. Let me nurse you back to health."

Erica shook her head, but stopped. The motion made her head throb and her stomach nauseous. "Tayler," her voice was low and sounded mechanical. "Thank you for saving my life tonight."

Tayler approached and put her arms around Erica. "What's wrong?" A moment of silence passed between them. "Talk to me, please."

"I've wished for this freedom for twelve years. And now that I've got it, I remain trapped."

"It'll take some time to adjust." Tayler offered. "No one can erase what you've been through. You've been under a tremendous strain these past years. But, your life is yours again."

Erica lowered her eyes. "The other night, you said I died years ago."

"I spoke those words in anger," Tayler said. "I'm sorry, I didn't mean to hurt you."

Erica stepped away from the embrace. "I fought falling in love with you, but I did. In many ways, your love gave me the courage to go on." Her voice was flat and labored. "I've come to the painful realization that the feelings we had for each other were a result of the tension, not love."

"What?" Tayler asked puzzled.

Erica sighed. "The more you knew about the curse, the farther away from me you went." Tears streamed down Erica's face. "I see now that you're in love with Ana."

"Erica—" Tayler looked into Erica's eyes.

"Ricah," Ana walked over to Erica. "I need to explain what happened."

"You owe me no explanation. Where love is concerned the only choice we have is to follow…" Erica hung her head, unable to finish.

"Erica, I'm not in love with Ana," Tayler said softly, her voice quivering. "When I met with Carmen she told me that the only way I could destroy the curse was through deception. Raven believed Ana and I had become lovers, but she also knew you were in love with me. That's why in the end she took on my appearance. It drove her insane to think that Ana and I had made love this morning, but we didn't. It was a cruel deception, I admit that, but that was Raven's weak spot. I don't know exactly what you told Raven, but by your cuts and bruises I knew she didn't like what you told her. She didn't know how to respond."

"Her anger became her weakness," Ana added.

"So when I saw the two of you—" Erica choked.

"It was part of the deception," Tayler interjected. "I had to turn the clock against Raven. She believed you. She believed that Ana and I had become lovers because you believed it." Tayler searched Erica's face for some indication that she understood. Finding nothing, she said, "I'm deeply in love with you, Erica."

The room became quiet. Erica walked toward the door, but stopped and turned around. "There's one thing I—I don't understand about tonight."

"What is it?" Tayler asked helplessly.

Erica's hands shook. "If you love me, why did you tell the panther to kill me?"

"The command was given only to kill. It wasn't given to kill you. As Raven walked around the room, I noticed that the panther got agitated when voices were raised. I also knew that as it got closer to midnight, Raven's illusions would begin to fall apart. I had just enough time to assume Raven's appearance. The panther got confused. When it saw the dagger in Raven's hand, I gave the command. Seeing Raven as the threat, it knocked you down and went for her. At midnight the entire illusion vanished."

Erica paced, her boots clicking on the floor. "I convinced myself that you were in love with Ana. It gave me the strength to meet Raven, but I was no match for her." Erica took a step toward Tayler, but retreated. "I didn't even have a plan to save myself. Me, the great architect, didn't have a blueprint of how to save my own soul. All I had was this," Erica pulled a dagger from her belt and placed it on the table.

"No, you had me. You brought me here to help you. Oh, Erica, I can't imagine life without you." Tayler's cheeks grew red. "I love you."

"Tayler, please don't. I need to leave."

"Erica, believe her, she's not deceiving you this time. She loves you and wants to be with you." Carmen got up from her chair. "Deception—whether used for good purposes or bad—has negative consequences. We all must learn to trust and we must swear to only tell the truth from this point on."

"My feelings are so confused. My grandmother didn't have a magic book, but she taught me that it's not the event we need to understand, but the feelings it evokes inside." Erica walked through the doorway and turned. "I know how to handle loneliness and fear. Now, I need to learn how to handle love."

Tayler couldn't stop her tears. She knew she couldn't ask Erica to put aside her right to heal. Erica had lost faith in herself and the people around her—she was the only one who could get it back. But the thought of Erica leaving Mexico without her was devastating. "How long, Erica? How long do you need?"

"I don't know…" Erica disappeared around the pillar.

twenty-six

Tayler sat at the Harbor Cafe waiting patiently for her mother. The restaurant held such wonderful memories for her. She wanted to feel again like she felt that October night with Erica. She had been back in Minneapolis for six weeks, but was having a difficult time keeping her mind on her work. Her days and nights in Mexico seemed so far away. It was a time she tried not to think about.

"Hello, dear," Christina bent and kissed the top of Tayler's head. "I'm sorry to keep you waiting."

"It's okay," Tayler sighed.

"My, that was enthusiastic." Christina sat down and took Tayler's hand. Her daughter's welfare was important to her and her own vacation in Europe had been plagued with apprehension for her daughter. After only one week in Paris, Catherine suggested they return to Minneapolis to wait for Tayler.

"Hey, I couldn't be happier." Tayler said sarcastically. "*The Narrator* is doing exceptionally well, I'm making an offer on a house, and I've actually had several dates."

Christina studied her daughter's face. After a brief hesitation, she said, "You can't forget her, can you?"

"You know me too well." A weak smiled appeared on Tayler's lips. "I've tried so hard to forget, to go on, but I can't."

"I know how it is. I've been there a few times myself," Christina smiled. The waiter appeared and took their order.

"You must think I'm crazy." Tayler had told Christina about the curse and Raven's attempts to kill her, but she did not tell her mother about her own powers.

"Why would I think that? You've told me some pretty strange things recently, but I never thought of you as crazy. If I hadn't been aware of Erica's mystical disposition, I think your story would have been more difficult for me to accept. But I've heard and seen some pretty unusual things in my time with Erica."

"It's more than that, Mom," Tayler wiggled in her chair. "It's not everyday that a daughter falls madly in love with her mother's former female lover."

Christina's eyebrows came together. She leaned toward Tayler and lowered her voice to a whisper. "Darling, be careful. If word gets out a national magazine may want to publish our story." Christina's eyes twinkled. "God, I can just see us on Oprah."

"Mother, I'm serious," Tayler pouted.

"As far as my past with Erica goes, it's over and done. Catherine and I are very happy together and still very much in love. Anyway, I have no patience for women on broomsticks."

"She doesn't ride a—oh, never mind," Tayler squeezed her mother's hand. Christina laughed.

"What's so funny?"

"I was just thinking about your father. If he knew his only daughter had fallen in love with a woman, he would have to be institutionalized."

"Mother, you're terrible." Tayler laughed. "Isn't it strange how things turn out?"

"Yes," Christina paused, "but that's why we need to live life to its fullest—or something like that." She looked out the window of the restaurant. Thanksgiving had come and gone and Christmas was only a week away. Outside, snowflakes began to cover the bushes and pine trees. Christina seemed lost in her thoughts.

"What are you thinking about?" Tayler asked.

"I wish I'd been there for you." Christina added matter-of-factly, "I'm not a very good mother."

"You are too." Tayler cocked her head to the side. "Why do you say that?"

"When Erica appeared, I was afraid she'd hurt you." Christina confessed. "I had some notion in my head that she'd use you to get back at me."

"She didn't."

"I know," Christina smiled. "But you know, the universe revolves around me."

Tayler laughed. Christina looked radiant against a backdrop of falling snow. Her cheeks glowed and she looked more content than Tayler had ever seen her. "But you let me go and I did get hurt. I don't get the feeling that you're angry with Erica."

"I'm not," Christina leaned closer. "From everything you've told me, it's obvious that Erica really is in love with you."

"Correction. Erica loved me."

"Counter-correction. She still is in love with you." Christina sat back in her chair.

"Then why is she moving to San Francisco?" Tayler looked past her mother and focused her gaze on the snow outside.

"What?" Christina blurted out.

Tayler handed her mother the morning paper and pointed to the featured article. "I rest my case."

As her mother read the article, other articles and photos flooded Tayler's thoughts. In the past month and a half, Erica appeared everywhere. She was designing buildings, making speeches and accepting awards. It seemed that her reluctance to be in the news was gone and the media loved it. In each new story, it became obvious to Tayler that Erica had regained her self-respect and confidence.

"Twin Cities to Say Farewell to Its Famous Architect," Christina read out loud. "But, it also states that Erica won't make her final decision public until the end of the week."

Tayler glanced back at Christina.

"So, is this the reason for the lunch invitation today?"

Tayler nodded. "I had to talk to you. No one would understand this whole mess like you would. I need your advice."

Christina's heart sank. "Honey, the best thing you can do is let her go."

"You're not saying what I want you to say."

"Let me put it this way. You left Mexico and came back here. Believe me, I've watched you struggle to forget what happened there. But you did and your life went on."

"Living with this emptiness isn't my definition of life."

"You just need to convince yourself that you're going to walk right back in and stand by your feelings. My god, you took on that horrible creature Raven. I would think your fight for Erica would be a little easier." Christina drummed her nails on the table. "At least, this time, you don't have to deal with a puma."

"Panther," Tayler corrected her mother. "Puma, panther—I suppose it doesn't matter. Technically, they both fall into the same category of leopard."

"Erica is a human being," Christina continued. "She's a woman who's put her emotional and physical needs aside for the past twelve years. Like you, she's been wise to walk away for a period of time. Closure helps us keep out the garbage from our past, so that our present and future relationships have a chance to succeed." Christina smiled. "Tayler, my dear, you need to lighten up. I've never seen you so anxious."

"You've never seen me fall head over heels for someone before," Tayler countered.

"True, and I hope this is the last." Christina laughed. "But what I'm getting at is this—Erica let down her defenses and let you in. You gave her a chance to experience today and see tomorrow. Now that she's had time to get acquainted with life again, she's probably noticing how empty it is without you."

Tayler nodded.

"There's only one you," Christina said drawing a few glances toward their table. "Maybe Erica needs to be reminded of that."

"Mother," Tayler got up and gave her mother a hug, "you're the greatest."

"Now that was enthusiastic."

twenty-seven

The falling snow placed a soft white blanket over the ground. It glittered in the evening light. Erica sat in her car and looked at the open space where her grandparent's house had stood. The ground was now level and a group of pine trees stood where the swimming pool had been. While she had been in Mexico, and on the west coast, the house destroyed by fire had been torn down and a landscaping company had restored the property to an approximation of its original natural state.

Tears filled Erica's eyes as she realized that a part of her had gone with that house—the house that Tayler had lived in. She was grateful that she had been gone when the house had been leveled, for it would have been too difficult to watch.

Unfortunately, Erica sighed, the landscape crew could do nothing to fill the void she felt in her life—to restore it to its original joy and wonder. With each passing day, the void seemed to grow deeper and deeper. She had stretched herself emotionally and physically ever since Halloween, using the destruction of the curse as a springboard to try to bring new meaning into her life. The response had been rewarding. Associates praised her renewed creativity, she was sought by a media who relished her new openness, and women lavished her with attention. For the first time in twelve years she felt in control of her destiny.

Though her days were filled with appointments, meetings and dates, the loneliness and emptiness that greeted her at the end of the day surprised her. The December wind rocked her car and the snow swirled around her. She started the engine and pulled out on to the road for the short trip home.

At the end of the long and winding road, the house waited patiently in the cold for her arrival. Through the bare branches she could see the lights that beckoned her. When she had it built, Erica had wanted to fill its rooms with laughter and love, but now she had to decide whether to leave what had become a fortress and start all over again. She was not the same woman who had left two months ago.

After her plane arrived in Minneapolis late that afternoon, Erica had gone to her office hoping to finalize her plans for the future, but the silence in her office only rekindled the loneliness. She sat at her desk too bewildered to move. After five hours of staring out the window, Erica left her office to confront her past and define her future.

Now, as she drove up the road to the house, everything looked so pristine. The tires crunched on the new snow and the black treads gripped the covered road. The only tracks on the driveway were hers.

On the stoop, Erica was surprised by the flood of memories. She exhaled and saw her breath in the cold night air. Her body ached wondering what Tayler was doing. The thought only heightened her despair. She had wanted to call Tayler a thousand times, but for a thousand reasons never did.

When she left Puerto Arista, Erica had flown straight to the Bahamas. She rented a house on the beach and spent the first few days trying to figure out how to begin living again. While out taking an evening stroll along the beach one night, a young woman approached her. At first Erica thought it was Tayler, or maybe she had prayed it was her, but it wasn't. Beyond the similarities in appearance, the woman was nothing like Tayler. They had gone to bed that night with little fanfare. Bored with Erica's lack of response, the woman left the following morning grumbling about "the beautiful rose with sharp thorns." Agitated and depressed, Erica closed herself in the house with a dreadful fear that the police were looking for her. Patricia Locksley's ghost kept her company hour after hour. At dusk she ventured out and sat under a palm tree and watched the sunset. Five hundred yards up the beach, she saw a woman collecting shells. Intrigued, Erica got up and began walking toward the woman. When she was halfway there she stopped in stunned silence. Erica fell to her knees. The water rushed around her legs and the sand rolled over her toes. Alarmed, the woman approached and helped Erica to her feet. Erica grew giddy. It was the same woman with whom she had spent the previous evening. Twelve hours after they had been intimate, the woman was still alive. She laughed, cried and played in the sand. She could hardly contain her joy. The befuddled woman walked away, shaking her head.

The curse, for her, was finally over and it was time for her to leave.

She went to San Francisco to take control of her destiny. Her business dealings with an architectural design firm in the city proved to be more than she had hoped. She dove back into her work with a renewed spirit. The merger that had been proposed in the months before she left for Mexico was finally going through. The papers were just waiting for her signature. The press conference wasn't scheduled to take place for three days.

"Erica," Candace Lanear squealed as she opened the door. "Hi, happy holidays.

"What are you doing out there in the cold? Come in, come in," Candace grabbed Erica's arm and pulled her into the house. She took Erica's coat and hung it up. When she came back she gave her employer a big hug. "It's so good to have you back. I've missed you."

"And I've missed you, Candace. The house looks great," Erica returned the hug, noticing the Christmas decorations behind them. The smell of fresh garland and baked cookies filled the air. Evergreen boughs were wrapped around the banister and red bows were placed at equal intervals. "It looks pretty festive in here." Erica walked to the double-doors, which opened to the living room, and saw a eight-foot tree decorated with colored lights, ornaments and tinsel. It brought back memories of the holidays Erica had spent with her grandparents. She turned and faced Candace. Tears threatened to reveal her pain.

"You didn't have to go through all this trouble," Erica said.

"You looked so down at the office today, your friends and coworkers went into action." Candace exclaimed excitedly.

"They're not all here are they?" Erica looked around.

"No, I sent them home before the snow got any deeper." Candace ushered Erica into the kitchen and pampered the tired traveler with warm spiced tea and sugar cookies fresh from the oven.

The tenderness touched her. Finally, Erica surrendered and let the tears fall. When her sobs subsided she stepped out of Candace's embrace. "Is everything set for the press conference?"

"Yup," Candace replied. She saw Erica frown.

"Good," Erica lied. "Candace, I want your opinion. Do you think I should go through with the merger?"

"Yes, I suppose, but first let me fill you in on some background. Your legal team has come up with a merger that allows you to keep your headquarters here in Minneapolis, while at the same time expanding your interests elsewhere." Candace replied confidently. "Second, the merger will provide more jobs by staying here—something that's important to you. Finally," Candace paused for effect, "you have no intention of moving to San Francisco."

"I see the logic, but really is it enough to keep me here?" Erica waited for Candace's response.

Candace removed a pan of cookies from the oven. "I know you're hurting and want to run away, but you're smart enough to know that your unhappiness will follow you. You're a survivor, Erica, you always have been. But, I have this sense that the confusion you feel tonight will be gone by the time your press conference takes place."

"Is that a prediction?" Erica teased and then laughed.

"Let's just say it's a woman's intuition."

"I hope you're right." Erica got up from her chair. They walked to the door of the library.

"Your messages are on your desk."

"Are there any from—"

"You're a very popular woman. You've also got a huge pile of magazines and newspapers to read."

Erica noticed how Candace had intentionally avoided letting Erica finish.

"I suggest that you get to bed as soon as you can. You look really tired." Candace looked at her watch. "And I've got a husband to get home to, so I'll see you tomorrow."

"Okay, good night, Candace, and thanks." Erica waved to Candace and walked into the library.

The familiar smell of leather filled her nostrils and she walked around the room touching everything—the desk, books, lamps— as if she were seeing them for the first time. As she stood behind her desk, however, the familiar pangs of loneliness and apprehension struck. She flipped through the stack of pink phone messages but, as she neared the end, the empty feeling inside began to swallow her. There were no calls from Tayler.

Erica sat down in her chair and put her head in her hands. Again she let the tears flow. She was in her own home and she was safe to cry the millions of tears she had held back for twelve years. She wondered where all the tears came from and if they would ever end. Erica wiped her nose and eyes. She stared at the phone, but she had no idea where to find Tayler. She picked up the receiver and dialed Christina, but the answering machine was the only voice in reply. Erica hung up. She picked up the phone again and dialed Tayler's office. It was after ten and the operator informed Erica that Tayler would be out of the office for a week. Again Erica left no message. The facts were clear to her, she had walked out of Tayler's life. How could she call Tayler and tell her that she was back and ready to pick up where they had left things on Halloween? She leaned back in her chair and closed her eyes.

Life had no meaning to her without Tayler.

The notes of her favorite song — *The Long and Winding Road* — floated through the open door. Through her tears Erica smiled. Candace was doing her best to ease Erica's pain by playing her favorite music. The music was comforting, yet haunting. The piano arrangement, one she had never heard before, was intriguing. At a slower measure the song seemed more compelling and elicited more emotion. She went to the door to listen.

The notes drifted down the hall from the conservatory and not the living room, where the stereo was located. Erica swallowed and leaned her head on the door frame. She made her way slowly down the hall to the conservatory.

In the doorway, she stood transfixed.

Tayler sat at the piano with her back to the door. Dressed in a black silk dress that clung to her body, Tayler seemed at ease at the piano. She was an accomplished pianist, blending mastery with magic. Erica shivered, remembering the strength in Tayler's hands.

From where she stood, Erica watched Tayler caress the black and white keys. Her hands seemed to glide above the keyboard producing an ivory sound of tranquility and splendor. Unwilling and unable to disturb the moment, Erica listened and let herself float within the enchanting rhythm of the music. The notes calmed Erica's heart and filled her soul with rapture.

The room glowed in candlelight and was filled with a wintry fragrance of pine cones, cinnamon and candle wax. The floor-length mirrors reflected the piano and Tayler, but from where she now stood, Erica knew that Tayler had not seen her yet. An evergreen wreath hung on the wall. Beyond the windows the light snow had been replaced with heavier flakes. With flakes the size of quarters, Erica knew there would be several feet of snow by morning.

Tayler poured her soul into her playing, giving freedom to her emotional turmoil. As Tayler reached the climax of the piece, Erica held her breath. Beautiful chords rose from the piano, bringing tears to her eyes. Tayler stopped and laid her hands on her lap.

"Welcome home," Tayler said softly without turning. She looked down at the keys.

Quietly, Erica approached and placed her hands lightly on Tayler's shoulders. Unable to resist, Erica touched Tayler's hair with her fingers. It felt like the velvet of rose petals. She moved Tayler's hair to the side, bent down and kissed the warm bare neck.

Tayler stood slowly, moved away from the bench and faced Erica for the first time since Halloween. Their hands sought each other and the two women moved closer until they were enclosed in each other's arms.

"I didn't know where to find you," Erica said breathlessly. "I hoped you would call and leave a number, but when I got home there were no messages from you."

Tayler broke their embrace and reached over to the piano. She picked up a stack of pink phone messages. They were all from Tayler, a message from every day in November leading up to the present day.

Erica looked at Tayler for a very long time. She slipped off her black suede jacket and threw it on the piano bench. The white blouse and black pants she wore accented her height and slender body. She put her hands on Tayler's waist. She could hardly believe that Tayler was here.

"My life has been so empty without you," Erica choked with emotion.

Their lips touched timidly at first, hesitating, like the awkwardness found in a first kiss. Erica ran her fingers over the silkiness of Tayler's dress. It was so soft and pleasurable.

"Let's go upstairs," Erica whispered into Tayler's ear. Her voice was soft, yet, confident and strong. She walked over to the piano and extinguished the candles.

Tears streamed down Erica's face as the dam overflowed with emotion, years of denial, and gratitude. For five minutes, the only sound that could be heard was her sobs. Tayler handed her several tissues. She wiped her eyes and looked at Tayler.

"I was that bad, huh?" Tayler grinned, her eyes filled with

tears.

"I guess you'll just have to practice some more," Erica laughed placing light kisses on Tayler's skin. She shuddered feeling Tayler's fingers caress her breasts.

"Okay, so every day we set aside time for practicing." Tayler responded, kissing Erica's lips. "But, I'm still curious about something," she whispered. Her voice was hoarse.

"What's that?" Erica bit her lip.

"I still don't understand why you ran into the house when it was on fire." Tayler's face was an inch from Erica's.

"I went in to get the crystal you've been wearing around your neck." Erica began to kiss Tayler's chest where the crystal hung. "It was a gift from my mother. When she gave it to me she said it had magical powers and it would protect whoever wore it. It was the last thing she gave me before she died. "

"Your mother was a wise woman." Tayler smiled. "Was she as beautiful as you?"

"As a child I thought she was the most beautiful woman in the world. Now, as an adult, I think I'll have to reconsider." Erica nibbled Tayler's ear.

"Ana has called me everyday since I left Puerto Arista. She's worried about you."

Erica sighed, "I was so angry with her. I don't do well with betrayal and deception, but I understand why you and Ana had to do what you did." Erica hung her head. "For all these years, I turned to Ana for support, but then I walked away when it was all over."

"She understands why you left," Tayler offered.

"I'll call her in the morning."

"She won't be there." Tayler stroked Erica's cheek. "She and Gabrielle will be flying in tomorrow night to spend the holidays with us."

"Wow, you work fast," Erica smiled, stretching in satisfaction beneath the crisp sheets.

"Oh, on the contrary. I can go...very...very...slowly...if I want," Tayler taunted, slipping her hand beneath the sheets.

When Erica reached for her, Tayler flipped her over, pinioning her hands beside her head. "You tease," she growled.

"No, I just want to remember every detail, every word and every touch. Tomorrow will come, but I want this first night to last forever." Tayler ran the tip of her tongue over her upper lip. Then she lowered her mouth to Erica's, welcoming Erica with passion.

epilogue

"No, absolutely not," Tayler shook her head.

"But I thought you'd jump at the chance." Erica placed another log on the fire, and returned to her seat near Tayler. The heat of the fire was in contrast to the cold, heavy snow falling beyond the balcony doors.

Tayler sat on the love seat in front of the fireplace watching Erica. The bedroom was quiet except for the crackling logs.

"I don't believe it. You don't want to cover the merger announcement even after my personal invitation?" Erica ran her fingers through her hair.

As Erica moved, Tayler caught a whiff of her perfume. The light, clean fragrance, mixed with the pleasant scent of burning logs, had a dizzying effect on her. But her heart was heavy.

"Erica, I don't want to cover the story of your departure. I watched you leave once. I don't have the strength to do it again."

Erica leaned forward and kissed Tayler lightly on the lips. "After Halloween, I roamed around feeling empty and alone. It was no different than what I had experienced during the curse.

With you in my life, I remembered how it felt to laugh. And I remembered how desire felt. The curse didn't seem so powerful. Time is as short or as long as we make it. No matter where I am, whether in Minneapolis or San Francisco, I know I can get through any obstacle as long as you're with me." Erica's eyes filled with tears.

The logs crackled in the background. Tayler tried to form her thoughts and emotions into words. "When you left Ana's that night I was devastated. For the past six weeks, everywhere I went I took you with me. I'll go wherever you go," Tayler kissed Erica.

"I'll have to spend some time out in California to work everything out, but I think it's important for you and I to be here." Erica's fingers lightly touched Tayler's face.

Tayler slowly exhaled, realizing suddenly that she had been holding her breath. Did "here" mean what Tayler hoped it meant?

"When I stayed with you after the fire, you didn't have a piano. Now you do, but you don't play." Tayler paused, and toyed with the pendant hanging from her neck. "Do you intend to move to piano to my house, or..."

Erica didn't let Tayler finish. "I want *this* to be your house ... our house." The look in Tayler's eyes was answer enough. They kissed fiercely, until Tayler broke away.

"Wait a minute. How could you be sure I'd come here tonight, or even at all?" Tayler's brow was furrowed.

"I didn't, but I figured that if the move to San Francisco didn't get your attention, then I'd spend all my lonely hours learning to play the piano." Erica said, gliding her fingers down Tayler's body. "But I'd rather play you instead."

Watch for part
two of the Raven
Delaire Curse
Trilogy in
2002!!

Beware the Kiss by **J. Alex Acker**

Front and Back Cover Images ©Digital Vision
Interior composed in Book Antiqua and Pepps-NO using Adobe
PageMaker 6.5
Printed by Thomson-Shore, Inc. on 60# Joy White Offset 444ppi

ORDER FORM

Complete the form below, providing credit card information or including check or money order, and mail to:

Women's Work Press, LLC
Attn: Orders
P.O. Box 10375
Burke, VA 22009 - 0375

Please Print:

Name _____

Address _____

City State Zip _____

Phone Number _____

Credit Card Number _____

Expiration _____

Signature (required) _____

Qty	Title	Price	Subtotal
	Beware the Kiss by J. Alex Acker	$12.95	
	Death Off Stage by Carlene Miller	$12.95	
	Cognate by RC Brojim	$14.95	
	Virginia residents, please add 4.5% sales tax		
	Shipping: $5 for first title, add $1 for each additional title ordered		
	Total enclosed		

On-line, secure ordering is also available at www.womensworkpress.com
We will never sell, rent, or share your personal information with anyone.

COGNATE

By R. C. Brojim

-꾳꾳-

The deafening harangue of the klaxon pounded through the haze of noxious yellow smoke cloaking the bridge of the *U.C.S.S. Boadicea*. Captain Danielle Artemis Forrest, rooted to the aft deck, strained to glimpse the flash of billowing gold sleeve that was all she could make out of Ma'at as the Nhavan rolled in battle with a giant reptilian creature.

The captain fought to push herself through the uproar of hand-to-hand combat waging on the bridge. The choking haze shifted deceptively before her eyes. As she moved, her legs grew heavier as though the gravity of a thousand planets dragged her down.

Ma'at cried out, "Dani, help me!"

Tears of despair leapt to Dani's eyes, blinding her. She would never reach Ma'at in time. Then the murk cleared. The lizard creature staggered up from the deck, its face a grinning mask. Beneath its feet, like a broken toy, lay the still body of Ma'at, the wo/man's blood spreading in a pool, making incarnadine the purple sash circling the intersexual's waist.

"Captain Forrest to the bridge, please."

Dani jerked upright in her bunk, drenched in sour-smelling sweat. A long shuddering moment passed before the specter of Ma'at's torn body faded from the screen of her inner vision. She made an effort to re-orient herself. What she had exaggerated into a cry of unspeakable anguish by Ma'at was only the measured tones of her First Officer signaling her over the intercom.

"Captain Forrest to the bridge -"

Dani punched the intercom button. "What is it, Ma'at?"

"Just a courtesy call, Captain. You requested we meet on the bridge at 1300."

"Damn. On my way, Ma'at." She forced her legs out of bed. Holy planets, but she was stiff! She massaged her calves with brisk kneading motions. Tired after only a few moments of exertion, she cradled her head in her hands and started to worry that she was sick. She hadn't slept solidly in a week. She'd thrown unappealing breakfasts back down the recycling chute the previous three mornings. This morning she hadn't had the guts, literally, to even venture into the mess.

She knew she wasn't pregnant. She knew because she hadn't slept with a man since her final year at the Academy - when she was still trying to prove she was heterosexual so she wouldn't be commissioned to serve in the Minority Fleet.

At first, she hadn't been. She had proudly, if furtively, begun her career as a command ensign aboard the dreadnought, *Christie May*. She'd gone on fooling her superiors for a few years, rising with speed to the rank of Lieutenant. Fooling them, that is, until Castle came into her life.

Castle, with her long willowy limbs, her skin the color of apricots, her eyes translucent gems of aquamarine. To touch Castle had been to melt into clouds and hear celestial choirs singing hymns. Castle had been irresistible, luscious...and not sufficiently discreet.

Dani tried to shake off the memory, but now the events flipped past her inner eye like an archaic album of analog snapshots, forcing her to view each miserable scene. She wondered why any of it still mattered and why, every so often, she felt compelled to torture herself with remembering.

When the scandal broke, Castle left the service in disgust, never looking back, never saying good-bye, never telling Dani what their affair had meant to her. To Dani, it had been love of the deep and painful kind, the kind she could not talk about. The kind she knew she would never find again.

Dani weathered the waves of gossip and, because she was a good officer, was shuffled quietly off to her first post in the

Minority Fleet, the *U.C.S.S. John Kettle*. Once aboard, she was promoted to Lieutenant Commander without any of the usual attendant fanfare: an ironic acknowledgment of her military ability shrouded by the shameful punishment meted out for her non-normativity.

She'd hated the 'Frying Pan', as everyone called the claustrophobic scout-class ship, hated herself, hated her gay shipmates and hated Explora Command for handicapping her career. For the first two years, the only sound that could penetrate the wall of outraged pride she had built around herself was the 'tsk-tsking' of her straight colleagues in the service.

But the years passed and, whether through sheer anger or sheer ability - and she was not sure, even now, which it had been - she was promoted again and assigned to the *U.C.S.S. Boadicea*, a genuine starship, albeit a Minority Fleet one. When its charismatic and beloved captain, Gary Steele, died six years later, she was appointed his able successor.

It had been a rigorous five years since, but she had stuck with it. Stuck with it through the High Command homophobia, the institutionalized misogyny, the close calls, the deaths of friends.

She'd long since made peace with her sexuality and even indulged it on occasion on shore leave, careful to ensure no one deeply touched her heart. What she had never made peace with was the military structure that had condemned her and others like her to a dimmer future than that countenanced by her heterosexual counterparts in Explora Command.

Dani pushed herself off the bunk, stripped off the smelly sleeping tunic, and stepped into the pulse shower. The water beat her neck and she wondered again at the unaccustomed soreness in her muscles. She stepped out of the shower, toweled her body dry and slipped into and sealed closed her spandex body suit, striped green and gold for command.

With the agility of years of practice, she French-braided her damp brunette hair. Her fingers didn't fly as they usually did. She looked in the mirror and decided that, except for the olive-dark circles under her hazel eyes, she was passable.

Ma'at would notice her exhaustion, but then Ma'at noticed everything. Dani experimentally flexed her shoulders. Playing *dankin* against the genetically stronger Ma'at three times a week kept her fit, even though she tended naturally toward the chunkier side of trim.

She just wished exercising could chase away her blues and ease her irritability. Goddess, but she hadn't been so irritable since those first lonely months aboard the Frying Pan. In the past week alone, she'd taken two innocent jokes personally and unfairly reprimanded their perpetrators. Strangely, the undercurrent of irrationality she felt had not passed away, but was growing stronger. She was even looking forward to the long-promised shore leave scheduled for *Boadicea,* which wasn't like her.

Dani eyed herself more critically in the mirror. She checked for fine wrinkles at the corners of her eyes and searched for strands of gray hair among the brunette, but didn't find any. If her sheer irritability was a sign of oncoming menopause, she was being spared the telltale physical signs. Besides, she had only just turned forty-two. Maybe Sly would recommend hormone therapy.

With an anxious frown creasing her brow, Captain Forrest stepped from her cabin.

-꘎꘎꘎-

Death Off Stage

by Carlene Miller

Tandy Byers emerged from her low-slung sports car like a long-limbed puppet responding to the tug of strings. Though she towered above the vehicle, the strong lines of her five-foot-ten-inch frame complimented the sweeping sleekness of the topaz car. She closed and locked the door while her dark eyes swept the parking lot till they spotted her parents' dusty sedan.

The parking lot was reserved for the employees of the Florida Citizens Bank a block distant. Its stern geometry of concrete and asphalt rectangles was softened by the yellow-green of new leaves filling out the border hedges of legustrum and the bright bursts of rich pink and striking white azalea bushes scattered randomly throughout the lot. The bank, calculating the value of good publicity during a period of low-yield interest rates, had offered use of their private parking area to those involved in the renovation of the old Palm movie theater into a community playhouse.

Before crossing the street, Tandy surveyed the exterior progress on the corner building half a small-town block in length. The front and side that she could see had been stripped of the marquee and billboards and sanded smooth for painting. Atop the building, the tanned backs and muscled arms of men repairing the roof glistened with sweat, even though it was only the first day of April.

The old entrance had been bricked up and plastered over. A large, uneven hole at the angle of the corner indicated later placement of a new opening. Quick strides took Tandy across the street against the traffic light, her thick, dark hair bouncing slightly and the pearl-white of a cowlick ridge glittering in the sun. Coming from late afternoon sunlight, she had to pause in the rough entrance to allow her eyes to adjust to the general gloom highlighted here and there with the blaze of work lamps.

"Miss." Tandy turned toward the voice. "One of those if you're going further." She nodded understanding at the workman's gesture and reached toward a slanting stack of yellow hard-hats.

The interior was nearly gutted of the original furnishings. Near the back exit were large mounds of old seats, jagged slats of wood, and crumbled brick. Scaffoldings of pipes rose against both sides. There was no escaping the grate and scrape and thud of demolition, punctuated with shouted orders and raucous returns.

Tandy was surprised by the number of workmen even though several local contractors had volunteered one or two men from their crews. Scanning the area for her parents, she lifted her head and a work light flashed across her high cheekbones. She liked believing those cheekbones and the thickness of her hair were genetic gifts from an Indian maiden or stalwart brave centuries in her past. The stodgy denial of such a possibility by her parents—who generally exhibited flamboyant theatrical personalities and behavior—amused Tandy.

Just as she spotted her mother and father near the old screen area and started forward, she had to skip sideways to avoid a large beam being hoisted toward the ceiling.

Neither parent noticed her approach. Iva Jane Byers' head, a froth of blond and gray curls, was bent low over her husband's hand. She was intent on removing a large splinter despite her husband's impassioned plea for care.

"Been playing workman, Dad?"

"Certainly not." Irwin J. Byers' quick smile for Tandy just as quickly reverted to an exaggerated grimace. "When I sold the farm, I vowed I would pamper myself from then on."

"Some pampering," his wife commented. "Tandy, I've pried up the point a little. See if you can pull it out."

Using rounded nails free of polish, Tandy extracted the

splinter while her father inhaled loudly through his teeth.

"A real chunk of wood, Dad. Where did you get it?" She held the culprit toward the light.

He gestured sweepingly. "Anywhere." He paused to suck on his thumb. "You know how I lean on everything if I have to stand very long. These sixty-plus legs do their share of fussing."

Immediately amusement brightened the trio's eyes and they laughed together remembering an opening night performance of two years before. Irwin Byers, playing Clarence Darrow in *Inherit the Wind*, had leaned against the judge's bench, obviously at some crucial point in its construction, causing it to collapse and revealing the actor playing the judge to be barefooted. All had continued valiantly until the scene was concluded and the curtain drawn.

"Hope no one's laughing at my auction idea." Wayne Littleton, managing director of the Royal Palm Community Theatre, nodded a hello at Tandy and raised his thick eyebrows to her mother as he tapped the hard-hat on the floor with a piece of decorative molding scooting it toward her feet.

"At such a good idea...of course not!" Iva Jane, shorter and stouter than her daughter, stretched on tiptoe to plant a theatrical kiss on Littleton's cheek. "You are going to make us a mint of money."

"Don't I wish. What do you think, I.J. He?"

Tandy had grown up hearing her parents referred to as I.J. He and I.J. She. The use of their similar initials was obvious, but neither would identify who had started the method of distinguishing them. The always precise and practical Tandy had sometimes sensed an unease in their responses to her questions.

"Auctions always bring in money." Irwin Byers' mobile face settled into an uncharacteristic frown. He retrieved his wife's hat and placed it on her head. Starting away from the group, he turned to nod at Tandy's orders to find a first-aid kit and sterilize the tear in his thumb.

"Something I said?" Littleton was honestly concerned.

"No, Wayne. Irwin and I grew up on neighboring farms in the Midwest. Both our fathers died in World War Two and our mothers had to return to their homes. Eventually we married and combined the places, but the farming blood had run thin in us. When the time was right, we auctioned off everything and moved here to Inland. Selling things priceless in memories and meanings shook Irwin more than he expected. He's more sentimental than I am."

"So Dad shies away from all auctions now," Tandy added.

"Well, there goes my first choice for auctioneer," Littleton said. "There's some pretty good stuff coming in. You should see the old sheet music Thelma Haynes brought to me."

"She brought it in herself!" Iva Jane exclaimed.

"You bet. Heaved herself around this mess on crutches that looked way too little to hold her weight. Threatened to break one over poor Brian Mullins' back just because he was trying to put a hard-hat on her head."

Iva Jane glanced over to where Mullins was stacking old wood near an exit door. "That hunk can put a hat on my head any day."

Littleton followed her look. "I don't know what you women see that's so great. I like Brian for those sets he helped with last year and all the time he's putting in here...otherwise he's just a guy."

"Just a guy built like a medium-class wrestler but graceful as a cat." Iva Jane drew out the last phrase dramatically. "His Elizabeth-Taylor eyes say you are all woman, but his manner says you are just as good as he is and it doesn't bother him one bit. And that is a real hat trick. But this idiot daughter of mine is immune."

"He's a good ten years younger than your idiot daughter." Tandy pretended indignation.

"And in a very short number of years, you will be pushing forty."

"Mother!" A dash of anger seasoned Tandy's deeper voice.

Littleton lifted an arm as though to ward off violence. "I'll leave you ladies to your discussion. But tell me first if you've seen Grady. I've already checked his office. I need his key to the storeroom."

Iva Jane answered, "He was in his office around mid-morning. I came by to bring in some old play posters for the auction. But I ended up leaving them outside his door."

"How come?" Littleton asked.

"Would you walk in on an argument between Verda Whitcomb and anyone else?"

"A real argument, Mother? Or the usual laying down of the law by Miss Verda?" Tandy emphasized the name.

"A real argument by the pitch of their voices. By the little I heard, I could tell it had to do with money. So I propped the posters up next to the door and skidooed. Came back a little while ago with Irwin to make certain they got put away. Irwin was off checking when he got that splinter and came back bleating like a lamb."

"Well, I'll check out back," Littleton said. "You ladies take care. This isn't the safest place to stand around. Mack Barnes has petitioned me to keep non-construction workers out of here. Said he already had Grady's permission."

Iva Jane frowned. "Did you remind him that Raymond Grady no longer is in charge of this building?"

Littleton moved off good naturedly shaking his head as Tandy chided, "Nor are you, Mother. And Mack is right. When he volunteered his time to foreman this job, I'm sure he didn't know that everyone of you connected with the theater group was going to be advising him. And under foot to boot."

"So just what are you doing here? Planning to paint the ceiling?" Sarcasm was Iva Jane's method for trying to regain control of a situation.

"Actually I am here on legitimate business with Mack himself. He needs to know how much money is available for the next materials purchase. But I also wanted to catch you and dad to see if you would eat with me tonight. My treat." Tandy watched her mother's defensiveness fade.

While she and her mother settled details concerning the evening, Tandy scanned the large, cluttered room looking for Mack Barnes. She touched her jacket pocket lightly to make sure of the small notebook of financial information, an oft-repeated gesture of which she had been unaware until Iva Jane had incorporated it into one of her roles. She spotted Barnes in conversation with Littleton along a side wall. Littleton had removed his hat to mop his balding head and the back of his white shirt was damp with sweat. By contrast, the foreman appeared cool and his workman's jumpsuit neat and clean.

Iva Jane's eyes, an alert blue, followed Tandy's gaze. She sighed, "Tandy, when are you going to date someone else?"

Tandy pulled her lips in against her teeth, exhaled a long, slow breath, and spoke deliberately, "Mack and I don't date. There are just things we both like to do so we do them together. He's not looking to get married. I'm not looking to get married."

"I suppose neither of you need sex either."

Tandy enjoyed her mother's banty-hen blustering. "I'm the fisherman in this family, Mother. One of the several things Mack and I enjoy together." Her slight emphasis on the 'several' stirred her mother into a pantomime of shaking her.

Tandy stood lost in herself as she watched her mother meander through the workmen, engaging each in a moment of conversation. She often wondered, but would never ask, if her parents really did not know she was a lesbian. She had known the day she came home from junior high to find her parents being visited by an old friend, a career soldier accompanied by the woman he had met and married on a tour of duty in Korea and their teenage daughter.

It was the daughter, skin a light brown and glowing black eyes dominating a face sculpted by an artist, who had engendered a stillness within Tandy that she had never experienced again. That night she had known the loneliness of wanting.

For weeks after that she had observed herself in her relationships. She liked several boys and they liked her, yet she had recognized it as the same teasing camaraderie that she saw often in the behavior of her girlfriends with their brothers and cousins. But it had been the jerk of her thighs and the spreading warmth in response to the accidental pressure of a firm breast against her bare arm when the young math teacher had bent over her and reached to point out an error in computation that had sealed her awareness and sent her on furtive book and magazine expeditions.

Still, even at that young age, she had been perceptive enough to play the heterosexual game throughout public school. Though, on the other side of things, she had the advantage of watching and listening to the drama students from the nearby college that had the use of an outlying Byers' barn for their productions since the time of her grandparents. And she learned early on that, unless the person was openly out, it was impossible to be sure who was gay and who was straight. It had made her feel more secure with herself, but it had also made her shy and hesitant about seeking that first encounter.

The gloom of the theater suddenly darkened even more as spring thunderclouds lessened the daylight spilling in through the various openings to the outside. Tandy approached Mack Barnes as Wayne Littleton walked away toward the back. Each smiled a greeting.

Barnes tugged at an ear lobe. "Hope your adding machine sends good news. Or should I say computer?"

"Adding machine. I know I'm out of step, but I like the sounds it makes. But I know I'll have to change over soon."

Barnes responded, "I know what you mean. I like the sound of a hand saw." Tandy pulled a notebook from her pocket and held it where both could see the numbers. "Here's the money available right now. The auction should pad it considerably."

"The more padding the better. A lot of wood and paint and blocks have been donated, but the real decorating is going to take money. Right now there's some trimwork I need to get

on hold. Littleton just showed me a piece of what he wants."
He looked at the nearby wall and at his feet. "He must have
carried it off with him. I need it as a sample. And speaking of
needs, I need to keep folks like I.J. He and She out of here."

Tandy returned the notebook to her pocket. "Good luck."

Barnes frowned. "I'm serious. Grady let it slip yesterday
that he's let the insurance on this building lapse. That's what I
was just going over with Littleton. I had asked him days ago
about keeping out regular people and that was before I knew
about the insurance."

"Didn't Grady promise he'd carry the insurance through
renovation?

"Right." Barnes nodded. "Wayne was pretty hot under the
collar about it. Said he was going to jam that promise down
Grady's throat."

Irwin Byers appeared in a lobby doorway and was joined
by his wife. He held out his bandaged thumb for her approval.
Together they got Tandy's attention and, through gestures, indicated that they were leaving.

Barnes said, "Your parents are a trip. Special people."

Before Tandy could respond, she saw his eyes react to something going on behind her. She turned.

Wayne Littleton was staggering along the edge of the pile
of old movie seats. In reaching to steady himself, he caused a
seat to clatter to the floor. The man with the broom rushed to
tug Littleton toward a clear area and braced him as he slid
down on one knee panting heavily.

Barnes and Tandy hurried down the slanting concrete floor.
Barnes leaned down. "Wayne, what is it?"

The president of the theatre group lifted his head, eyes darting from face to face. The movements of tongue and lips pro-
duced no sound until he took a deep breath and exhaled loudly.
"Back...back there."

Tandy was a good four strides ahead of Mack Barnes as
she passed through the jagged opening leading to an area

planned for dressing rooms and storage. She ignored the foreman's "Tandy, wait..."

A wedge of artificial light from an open door drew her. Barnes collided with her suddenly rigid body and both stared at the male figure sprawled in the center of the narrow room, his head half surrounded by a spill of darkened blood. The foreman maneuvered her gently aside.

"Raymond Grady," Tandy said tonelessly. "He looks dead."

About Women's Work Press

Women's Work Press, LLC is an independent press devoted to publishing works by, for, and about lesbians. We're in business for a very simple reason: a majority of the books published today do not reflect our lives. Many of those that *do* speak to our experience are poorly written, trite, or formulaic. We're changing that — one book at a time.

We want to create a literary world where there is no need for publishers like us because lesbians are so - dare we say it - commonplace we don't merit putting the adjective "lesbian" in front of everything we do (lesbian chic, lesbian sex, lesbian music, etc.).

We intend to produce romances, sure. Romances that are longer, with more interesting characters and plots that move beyond the "Am I or aren't I?" dilemma. We also intend to bring you works of science fiction, adventure, fantasy, mystery and horror. It's a big world out there, and there's a place for us in it...Let's show ourselves and the world at large that our place is not in the closet, or between the pages of a cheesy lesbian sexcapade, or in those made-for-boys lesbian sex flicks.

That's why we want to hear from you. Our on-line questionnaire, located at http://www.womensworkpress.com is available for feedback and comments. Or, you can send us a SASE, and we'll send you a copy.

Did you like *Beware the Kiss*? Let us know! Send us an e-mail at feedback@womensworkpress.com. To contact J. Alex Acker directly, e-mail her at jaacker@womensworkpress.com. We welcome all opinions, so don't hold back.

To comment the old-fashioned way, drop us a line at:

Women's Work Press, LLC

Attention: Feedback

P.O. Box 10375

Burke, Virginia 22009-0375

We'll be posting reviews on the web site, and who knows - your comments might appear on a book cover some day!

Thank you for giving us this chance to entertain you. We hope we've exceeded your expectations!

What are you reading?

Find our books at
Amazon.com,
at our web site
womensworkpress.com or at
your local bookstore.

If they don't carry them,
please ask them to!!